LONDON TRANSPORTS

Maeve Binchy

LONDON
TRANSPORTS

WHEELER
PUBLISHING, INC.
ROCKLAND, MA

★ AN AMERICAN COMPANY ★

Copyright © 1978, 1979, 1980, 1982 by Maeve Binchy

Published in Large Print by arrangement with
Dell Publishing, a division of Bantam Doubleday Dell
Publishing Group, Inc.
in the United States and Canada.

Wheeler Large Print Book Series.

Set in 16 pt. Plantin.

Library of Congress Cataloging-in-Publication Data

Binchy, Maeve
    London transports / Maeve Binchy.
        p.   cm.—(Wheeler large print book series)
      ISBN 1-56895-226-0 (softcover)
    1. Large type books. I. Title. II. Series.
    [PR6052.I7728L65   1995]
    813'.914—dc20   95-16438
                                                              CIP

For dear Gordon,
with love and thanks

Contents

Shepherd's Bush

People looked very weary, May thought, and shabbier than she had remembered Londoners to be. They reminded her a little of those news-reel pictures of crowds during the war or just after it, old raincoats, brave smiles, endless patience. But then this wasn't Regent Street, where she had wandered up and down looking at shops on other visits to London, it wasn't the West End, with lights all glittering and people getting out of taxis full of excitement and wafts of perfume. This was Shepherd's Bush, where people lived. They had probably set out from here early this morning and fought similar crowds on the way to work. The women must have done their shopping in their lunch hour because most of them were carrying plastic bags of food. It was a London different to the one you see as a tourist.

And she was here for a different reason, although she had once read a cynical article in a magazine which said that girls coming to London for abortions provided a significant part of the city's tourist revenue. It wasn't something you could classify under any terms as a holiday. When she filled in the card at the airport she had written "Business" in the section where it said "Purpose of journey."

The pub where she was to meet Celia was near the tube station. She found it easily and settled herself in. A lot of the accents were Irish, workmen having a pint before they went home to their English wives and their television programmes. Not drunk tonight, it was only Monday, but obviously regulars. Maybe not so welcome as regulars on Friday or Saturday nights, when they would remember they were Irish and sing anti-British songs.

Celia wouldn't agree with her about that. Celia had rose-tinted views about the Irish in London, she thought they were all here from choice, not because there was no work for them at home. She hated stories about the restless Irish, or Irishmen on the lump in the building trade. She said people shouldn't make such a big thing about it all. People who came from much farther away settled in London, it was big enough to absorb everyone. Oh well, she wouldn't bring up the subject, there were enough things to disagree with Celia about . . . without searching for more.

Oh why of all people, of all the bloody people in the world, did she have to come to Celia? Why was there nobody else whom she could ask for advice? Celia would give it, she would give a lecture with every piece of information she imparted. She would deliver a speech with every cup of tea, she would be cool, practical, and exactly the right person, if she weren't so much the wrong person. It was handing Celia a whole box of ammunition about Andy. From now on Celia could say that Andy was a rat, and May could no longer say she had no facts to go on.

Celia arrived. She was thinner, and looked a little tired. She smiled. Obviously the lectures weren't going to come in the pub. Celia always knew the right place for things. Pubs were for meaningless chats and bright, nonintense conversation. Home was for lectures.

"You're looking marvellous," Celia said.

It couldn't be true. May looked at her reflection in a glass panel. You couldn't see the dark lines under her eyes there, but you could see the droop of her shoulders, she wasn't a person that could be described as looking marvellous. No, not even in a pub.

"I'm okay," she said. "But you've got very slim, how did you do it?"

"No bread, no cakes, no potatoes, no sweets," said Celia in a businesslike way. "It's the old rule but it's the only rule. You deny yourself everything you want and you lose weight."

"I know," said May, absently rubbing her waistline.

"Oh I didn't mean *that*," cried Celia, horrified. "I didn't mean that at all."

May felt weary, she hadn't meant that either, she was patting her stomach because she had been putting on weight. The child that she was going to get rid of was still only a speck, it would cause no bulge. She had put on weight because she cooked for Andy three or four times a week in his flat. He was long and lean. He could eat forever and he wouldn't put on weight. He didn't like eating alone so she ate with him. She reassured Celia that there was no offence and when Celia had gone, twittering with rage at herself, to the counter, May wondered whether she had explored every avenue before coming to Celia and Shepherd's Bush for help.

She had. There were no legal abortions in Dublin, and she did not know of anyone who had ever had an illegal one there. England and the ease of the system were less than an hour away by plane. She didn't want to try and get it

3

on the National Health, she had the money, all she wanted was someone who would introduce her to a doctor, so that she could get it all over with quickly. She needed somebody who knew her, somebody who wouldn't abandon her if things went wrong, somebody who would lie for her, because a few lies would have to be told. May didn't have any other friends in London. There was a girl she had once met on a skiing holiday, but you couldn't impose on a holiday friendship in that way. She knew a man, a very nice, kind man who had stayed in the hotel where she worked and had often begged her to come and stay with him and his wife. But she couldn't go to stay with them for the first time in this predicament, it would be ridiculous. It had to be Celia.

It might be easier if Celia had loved somebody so much that everything else was unimportant. But stop, that wasn't fair. Celia loved that dreary, boring, selfish Martin. She loved him so much that she believed one day he was going to get things organized and make a home for them. Everyone else knew that Martin was the worst possible bet for any punter, a Mamma's boy who had everything he wanted now, including a visit every two months from Celia, home from London, smartly dressed, undemanding, saving away for a day that would never come. So Celia did understand something about the nature of love. She never talked about it. People as brisk as Celia don't talk about things like unbrisk attitudes in men, or hurt feelings or broken hearts. Not when it refers to themselves, but they are very good at pointing out the foolish attitudes of others.

4

Celia was back with the drinks.

"We'll finish them up quickly," she said.

Why could she never, never take her ease over anything? Things always had to be finished up quickly. It was warm and anonymous in the pub. They could go back to Celia's flat, which May felt sure wouldn't have even a comfortable chair in it, and talk in a businesslike way about the rights and wrongs of abortion, the procedure, the money, and how it shouldn't be spent on something so hopeless and destructive. And about Andy. Why wouldn't May tell him? He had a right to know. The child was half his, and even if he didn't want it he should pay for the abortion. He had plenty of money, he was a hotel manager. May had hardly any, she was a hotel receptionist. May could see it all coming, she dreaded it. She wanted to stay in this warm place until closing time, and to fall asleep, and wake up there two days later.

Celia made walking-along-the-road conversation on the way to her flat. This road used to be very quiet and full of retired people, now it was all flats and bedsitters. That road was nice, but noisy, too much through traffic. The houses in the road over there were going for thirty-five thousand, which was ridiculous, but then you had to remember it was fairly central and they did have little gardens. Finally they were there. A big Victorian house, a clean, polished hall, and three flights of stairs. The flat was much bigger than May expected, and it had a sort of divan on which she sat down immediately and put up her legs while Celia fussed about a bit, opening a bottle of wine and putting a dish of four small lamb chops into the oven. May braced herself for the lecture.

It wasn't a lecture, it was an information sheet. She was so relieved that she could feel herself relaxing, and filled up her wineglass again.

"I've arranged with Dr. Harris that you can call to see him tomorrow morning at eleven. I told him no lies, just a little less than the truth. I said you were staying with me. If he thinks that means you are staying permanently, that's his mistake not mine. I mentioned that your problem was . . . what it is. I asked him when he thought it would be . . . em . . . done. He said Wednesday or Thursday, but it would all depend. He didn't seem shocked or anything; it's like tonsillitis to him, I suppose. Anyway he was very calm about it. I think you'll find he's a kind person and it won't be upsetting . . . that part of it."

May was dumbfounded. Where were the accusations, the I-told-you-so sighs, the hope that now, finally, she would finish with Andy? Where was the slight moralistic bit, the heavy wondering whether or not it might be murder? For the first time in the eleven days since she had confirmed she was pregnant, May began to hope that there would be some normality in the world again.

"Will it embarrass you, all this?" she asked. "I mean, do you feel it will change your relationship with him?"

"In London a doctor isn't an old family friend like at home, May. He's someone you go to, or I've gone to anyway, when I've had to have my ears syringed, needed antibiotics for flu last year, and a medical certificate for the time I sprained my ankle and couldn't go to work. He hardly knows me except as a name on his register. He's

6

nice though, and he doesn't rush you in and out. He's Jewish and small and worried-looking."

Celia moved around the flat, changing into comfortable sitting-about clothes, looking up what was on television, explaining to May that she must sleep in her room and that she, Celia, would use the divan.

No, honestly, it would be easier that way, she wasn't being nice, it would be much easier. A girl friend rang and they arranged to play squash together at the week-end. A wrong number rang; a West Indian from the flat downstairs knocked on the door to say he would be having a party on Saturday night and to apologize in advance for any noise. If they liked to bring a bottle of something, they could call in themselves. Celia served dinner. They looked at television for an hour, then went to bed.

May thought what a strange empty life Celia led here far from home, miles from Martin, no real friends, no life at all. Then she thought that Celia might possibly regard her life too as sad, working in a second-rate hotel for five years, having an affair with its manager for three years. A hopeless affair because the manager's wife and four children were a bigger stumbling block than Martin's mother could ever be. She felt tired and comfortable, and in Celia's funny, characterless bedroom she drifted off and dreamed that Andy had discovered where she was and what she was about to do, and had flown over during the night to tell her that they would get married next morning, and live in England and forget the hotel, the family, and what anyone would say.

Tuesday morning, Celia was gone. Dr. Harris's address was neatly written on the pad by the phone with instructions how to get there. Also Celia's phone number at work, and a message that May never believed she would hear from Celia. "Good luck."

He was small, and Jewish, and worried, and kind. His examination was painless and unembarrassing. He confirmed what she knew already. He wrote down dates, and asked general questions about her health. May wondered whether he had a family, there were no pictures of wife or children in the surgery. But then there were none in Andy's office, either. Perhaps his wife was called Rebecca and she, too, worried because her husband worked so hard, they might have two children, a boy who was a gifted musician, and a girl who wanted to get married to a Christian. Maybe they all walked along these leafy roads on Saturdays to synagogue and Rebecca cooked all those things like gefilte fish and bagels.

With a start, May told herself to stop dreaming about him. It was a habit she had gotten into recently, fancying lives for everyone she met, however briefly. She usually gave them happy lives with a bit of problem-to-be-solved thrown in. She wondered what a psychiatrist would make of that. As she was coming back to real life, Dr. Harris was saying that if he was going to refer her for a termination he must know why she could not have the baby. He pointed out that she was healthy, and strong, and young. She should have no difficulty with pregnancy or birth. Were there emotional reasons? Yes, it would kill her parents, she wouldn't be able to look after the baby, she didn't want to look after one on her own either, it wouldn't be fair on her or the baby.

"And the father?" Dr. Harris asked.

8

"Is my boss, is heavily married, already has four babies of his own. It would break up his marriage, which he doesn't want to do . . . yet. No, the father wouldn't want me to have it either."

"Has he said that?" asked Dr. Harris as if he already knew the answer.

"I haven't told him, I can't tell him, I won't tell him," said May.

Dr. Harris sighed. He asked a few more questions; he made a telephone call; he wrote out an address. It was a posh address near Harley Street.

"This is Mr. White. A well-known surgeon. These are his consulting rooms, I have made an appointment for you at two-thirty this afternoon. I understand from your friend Miss . . ." He searched his mind and his desk for Celia's name and then gave up. "I understand anyway that you are not living here, and don't want to try and pretend that you are, so that you want the termination done privately. That's just as well, because it would be difficult to get it done on the National Health. There are many cases that would have to come before you."

"Oh I have the money," said May, patting her handbag. She felt nervous but relieved at the same time. Almost exhilarated. It was working, the whole thing was actually moving. God bless Celia.

"It will be around £180 to £200, and in cash, you know that?"

"Yes, it's all here, but why should a well-known surgeon have to be paid in cash, Dr. Harris? You know it makes it look a bit illegal and sort of underhand, doesn't it?"

Dr. Harris smiled a tired smile. "You ask me

9

why he has to be paid in cash. Because he says so. Why he says so, I don't know. Maybe it's because some of his clients don't feel too like paying him after the event. It's not like plastic surgery or a broken leg, where they can see the results. In a termination you see no results. Maybe people don't pay so easily then. Maybe also Mr. White doesn't have a warm relationship with his income tax people. I don't know."

"Do I owe you anything?" May asked, putting on her coat.

"No, my dear, nothing." He smiled and showed her to the door.

"It feels wrong. I'm used to paying a doctor at home or they send bills," she said.

"Send me a picture postcard of your nice country sometime," he said. "When my wife was alive she and I spent several happy holidays there before all this business started." He waved a hand to take in the course of Anglo-Irish politics and difficulties over the last ten years.

May blinked a bit hard and thanked him. She took a taxi which was passing his door and went to Oxford Street. She wanted to see what was in the shops because she was going to pretend that she had spent £200 on clothes and then they had all been lost or stolen. She hadn't yet worked out the details of this deception, which seemed unimportant compared to all the rest that had to be gone through. But she would need to know what was in the shops so that she could say what she was meant to have bought.

Imagining that she had this kind of money to spend, she examined jackets, skirts, sweaters, and the loveliest boots she had ever seen. If only she didn't have to throw this money away, she could have these things. It was her savings over ten months, she put by £30 a month with difficulty. Would Andy have liked her in the boots? She didn't know. He never said much about the way she looked. He saw her mostly in uniform when she could steal time to go to the flat he had for himself in the hotel. On the evenings when he was meant to be working late, and she was in fact cooking for him, she usually wore a dressing gown, a long velvet one. Perhaps she might have bought a dressing gown. She examined some, beautiful Indian silks, and a Japanese satin one in pink covered with little black butterflies. Yes, she would tell him she had bought that, he would like the sound of it, and be sorry it had been stolen.

She had a cup of coffee in one of the big shops and watched the other shoppers resting between bouts of buying. She wondered, did any of them look at her, and if so, would they know in a million years that her shopping money would remain in her purse until it was handed over to a Mr. White so that he could abort Andy's baby? Why did she use words like that, why did she say things to hurt herself, she must have a very deep-seated sense of guilt. Perhaps, she thought to herself with a bit of humour, she should save another couple of hundred pounds and come over for a few sessions with a Harley Street shrink. That should set her right.

It wasn't a long walk to Mr. White's rooms, it wasn't a pleasant welcome. A kind of girl that May had before only seen in the pages of fashion magazines, bored, disdainful, elegant, reluctantly admitted her.

"Oh yes, Dr. Harris's patient," she said, as

if May should have come in some tradesman's entrance. She felt furious, and inferior, and sat with her hands in small tight balls, and her eyes unseeing in the waiting room.

Mr. White looked like a caricature of a diplomat. He had elegant grey hair, elegant manicured hands. He moved very gracefully, he talked in practised, concerned clichés, he knew how to put people at their ease, and despite herself, and while still disliking him, May felt safe.

Another examination, another confirmation, more checking of dates. Good, good, she had come in plenty of time, sensible girl. No reasons she would like to discuss about whether this was the right course of action? No? Oh well, grown-up lady, must make up her own mind. Absolutely certain then? Fine, fine. A look at a big leather-bound book on his desk, a look at a small note-book. Leather-bound for the tax people, small notebook for himself, thought May viciously. Splendid, splendid. Tomorrow morning then, not a problem in the world, once she was sure, then he knew this was the best, and wisest, thing. Very sad the people who dithered.

May could never imagine this man having dithered in his life. She was asked to see Vanessa on the way out. She knew that the girl would be called something like Vanessa.

Vanessa yawned and took £194 from her. She seemed to have difficulty in finding the six pounds in change. May wondered wildly whether this was meant to be a tip. If so, she would wait for a year until Vanessa found the change. With the note came a discreet printed card advertising a nursing home on the other side of London.

"Before nine, fasting, just the usual overnight things," said Vanessa helpfully.

"Tomorrow morning?" checked May.

"Well yes, naturally. You'll be out at eight the following morning. They'll arrange everything like taxis. They have super food," she added as an afterthought.

"They'd need to have for this money," said May spiritedly.

"You're not just paying for the food," said Vanessa wisely.

It was still raining. She rang Celia from a public phone box. Everything was organized, she told her. Would Celia like to come and have a meal somewhere, and maybe they could go on to a theatre?

Celia was sorry, she had to work late, and she had already bought liver and bacon for supper. Could she meet May at home around nine? There was a great quiz show on telly, it would be a shame to miss it.

May went to a hairdresser and spent four times what she would have spent at home on a hairdo.

She went to a cinema and saw a film which looked as if it were going to be about a lot of sophisticated witty French people on a yacht and turned out to be about a sophisticated witty French girl who fell in love with the deckhand on the yacht and when she purposely got pregnant, in order that he would marry her, he laughed at her and the witty sophisticated girl threw herself overboard. Great choice that, May said glumly, as she dived into the underground to go back to the smell of liver frying.

Celia asked little about the arrangements for the morning, only practical things like the address

13

so that she could work out how long it would take to get there.

"Would you like me to come and see you?" she asked. "I expect when it's all over, all finished you know, they'd let you have visitors. I could come after work."

She emphasized the word "could" very slightly. May immediately felt mutinous. She would love Celia to come, but not if it was going to be a duty, something she felt she had to do, against her principles, her inclinations.

"No, don't do that," she said in a falsely bright voice. "They have telly in the rooms apparently, and anyway, it's not as if I were going to be there for more than twenty-four hours."

Celia looked relieved. She worked out taxi times and locations and turned on the quiz show.

In the half-light May looked at her. She was unbending, Celia was. She would survive everything, even the fact that Martin would never marry her. Christ, the whole thing was a mess. Why did people start life with such hopes, and as early as their mid-twenties become beaten and accepting of things. Was the rest of life going to be like this?

She didn't sleep so well, and it was a relief when Celia shouted that it was seven o'clock.

Wednesday. An ordinary Wednesday for the taxi driver, who shouted some kind of amiable conversation at her. She missed most of it, because of the noise of the engine, and didn't bother to answer him half the time except with a grunt.

The place had creeper on the walls. It was a big house, with a small garden, and an attractive brass handle on the door. The nurse who opened

14

it was Irish. She checked May's name on a list. Thank God it was O'Connor, there were a million O'Connors. Suppose she had had an unusual name, she'd have been found out immediately.

The bedroom was big and bright. Two beds, flowery covers, nice furniture. A magazine rack, a bookshelf. A television, a bathroom.

The Irish nurse offered her a hanger from the wardrobe for her coat as if this were a pleasant family hotel of great class and comfort. May felt frightened for the first time. She longed to sit down on one of the beds and cry, and for the nurse to put her arm around her and give her a cigarette and say that it would be all right. She hated being so alone.

The nurse was distant.

"The other lady will be in shortly. Her name is Miss Adams. She just went downstairs to say good-bye to her friend. If there's anything you'd like, please ring."

She was gone, and May paced the room like a captured animal. Was she to undress? It was ridiculous to go to bed. You only went to bed in the daytime if you were ill. She was well, perfectly well.

Miss Adams burst in the door. She was a chubby, pretty girl about twenty-three. She was Australian, and her name was Hell, short for Helen.

"Come on, bedtime," she said, and they both put on their nightdresses and got into beds facing each other. May had never felt so silly in her whole life.

"Are you sure we're meant to do this?" she asked.

"Positive," Helen announced. "I was here last

15

year. They'll be in with the screens for modesty, the examination, and the premed. They go mad if you're not in bed. Of course that stupid Paddy of a nurse didn't tell you, they expect you to be inspired."

Hell was right. In five minutes, the nurse and Mr. White came in. A younger nurse carried a screen. Hell was examined first, then May, for blood pressure and temperature, and that kind of thing. Mr. White was charming. He called her Miss O'Connor, as if he had known her all his life.

He patted her shoulder and told her she didn't have anything to worry about. The Irish nurse gave her an unsmiling injection which was going to make her drowsy. It didn't immediately.

Hell was doing her nails.

"You were really here last year?" asked May in disbelief.

"Yeah, there's nothing to it. I'll be back at work tomorrow."

"Why didn't you take the Pill?" May asked.

"Why didn't you?" countered Hell.

"Well, I did for a bit, but I thought it was making me fat, and then anyway, you know, I thought I'd escaped for so long before I started the Pill that it would be all right. I was wrong."

"I know." Hell was sympathetic. "I can't take it. I've got varicose veins already and I don't really understand all those things they give you in the family planning clinics, jellies, and rubber things, and diaphragms. It's worse than working out income tax. Anyway, you never have time to set up a scene like that before going to bed with someone, do you? It's like preparing for a battle."

May laughed.

16

"It's going to be fine, love," said Hell. "Look, I know, I've been here before. Some of my friends have had it done four or five times. I promise you, it's only the people who don't know who worry. This afternoon you'll wonder what you were thinking about to look so white. Now if it had been terrible, would I be here again?"

"But your varicose veins?" said May, feeling a little sleepy.

"Go to sleep, kid," said Hell. "We'll have a chat when it's all over."

Then she was getting onto a trolley, half asleep, and going down corridors with lovely prints on the walls to a room with a lot of light, and transferring onto another table. She felt as if she could sleep forever and she hadn't even had the anaesthetic yet. Mr. White stood there in a coat brighter than his name. Someone was dressing him up the way they do in films.

She thought about Andy. "I love you," she said suddenly.

"Of course you do," said Mr. White, coming over and patting her kindly without a trace of embarrassment.

Then she was being moved again, she thought they hadn't got her right on the operating table, but it wasn't that, it was back into her own bed and more sleep.

There was a tinkle of china. Hell called over from the window.

"Come on, they've brought us some nice soup. Broth they call it."

May blinked.

"Come on, May. I was done after you and I'm wide awake. Now didn't I tell you there was nothing to it?"

May sat up. No pain, no tearing feeling in her insides. No sickness.

"Are you sure they did me?" she asked.

They both laughed.

They had what the nursing-home called a light lunch. Then they got a menu so that they could choose dinner.

"There are some things that England does really well, and this is one of them," Hell said approvingly, trying to decide between the delights that were offered. "They even give us a small carafe of wine. If you want more you have to pay for it. But they kind of disapprove of us getting pissed."

Hell's friend Charlie was coming in at six when he finished work. Would May be having a friend, too, she wondered? No. Celia wouldn't come.

"I don't mean Celia," said Hell. "I mean the bloke."

"He doesn't know, he's in Dublin, and he's married," said May.

"Well, Charlie's married, but he bloody knows, and he'd know if he were on the moon."

"It's different."

"No, it's not different. It's the same for everyone, there are rules, you're a fool to break them. Didn't he pay for it either, this guy?"

"No. I told you he doesn't know."

"Aren't you noble," said Hell scornfully. "Aren't you a real Lady Galahad. Just visiting London for a day or two, darling, just going to see a few friends, see you soon. Love you, darling. Is that it?"

"We don't go in for so many darlings as that in Dublin," said May.

"You don't go in for much common sense

18

either. What will you gain, what will he gain, what will anyone gain? You come home penniless, a bit lonely. He doesn't know what the hell you've been doing, he isn't extrasensitive and loving and grateful because he doesn't have anything to be grateful about as far as he's concerned."

"I couldn't tell him. I couldn't. I couldn't ask him for £200 and say what it was for. That wasn't in the bargain, that was never part of the deal."

May was almost tearful, mainly from jealousy she thought. She couldn't bear Hell's Charlie to come in, while her Andy was going home to his wife because there would be nobody to cook him something exciting and go to bed with him in his little manager's flat.

"When you go back, tell him. That's my advice," said Hell. "Tell him you didn't want to worry him, you did it all on your own because the responsibility was yours since you didn't take the Pill. That's unless you think he'd have wanted it?"

"No, he wouldn't have wanted it."

"Well then, that's what you do. Don't ask him for the money straight out, just let him know you're broke. He'll react some way then. It's silly not to tell them at all. My sister did that with her bloke back in Melbourne. She never told him at all, and she got upset because he didn't know the sacrifice she had made, and every time she bought a drink or paid for a cinema ticket she got resentful of him. All for no reason, because he didn't bloody know."

"I might," said May, but she knew she wouldn't.

Charlie came in. He was great fun, very fond of Hell, wanting to be sure she was okay, and no

19

problems. He brought a bottle of wine which they shared, and he told them funny stories about what had happened at the office. He was in advertising. He arranged to meet Hell for lunch next day and joked his way out of the room.

"He's a lovely man," said May.

"Old Charlie's smashing," agreed Hell. He had gone back home to entertain his wife and six dinner guests. His wife was a marvellous hostess apparently. They were always having dinner parties.

"Do you think he'll ever leave her?" asked May.

"He'd be out of his brains if he did," said Hell cheerfully.

May was thoughtful. Maybe everyone would be out of their brains if they left good, comfortable, happy home setups for whatever the other woman imagined she could offer. She wished she could be as happy as Hell.

"Tell me about your fellow," Hell said kindly.

May did, the whole long tale. It was great to have somebody to listen, somebody who didn't say she was on a collision course, somebody who didn't purse up lips like Celia, someone who said, "Go on, what did you do then?"

"He sounds like a great guy." said Hell, and May smiled happily.

They exchanged addresses, and Hell promised that if ever she came to Ireland she wouldn't ring up the hotel and say, "Can I talk to May, the girl I had the abortion with last winter?" and they finished Charlie's wine, and went to sleep.

The beds were stripped early next morning when the final examination had been done, and both were pronounced perfect and ready to leave.

May wondered fancifully how many strange life stories the room must have seen.

"Do people come here for other reasons apart from . . . er, terminations?" she asked the disapproving Irish nurse.

"Oh certainly they do, you couldn't work here otherwise," said the nurse. "It would be like a death factory, wouldn't it?"

That puts me in my place, thought May, wondering why she hadn't the courage to say that she was only visiting the home, she didn't earn her living from it.

She let herself into Celia's gloomy flat. It had become gloomy again, like the way she had imagined it before she saw it. The warmth of her first night there was gone. She looked around and wondered why Celia had no pictures, no books, no souvenirs.

There was a note on the telephone pad.

"I didn't ring or anything, because I forgot to ask if you had given your real name, and I wouldn't know who to ask for. Hope you feel well again. I'll be getting some chicken pieces so we can have supper together around 8. Ring me if you need me. C."

May thought for a bit. She went out and bought Celia a casserole dish, a nice one made of cast iron. It would be useful for all those little high-protein, low-calorie dinners Celia cooked. She also bought a bunch of flowers, but could find no vase when she came back and had to use a big glass instead. She left a note thanking her for the hospitality, warm enough to sound properly grateful, and a genuinely warm remark about how glad she was that she had been able to do it all through nice Dr. Harris. She said nothing about

21

the time in the nursing home. Celia would prefer not to know. May just said that she was fine, and thought she would go back to Dublin tonight. She rang the airline and booked a plane.

Should she ring Celia and tell her to get only one chicken piece? No, damn Celia, she wasn't going to ring her. She had a fridge, hadn't she?

The plane didn't leave until the early afternoon. For a wild moment she thought of joining Hell and Charlie in the pub where they were meeting, but dismissed the idea. She must now make a list of what clothes she was meant to have bought and work out a story about how they had disappeared. Nothing that would make Andy get in touch with police or airlines to find them for her. It was going to be quite hard, but she'd have to give Andy some explanation of what she'd been doing, wouldn't she? And he would want to know why she had spent all that money. Or would he? Did he know she had all that money? She couldn't remember telling him. He wasn't very interested in her little savings, they talked more about his investments. And she must remember that if he was busy or cross tonight or tomorrow she wasn't to take it out on him. Like Hell had said, there wasn't any point in her expecting a bit of cosseting when he didn't even know she needed it.

How sad and lonely it would be to live like Celia, to be so suspicious of men, to think so ill of Andy. Celia always said he was selfish and just took what he could get. That was typical of Celia, she understood nothing. Hell had understood more, in a couple of hours, than Celia had in three years. Hell knew what it was like to love someone.

But May didn't think Hell had got it right about

telling Andy all about the abortion. Andy might be against that kind of thing. He was very moral in his own way, was Andy.

Holland Park

Everyone hated Malcolm and Melissa out in Greece last summer. They pretended they thought they were marvellous, but deep down we really hated them. They were too perfect, too bright, intelligent, witty, and aware. They never monopolized conversations in the taverna, they never seemed to impose their will on anyone else, but somehow we all ended up doing what they wanted to do. They didn't seem lovey-dovey with each other, but they had a companionship which drove us all to a frenzy of rage.

I nearly fainted when I got a note from them six months later. I thought they were the kind of people who wrote down addresses as a matter of courtesy, and you never heard from them again.

"I hate trying to recreate summer madness," wrote Melissa. "So I won't gather everyone from the Hellenic scene, but Malcolm and I would be thrilled if you could come to supper on the twentieth. Around eightish, very informal and everything. We've been so long out of touch that I don't know if there's anyone I should ask you to bring along; if so, of course the invitation is for two. Give me a ring sometime so that I'll know how many strands of spaghetti to put in the pot. It will be super to see you again."

I felt that deep down she knew there was

nobody she should ask me to bring along. She wouldn't need to hire a private detective for that, Melissa would know. The wild notion of hiring someone splendid from an escort agency came and went. In three artless questions Melissa would find out where he was from, and think it was a marvellous fun thing to have done.

I didn't believe her about the spaghetti, either. It would be something that looked effortless but would be magnificent and unusual at the same time. Perhaps a perfect Greek meal for nostalgia, where she would have made all the hard things like pita and hummus and feta herself, and laugh away the idea that it was difficult. Or it would be a dinner around a mahogany table with lots of cut-glass decanters, and a Swiss darling to serve it and wash up.

But if I didn't go, Alice would kill me, and Alice and I often had a laugh over the perfection of Malcolm and Melissa. She said I had made them up, and that the people in the photos were in fact models who had been hired by the Greek Tourist Board to make the place look more glamorous. Their names had passed into our private shorthand. Alice would describe a restaurant as a "Malcolm and Melissa sort of place," meaning that it was perfect, understated, and somehow irritating at the same time. I would say that I had handled a situation in a "Malcolm and Melissa way," meaning that I had scored without seeming to have done so at all.

So I rang the number and Melissa was delighted to hear from me. Yes, didn't Greece all seem like a dream nowadays, and wouldn't it be foolish to go to the same place next year in case it wasn't as good, and no, they hadn't really decided where to go next year, but Malcolm had seen this advertisement about a yacht party which wanted a few more people to make up the numbers, and it might be fun, but one never knew and one was a bit trapped on a yacht if it was all terrible. And super that I could come on the twentieth, and then with the voice politely questioning, would I be bringing anyone else?

In one swift moment I made a decision. "Well, if it's not going to make it too many I would like to bring this friend of mine, Alice," I said, and felt a roaring in my ears as I said it. Melissa was equal to anything.

"Of course, of course, that's lovely, we look forward to meeting her. See you both about eightish then. It's not far from the tube, but maybe you want to get a bus. I'm not sure. . . ."

"Alice has a car," I said proudly.

"Oh, better still. Tell her there's no problem about parking, we have a bit of waste land around the steps. It makes life heavenly in London not to have to worry about friends parking."

Alice was delighted. She said she hoped they wouldn't turn out to have terrible feet of clay and that we would have to find new names for them. I was suddenly taken with a great desire to impress her with them, and an equal hope that they would find her as funny and witty as I did. Alice can be eccentric at times, she can go into deep silences. We giggled a lot about what we'd wear, Alice said that we should go in full evening dress, with capes, and embroidered handbags, and cigarette holders, but I said that would be ridiculous.

"It would make her uneasy," said Alice with an evil face.

25

"But she's not horrible, she's nice. She's asked us to dinner, she'll be very nice," I pleaded.

"I thought you couldn't stand her," said Alice, disappointed.

"It's hard to explain. She doesn't mean any harm, she just does everything too well." I felt immediately that I was taking the myth away from Malcolm and Melissa and wished I'd never thought of asking Alice.

Between then and the twentieth, Alice thought that we should go in boiler suits, in tennis gear, dressed as Greek peasants, and at one stage that we should dress up as nuns and tell her that this was what we were in real life. With difficulty I managed to persuade her that we were not to look on the evening as some kind of search-and-destroy mission, and Alice reluctantly agreed.

I don't really know why we had allowed the beautiful couple to become so much a part of our fantasy life. It wasn't as if we had nothing else to think about. Alice was a solicitor with a busy practice consisting mainly of battered wives, worried one-parent families faced with eviction, and a large vocal section of the female population who felt that they had been discriminated against in their jobs. She had an unsatisfactory love life going on with one of the partners in the firm, usually when his wife was in hospital, which didn't make her feel at all guilty, she saw it more as a kind of service that she was offering. I work in a theatre writing publicity handouts and arranging newspaper interviews for the stars, and in my own way I meet plenty of glittering people. I sort of love a hopeless man who is a good writer but a bad person to love, since he loves too many people, but it doesn't break my heart.

I don't suppose that deep down Alice and I want to live in a big house in Holland Park, and be very beautiful and charming, and have a worthy job like Melissa raising money for a good cause, and be married to a very bright, sunny-looking man like Malcolm, who runs a left-wing bookshop that somehow has made him a great deal of money. I don't *suppose* we could have been directly envious. More indirectly irritated, I would have thought.

I was very irritated with myself on the night of the twentieth because I changed five times before Alice came to collect me. The black sweater and skirt looked too severe, the gingham dress, mutton dressed as lamb, the yellow too garish, the pink too virginal. I settled for a tapestry skirt and a cheap cotton top.

"Christ, you look like a suite of furniture," said Alice when she arrived.

"Do I? Is it terrible?" I asked, anxious as a sixteen-year-old before a first dance.

"No, of course it isn't," said Alice. "It's fine, it's just a bit sort of sofa coverish if you know what I mean. Let's hope it clashes with her decor."

Tears of rage in my eyes, I rushed into the bedroom and put on the severe black again. Safe is what magazines call black. Safe I would be.

Alice was very contrite.

"I'm sorry, I really am. I don't know why I said that, it looked fine. I've never given two minutes' thought to clothes, you know that. Oh for God's sake wear it, please. Take off the mourning gear and put on what you were wearing."

"Does this look like mourning then?" I asked, riddled with anxiety.

"Give me a drink," said Alice firmly. "In ten years of knowing each other we have never had to waste three minutes talking about clothes. Why are we doing it tonight?"

I poured her a large Scotch and one for me, and put on a jokey necklace which took the severe look away from the black. Alice said it looked smashing.

Alice told me about a client whose husband had put Vim in her tin of tooth powder and she had tried to convince herself that he still wasn't too bad. I told Alice about an ageing actress who was opening next week in a play, and nobody, not even the man I half love, would do an interview with her for any paper because they said, quite rightly, that she was an old bore. We had another Scotch to reflect on all that.

I told Alice about the man I half loved having asked me to go to Paris with him next weekend, and Alice said I should tell him to get stuffed, unless, of course, he was going to pay for the trip, in which case I must bring a whole lot of different judgements to bear. She said she was going to withdraw part of her own services from her unsatisfactory partner, because the last night they had spent together had been a perusal of *The Home Doctor* to try and identify the nature of his wife's illness. I said I thought his wife's illness might be deeply rooted in drink, and Alice said I could be right but it wasn't the kind of thing you said to someone's husband. Talking about drink reminded us to have another and then we grudgingly agreed it was time to go.

There were four cars in what Melissa had described as a bit of waste land, an elegantly paved semicircular courtyard in front of the twelve steps up to the door. Alice commented that they were all this year's models, and none of them cost a penny under three thousand. She parked her battered 1969 Volkswagen in the middle, where it looked like a small child among a group of elegant adults.

Malcolm opened the door, glass in hand. He was so pleased to see us that I wondered how he had lived six months without the experience. Oh come on, I told myself, that's being unfair, if he wasn't nice and welcoming I would have more complaints. The whole place looked like the film set for a trendy frothy movie on gracious modern living. Melissa rushed out in a tapestry skirt, and I nearly cried with relief that I hadn't worn mine. Melissa is shaped like a pencil rather than a sofa; the contrast would have been mind-blowing.

We were wafted into a sitting room, and wafted is the word. Nobody said "come this way" or "let me introduce you" but somehow there we were with drinks in our hands, sitting between other people, whose names had been said clearly, a Melissa would never mutter. The drinks were good and strong, a Malcolm would never be mean. Low in the background a record player had some nostalgic songs from the sixties, the time when we had all been young and impressionable, none of your classical music, nor your songs of the moment. Malcolm and Melissa couldn't be obvious if they tried.

And it was like being back in Andrea's Taverna again. Everyone felt more witty and relaxed because Malcolm and Melissa were there, sort of in charge of things without appearing to be. They sat and chatted, they didn't fuss, they never tried to drag anyone into the conversation or to force some grounds of common interest. Just because we were all there together under their roof . . . that was enough.

And it seemed to be enough for everyone. A great glow came over the group in the sunset, and the glow deepened when a huge plate of spaghetti was served. It was spaghetti, damn her. But not the kind that you and I would ever make. Melissa seemed to be out of the room only three minutes, and I know it takes at least eight to cook the pasta. But there it was, excellent, mountainous, with garlic bread, fresh and garlicky, not the kind that breaks your teeth on the outside and then is soggy within. The salad was like an exotic still-life, it had everything in it except lettuce. People moved as if in a dance to the table. There were no cries of praise and screams of disclaimer from the hostess. Why then should I have been so resentful of it all?

Alice seemed to be loving every minute of her evening, she had already fought with Malcolm about the kind of women's literature he sold, but it was a happy fight where she listened to the points he was making and answered them. If she didn't like someone she wouldn't bother to do this. She had been talking to Melissa about some famous woman whom they both knew through work, and they were giggling about the famous woman's shortcomings. Alice was forgetting her role, she was breaking the rules. She had come to understand more about the Melissa and Malcolm people so that we could laugh at them. Instead, she looked in grave danger of getting on with them.

I barely heard what someone called Keith was saying to me about my theatre. I realized with a great shock that I was jealous. Jealous that Alice was having such a nice time, and impressing Melissa and Malcolm just because she was obviously not trying to.

This shock was so physical that a piece of something exotic, avocado maybe, anyway something that shouldn't be in a salad, got stuck in my throat. No amount of clearing and hurrumphing could get rid of it and I stood up in a slight panic.

Alice grasped at once.

"Relax and it will go down," she called. "Just force your limbs to relax, and your throat will stop constricting. No, don't bang her, there's no need."

She spoke with such confidence that I tried to make my hands and knees feel heavy, and miracles it worked.

"That's a good technique," said Malcolm admiringly, when I had been patted down and, scarlet with rage, assured everyone I was fine.

"It's very unscientific," said the doctor amongst us, who would have liked the chance to slit my throat and remove the object to cries of admiration.

"It worked," said Alice simply.

The choking had gone away but not the reason for it. Why did I suddenly feel so possessive about Alice, so hurt when she hadn't liked my dress, so jealous and envious that she was accepted here on her own terms and not as my friend? It was ridiculous. Sometimes I didn't hear from Alice for a couple of weeks; we weren't soul mates over everything, just long-standing friends.

". . . have you had this flat in the City long?" asked Keith politely.

"Oh that's not my flat, that's Alice's," I said.

Alice was always unusual. She had thought that since the City would be deserted at weekends, the time she wanted a bit of peace, that's where she should live. And of course it worked. Not a dog barked, not a child cried, not a car revved up when Alice was sleeping till noon on a Sunday.

"No, I live in Fulham," I said, thinking how dull and predictable it sounded.

"Oh I thought . . ." Keith didn't say what he thought but he didn't ask about my flat in Fulham.

Malcolm was saying that Alice and I should think about the yachting holiday. Keith and Rosemary were thinking about it, weren't they? They were, and it would be great fun if we went as a six, then we could sort of take over in case the other people were ghastly.

"It sounds great," I said dishonestly and politely. "Yes, you must tell me more about it."

"Weren't you meant to be going on holiday with old Thing?" said Alice practically.

"That was very vague," I snapped. "The weekend in Paris was definite but the holiday . . . nothing was fixed. Anyway weren't you meant to be going to a cottage with your Thing . . .?"

Everyone looked at me, it was as if I had belched loudly or taken off my blouse unexpectedly. They were waiting for me to finish and in a well-bred way rather hoping that I wouldn't. Their eyes were like shouts of encouragement.

"You said that if his wife was put away for another couple of weeks you might go to their very unsocialistic second home? Didn't you?"

Alice laughed, everyone else looked stunned.

Melissa spooned out huge helpings of a ten-thousand-calorie ice cream with no appearance of having noticed a social gaffe.

"Well, when the two of you make up your minds, do tell us," she said. "It would be great fun, and we have to let these guys know by the end of the month, apparently. They sound very nice actually. Jeremy and Jacky they're called, he makes jewellery and Jacky is an artist. They've lots of other friends going too, a couple of girls who work with Jeremy and their boy friends, I think. It's just Jeremy and Jacky who are . . . who are organizing it all."

Like a flash I saw it. Melissa thought Alice and I were lesbians. She was being her usual tolerant liberated self over it all. If you like people, what they do in bed is none of your business. HOW could she be so crass as to think that about Alice and myself? My face burned with rage. Slowly like heavy flowers falling off a tree came all the reasons. I was dressed so severely, I had asked could I bring a woman, not a man, to her party. I had been manless in Greece when she met me the first time, I had just put on this appalling show of spitely spiteful dikey jealousy about Alice's relationship with a man. Oh God. Oh God.

I knew little or nothing about lesbians. Except that they were different. I never was friendly with anyone who was one. I knew they didn't wear bowler hats, but I thought that they did go in for this aggressive sort of picking on one another in public. Oh God.

Alice was talking away about the boat with interest. How much would it cost? Who decided where and when they would stop? Did Jeremy and Jacky sound madly camp and would they drive everyone mad looking for sprigs of tarragon in case the pot au feu was ruined?

Everyone was laughing, and Malcolm was being liberated and tolerant and left-wing.

"Come on, Alice, nothing wrong with tarragon, nothing wrong with fussing about food, we all fuss about something. Anyway, they didn't say anything to make us think that they would fuss about food, stop typecasting."

He said it in a knowing way. I felt with a sick dread that he could have gone on and said, "After all, I don't typecast you and expect you to wear a hairnet and military jacket."

I looked at Alice, her thin white face all lit up laughing. Of course I felt strongly about her, she was my friend. She was very important to me. I didn't need to act with Alice. I resented the way the awful man with his alcoholic wife treated her, but was never jealous of him because Alice didn't really give her mind to him. And as for giving anything else . . . well I suppose they made a lot of love together but so did I and the unsatisfactory journalist. I didn't want Alice in that way. I mean that was madness, we wouldn't even know what to do. We would laugh ourselves silly.

Kiss Alice?

Run and lay my head on Alice's breast?

Have Alice stroke my hair?

That's what people who were in love did. We didn't do that.

Did Alice need me? Yes, of course she did. She often told me that I was the only bit of sanity in her life, that I was safe. I had known her for ten years, hardly anyone else she knew nowadays went back that far.

Malcolm filled my coffee cup.

"Do persuade her to come with us," he said gently to me. "She's marvellous really, and I know you'd both enjoy yourselves."

I looked at him like a wild animal. I saw us fitting into their lives, another splendid liberal concept, slightly racy, perfectly acceptable. "We went on holiday with that super gay couple, most marvellous company, terribly entertaining." Which of us would he refer to as the He? Would there be awful things like leaving us alone together, or nodding tolerantly over our little rows?

The evening and not only the evening stretched ahead in horror. Alice had been laying into the wine, would she be able to drive? If not, oh God, would they offer us a double bed in some spare room in this mansion? Would they suggest a taxi home to Fulham since my place was nearer? Would they speculate afterwards why we kept two separate establishments in the first place?

Worse, would I ever be able to laugh with Alice about it or was it too important? I might disgust her, alarm her, turn her against me. I might unleash all kinds of love that she had for me deep down, and how would I handle that?

Of course I loved Alice, I just didn't realize it. But what lover, what poor unfortunate lover in the history of the whole damn thing, ever had the tragedy of Coming Out in Malcolm and Melissa's lovely home in Holland Park?

Notting Hill Gate

Everyone knew that Daphne's friend Mike was a shit and to give us our due most of us said so. But she laughed and said we were full of rubbish. She agreed, still laughing, to take the address of the battered-wife place, just in case, then we gave her a lovely fur jacket that Mike wouldn't be able to share, and she left us and married him. We never saw her again. But we had to find a new secretary.

Nowadays nobody thinks anymore that you meet a lot of interesting people on a newspaper, so you don't have breathless, overeducated, anxious-to-please Oxford graduates rushing around doing all the dirty work willingly as well as all the ordinary work efficiently. Nowadays you have temps earning a fortune, but with no security, and no plans, and no interest in what they're doing. My woolly, right-minded, left-thinking views thought that this was unfair on the girls . . . they had no career structure, no dignity, and the agencies made all the money. But then from time to time my wrong-minded right-wing views made me wonder what the country was coming to when you couldn't get a girl who could spell, read, take orders, and be grateful for a good job. It was a month of temps before Rita came.

Rita was big and black and tough about luncheon vouchers, and wanted us to buy her a season ticket on the tube. She walked not like other people walk . . . she rolled along as if she had wheels in her shoes. She had a lot of low-cut purple or green blouses and she wore a series of desperately tight orange or yellow skirts. Marian, who deals with readers' letters, said she thought that Rita's skirts might rip open every evening after the strain of the day, and she would throw them away.

She looked slow and lazy, and as if she was thinking of something else almost all the time, but she was far better than anyone we had had up until then. You didn't have to tell Rita twice that there were ten hopeless people who kept coming into the office with ideas for stories, and that none of the ideas were ever any use. Rita just nodded vaguely, but she knew how to deal with them. She would write down what they said, type it out, and put it in a file. The people would go away satisfied that things were under way, and Rita had all the ideas neatly put in the H file, under Hopeless.

After three weeks, we realized two things: firstly that Rita was still there, that she hadn't walked out at 11 A.M. one day like the other temps were in the habit of doing, and secondly that she didn't need to be watched and advised all the time. Martin, the features editor, asked her if she would like a permanent job, and Rita looked as if she had been offered a potato crisp at a bus stop, and said she might as well. But only if he would pay for a monthly ticket on the underground for her.

Rita lived in Notting Hill but that's all she said. This was a change, too, because normally whoever sat in that desk seemed to unburden themselves of a long and complicated life history. There was nothing about Daphne's Mike that we didn't know, his deprived childhood, his poor relationship with Daphne's mother, his disastrous early marriage . . . even Daphne's black eyes were explained away by some incredible misunderstanding, some terrible mistake for which Mike was now heartbroken. All the useless temps had told us tales about their flats being too far out, or their fellows thinking they owned them, or distant boyfriends in Cumbria or on sheep stations in Australia who wanted them to throw up the job and come home and marry them. Rita never told us anything.

"Do you live in a flat or with your family?" Marian asked her once.

"Why?" asked Rita.

"Oh well I just wondered," said Marian, a bit confused.

"Oh that's all right," said Rita quite happily, but didn't answer the question.

She used her luncheon vouchers to buy a huge sandwich and a carton of milk, and she ate it quietly reading a trashy magazine, or at least one that was marginally more trashy than our own features pages. Because she was so uncommunicative, I suppose we were more interested in her. She got the odd phone call, and I found myself listening to her side of the conversation with all the attention of a village postmistress. She would speak in her slow flat tone, smiling only rarely, and seemed to be agreeing with whoever was on the other end about some course of action.

Once she said, "He's a bad bastard I tell you, he used to be a friend of my husband . . . get out of it if you can." Full of secret information, I told Marian and the others that Rita had a husband. Martin said he had always supposed she did;

nothing about Rita would suggest she was a lonely girl who went home to an empty bed, she was too sexy. We had long arguments about his attitudes, like that only sexy women had husbands and that all single women went home to empty beds . . . but it was an old and well-worn line of argument. I was more interested that he thought Rita sexy. I thought she was overblown, and fat, and very gaudily dressed, but assumed that West Indians might like brighter colours than we would because of all their bright sunlight back home. Sexy. No.

I was waiting one night in a pub for my sister, who's always late, and I had forgotten to bring anything to read. So I looked around hopefully in case anyone had abandoned an evening paper. There was one on the floor near a very good-looking blond lad and I went over to pick it up. He put his foot on it immediately.

"That's mine," he said.

He was very drunk. When someone's very drunk you don't make an issue about nicking their evening paper. I apologized and said I thought it was one that someone had finished with. He looked at me coldly and forgave me. Irritated, I went back to my seat and wished that my sister could for once in her life turn up at something approaching the time arranged. The blond boy now stumbled over to my table and in exaggerated gestures began to present me the paper. He managed to knock my gin and tonic over my skirt and the contents of the ashtray on top of that. I could have killed him I was so annoyed, but before I had time to do anything, a big shadow fell on the whole scene. It was of all people Rita.

She didn't seem embarrassed, surprised, or apologetic. She said, "You drunken bum," pulled him away back to a distant seat, ordered me another gin and tonic, brought a cloth, and a lot of paper napkins, all in what looked like slow movements, but they only took a minute or two all the same.

I was so surprised to see her that I forgot about the disgusting mess seeping into my best cream-coloured linen skirt. What was even more amazing, she offered no explanation. I'd have said I was sorry about my friend, or made some nervous joke about it being a small world. Rita just said, "Hot water, and if that doesn't work, dry cleaning tomorrow, I suppose." She said it in exactly the same way she'd say, "We can try the usual photographer for the fashion pictures, and if he's busy get the agency ones I suppose." With no involvement at all.

Hot water didn't work very well, the whole skirt now looked appalling. When my sister Trudy came in I was in such a temper that it frightened her.

"You can wear a coat," she said, trying to placate me.

"I haven't got a bloody coat," I said. "It's the middle of bloody summer. My coat's at home on the other side of London, isn't it?"

Rita asked with the mild concern of a bystander and not the sense of responsibility of someone whose drunken boyfriend had just ruined an expensive skirt:

"Do you want something to wear? I'll give you something."

Trudy thought she was an innocent concerned

bystander and started to gush that it would be perfectly all right thank you. . . .

Rita said, "I live upstairs, you can come up and choose what you'd like."

Now this was too good to miss. Firstly I had discovered that Rita had a white boyfriend who looked like a Greek god, that he was as drunk as a maggot, and that Rita lived over a pub. Now I was going to see her place . . . this would be a great dossier for the office.

"Thanks, Rita," I said ungraciously, and left Trudy open-mouthed behind me.

As we went out the pub door and almost immediately through another, I wondered, Was I mad? Rita's clothes would go around me four times. How could she or I think that any skirt of hers would fit me?

She opened the door of a cheaply furnished, but neat and bright, apartment. Two small and very pig-tailed girls sat on a big cushion looking at a big colour telly.

"This is Miss that I work with," said Rita.

"Hallo, Miss," they chorused, and went back to looking at bionic things on the screen.

We walked into a bedroom also very neat and bright, and Rita opened a cupboard. She took out what looked like two yards of material with a ribbon around the top.

"It's a wrap-around skirt, it fits any size," she said. I got out of the dirty dishcloth I was wearing, and wrapped it around, and tied the ribbon. It looked fine.

"Thank you very much indeed, Rita," I said, trying at the same time to take in every detail for the telling tomorrow in the pub, while Rita would be sitting at her desk. There were big prints on

41

the wall, Chinese girls, and horses with flying manes. The bed had a beautiful patchwork quilt, it looked as if it could sleep four people comfortably.

"Are those your little girls?" I asked, a question brought on indirectly by the bed I suppose.

"They're Martie and Anna, they live here," said Rita.

I realized immediately she hadn't told me whether they were her daughters, her sisters, her nieces, or her friends. And I also realized that I wasn't going to ask any more.

"You can leave the other skirt," said Rita and then, for the very first time volunteering some information, she added, "Andrew has quite enough money to pay to have it dry-cleaned, and I'll bring it into the office for you on Friday."

Oh, so he was called Andrew, the young beautiful boy, and he had plenty of money, oh ho. I was learning something anyway. I didn't dare to ask her whether he was her boyfriend. It wasn't that Rita was superior or distant, but she drew a shutter down like someone slamming a door, and didn't find it rude or impolite. It left you feeling rude and impolite instead.

I thanked her for the skirt. Martie and Anna said "Goodbye, Miss" without removing their eyes from the screen. Somehow *they* seemed so much at ease with the goings-on that it made me very annoyed with myself for feeling diffident because this was a black house and I was a white woman. Who creates these barriers anyway? I argued with myself, and, taking a deep breath, said to Rita on the stairs:

"Why do they wear their hair in those tight

little pigtails? They'd be much prettier if their hair was loose."

"Maybe," Rita shrugged, as if I had asked her why she didn't move the coffee percolator to another table in the office to give herself more room. "Yeah maybe," she agreed.

"Do you like them with their hair all tied up like that?" I asked courageously.

"Oh it has nothing to do with me," she said, and we were out on the street and into the pub again.

Trudy had a face like thunder when I came back but she greeted Rita pleasantly enough, and asked her if she would like to join us.

Rita shook her head. "This drunken baby has to be taken to bed," she said enigmatically, and she frog-marched the handsome Andrew out the door without a good-bye. I ran to the window to see whether she was taking him up to her own flat, but they had gone too quickly. There was no way of knowing whether they had gone in her door or turned the corner, and I didn't really want to run out into the street to check.

Trudy wasn't very interested in my speculation.

"I don't suppose I should have been so surprised to see her," I reflected. "I knew she lived in Notting Hill. This is a very black area around here, too, I suppose."

"Quite a few white people live here as well," said Trudy acidly, and I forgot that she had just paid what seemed like an enormous sum of money for a very small, very twee house around the corner.

The others were interested at lunchtime the

next day. They wanted to know what Andrew looked like.

"Like that actor who plays the part of Henry in that serial," I said, meaning an actor whose dizzying looks had sent people of all ages into some kind of wistful speculation as to what a future with him might be like.

"You mean Andy Sparks," said Marian, and with a thud I realized it *was* Andy Sparks. It was just that his face seemed so contorted, and he hadn't worn the boyish eager look nor the boyish eager anorak he always wore in the serial.

"My God, it was definitely him," I said. By this time the others were losing interest, they thought I had gone into fantasy. Large lumbering black Rita, who read rubbishy magazines, who never seemed interested in anything, not even herself . . . she could never have been the *petite amie* of Andy Sparks.

"We did a feature on him about three weeks ago," said Martin. "No, it can't have been the same guy, you only think so because they had the same name."

"You did say Rita was sexy," I pointed out, trying to bolster up my claim that she might be so sexy that she could have been seen with the superstar of the moment.

"Not *that* sexy," said Martin, and they began to talk about other things.

"Don't tell her I told you," I said. I felt it was important that Rita shouldn't think I had been blabbing about her. It was as if I had gone into her territory by being in that pub, and I shouldn't be carrying back tales from it.

I looked up the back pages surreptitiously. It *was* the same guy. He had looked unhappy and drawn compared to the pictures we used of him, but it was the same Andrew.

On Friday Rita handed me a parcel and an envelope. The parcel was my skirt, which she said the cleaners had made a lovely balls of. They were sorry but with a stain like that it was owner's risk only, and she had alas agreed to owner's risk. They were, she said, the best cleaners around. I looked at the docket and saw she was right. I also saw the name on the docket. It said "A. Sparks." She took the docket away and gave me the envelope. It was a gift-token for almost exactly what the skirt had cost, and it was from the shop where I had in fact bought it. Not a big chain-store but a boutique.

"I can't take it," I said.

"You might as well, he can afford it." She shrugged.

"But if it had been a stranger, not a . . . er . . . well someone you knew, then I wouldn't have got it replaced," I stammered.

"That's your good luck, then," said Rita and went back to her desk. She hadn't even left me the docket so that I could show the others I was right about the name.

At lunchtime I invited Rita out with me.

"I thought you were having lunch with that woman who wrote the book about flowers," she said, neither interested nor bored, just stating a fact.

"She rang and cancelled," I said.

"I didn't put her through to you," said Rita.

"No, well I rang her on the direct line actually," I said, furious to have my gesture of taking her out to lunch made into an issue. "I didn't feel like talking to her."

"And you feel like talking to me?" asked Rita with one of her rare smiles.

"I'd like to buy you a nice lunch and relax with you and thank you for going to all that trouble over my skirt," I snapped. It sounded the most ungracious invitation to lunch ever given.

Even if I had been down on my knees with roses I don't think Rita would have reacted differently.

"Thanks very much, but I don't think I will. I don't like long boozy lunches. I have too much work to do in the afternoons here anyway."

"For Christ's sake it doesn't have to be long and boozy, and though you may not have noticed it, I work here in the afternoons myself," I said like a spoiled child.

"Okay then," she said, took up her shoulder bag, and with no coat to cover her fat bouncing bottom and half-exposed large black breasts, she rolled down the corridor with me, into the lift, and out into the street.

I chose a fairly posh place, I wasn't going to have her say I went to less expensive places with her than with the journalists or people I interviewed.

She looked at the menu as if it were a list of cuttings we needed her to get from the library. I asked her if she would like pâté and said that they made it very well here.

"Sure," she said.

I could see it was going to be hard going.

We ordered one glass of wine each, she seemed to accept that, too, as if it were extra dictation. The few starts I made were doomed. When I asked her whether she found the work interesting in the office, she said it was fine. Better than where she had worked before? Oh yes she

46

supposed so. Where had that been? Hadn't I seen it on her application? She'd been with a lot of firms as a temp. I was driven to talk about the traffic in London, the refuge of all who run out of conversation.

Just then a birdbrained rival of mine on another newspaper came over. Normally I would have walked under buses to avoid her. Today she seemed like a rescue ship sent to a desert island.

She sat down, had a glass of wine, wouldn't eat because of some new diet, wouldn't take her coat off because she was in a hurry, and looked at Rita with interest. I introduced them just name by name without saying where either worked.

"I expect you're being interviewed," the bird-brain, highly paid writer said to Rita. Rita shrugged. She wasn't embarrassed, she wasn't waiting for me to give her a lead. She shrugged because she couldn't be bothered to say anything.

At least now I didn't have to do all the talking. Rita and I heard how hard life was, how long it took to get anywhere these days because of the traffic, how hopeless hairdressers were, how they never listened to what you wanted done, how silly the new summer clothes were, how shoes didn't last three months, how selfish show-biz people were making big productions out of being interviewed, instead of being so grateful for all the free publicity. Then her eyes brightened.

"I'm doing Andy Sparks," she said. "Yes I know, your lot had him last week, but he's promised to tell me all about his private life. I'm taking him to dinner in a little club I've just joined, so that people won't keep coming over to disturb us. He's meant to be absolutely as dumb as anything, only intelligent when he gets lines to read.

Anyway we'll see, we can't go far wrong if he tells a bit about the loves of his life. I only hope it won't be religion or his mother or a collie dog or something."

Rita sat half listening as she had been doing all along. I started to say about three different things and got a coughing fit. Finally it dawned on the world's most confident bad writer that she was losing her audience so she excused herself on the grounds that she wanted to go and get herself smartened up at the hairdresser, just in case this beautiful man by some lovely chance wasn't in love with his mother or the man who directed the series.

"Do people usually talk about him like that?" I asked Rita.

"About who?" she said.

"About Andy Sparks," I said relentlessly.

"Oh, I suppose they do," she said uncaringly. "I mean he's quite famous really, isn't he? In everyone's homes every night—as they say."

"Did you know him before he was a star?" I asked.

"No, I only got to know him a couple of years ago," she said.

"Are you fond of each other?" I asked, again amazed at my bravery.

"Why?" she said.

"Well, I thought that he seemed very dependent on you the other night."

"Oh, he was just pissed the other night," she said.

There was a silence.

"Look," I said. "I don't want to talk about him if you don't. I just thought it was interesting, there you are knowing him very well while we

48

just had to do bits and pieces about him to make up that feature. I suppose I wonder why you didn't say anything."

"And have my picture in the paper you mean? Like Andy Sparks and the girl he can't have . . . that sort of thing."

"No, of course we wouldn't have done anything like . . ."

"Of course you would," she said flatly. "You work on a newspaper."

"There might have been a bit of pressure, yes, but in the end it would have been up to you. Come on, Rita, you work with us, you're part of our team, we wouldn't rat on you that way."

"Maybe," she said.

"But why can't he have you . . .?" I went on. "You said Andy Sparks and the girl he can't have."

"Oh well, I'm married to someone else," she said.

"I see," I said, though I didn't.

Another silence.

"And does he want to marry you, Andy, I mean?"

"Oh yes, I think Andrew would like to, but I don't think he really knows what he wants."

"Do you not want to leave your husband?" I asked, remembering suddenly that there had been no sign of a man around that little flat.

"He's inside, served four years of fifteen, he'll probably have to do two more anyway."

"Oh God, I'm sorry I asked."

"No you're not, if you hadn't asked you wouldn't know. You want to know, it's partly you yourself, it's partly your job. You all like to know things."

49

It was the longest speech I'd heard her make. I didn't know what to say.

She went on.

"Listen, I'm not coming back to the office. I don't want to go back now, because everyone already knows I know him. Oh yes they do, you told them, but you told them not to mention it, I'm not a fool. I can't bear offices where everyone knows everything about everyone else, that's why I stayed so long with you lot . . . you didn't talk too much about your own lives, and you didn't pry into mine. I thought you'd like me being fairly buttoned up . . . but no, it's all of you who've been doing the prying. . . ."

"I understand what you mean, Rita, honestly I do. The girls who did your job before were always so boring about their boyfriends and their life's history . . . but seriously I understand if . . ."

She looked at me.

"You understand nothing if I may say so. You don't understand the first little thing. And because it isn't clear to you at once, you turn it all into a little mystery and have to solve it. You don't understand why Andrew fancies me, you don't understand why I wait for a husband to come out of prison, you don't understand whether those kids Martie and Anna are mine or not."

"It's none of my business," I said, distressed and unable to cope with the articulate and very, very angry Rita. "I can't say anything right now."

Rita calmed down. Her eyes didn't flash, but they were not back to the dead dull look they normally held.

"Well, I could tell you a few things which would give you information, but you still

50

wouldn't *understand*. Martie and Anna aren't my girls, they're Nat's. Nat is my husband. Nat is in gaol because he beat Myrtle to death. Myrtle was my best friend. Myrtle always loved Nat. Nat never loved Myrtle but he had two children by her. Even after he married me, he would see Myrtle. I knew, I didn't mind, that's the way Nat was. I knew it at the time, I know it now. Myrtle found this other fella, he wanted to marry her, take the kids and all he would. Myrtle told Nat, Nat said no, he didn't want another man raising his kids. Myrtle asked me what she should do. I said I thought she should marry the other fella, but then my advice was prejudiced.

"Myrtle said I was right, and she told Nat. They had a great row. Nat he lost his temper and he beat Myrtle and he beat her, and she died. I telephoned the police and they came, and they took him, and he got fifteen years and I look after Anna and Martie."

She paused and took a drink of her wine, and though I didn't understand I could approach an understanding of how strong she must have been, must still be.

"And you won't understand either why Andrew wants me to go away with him. He just needs me. I don't know whether he loves me or not, or whether he knows what love is, but he needs me, because I . . . well I'm what he needs. And he doesn't understand either, he can't understand that Nat don't mind me seeing him. He knows that Nat has a lot of friends who tell him or his friends what's going on. But Nat doesn't mind me going about with a white man, a white actor from the television. Nat thinks that's

51

just company for me. Now can you understand any of that at all?"

At the end of the week when the birdbrain's story appeared it was pretty tame stuff. She did have an angle that Andy Sparks had some mystery woman in his life, someone he leaned on, someone he needed, but was not prepared to discuss.

Rita came around that day to collect some things she'd left in the drawer of her desk, and to pick up her salary. She came at lunchtime when there was nobody there, except her replacement, who was full of chat and said that she had told Rita all about her fiancé being mean with money. She asked Rita if she thought that was a bad omen. Rita had said that she couldn't care less.

"Odd sort of woman, I thought," said the replacement. "Very untidy, sort of trampishly dressed really. Funny that she wasn't more pleasant. Black people are usually happy-looking, I always think."

Queensway

Pat wished that she didn't have such a lively imagination when she was reading the advertisements. When she saw something like "Third girl wanted for quiet flat. Own room, with central heating" she had dark fears that it might be a witches' coven looking for new recruits. Why mention that the flat was quiet? Could central heating be some code for bonfires? But she couldn't afford a flat of her own, and she didn't know anyone who wanted to share, so it was either this or stay forever in the small hotel which was eating into her savings.

She dreaded going for the interview, which was why she kept putting off answering any of the offers. What would they ask her? Would they give her a test to see whether she was an interesting conversationalist? Might they want to know all about her family background? Did they ask things like her attitude towards promiscuity, or spiritualism, or the monarchy? Or would it be a very factual grilling, like could she prove that she wouldn't leave a ring around the bath or use the phone without paying for her calls?

There were about twenty women working in the bank, why did none of them want to share? she complained to herself. At least she knew something about them, that they were normal during the daytime anyway. But no, they were all well established in London, married to men who wouldn't do the shopping, or living with blokes who wouldn't wash their own socks, or sharing flats with girls who wouldn't clean up the kitchen after them. There was no place in any of their lives for Pat.

Three months was all she was going to allow herself in the hotel, three months to get over the breakup of her home, to calm herself down about Auntie Delia being taken away to hospital and not recognizing anyone ever again. It was better, the doctors said, that Pat should go right away, because Auntie Delia really didn't know who she was anymore, and would never know. She wasn't unhappy, she was just, well there were many technical terms for it, but she was in a world of her own.

If you have worked in a bank in Leicester, you can usually get a job working in a bank in London. But if you've lived with Auntie Delia, funny, eccentric, fanciful, generous, undemanding, for years and years, it's not so easy to find a new home.

"What should I ask them?" she begged the small, tough Terry who knew everything, and who had no fears about anything in this life. "I'll feel so stupid not knowing the kind of questions that they'll expect *me* to ask."

Terry thought it was so simple that it hardly needed to be stated.

"Money, housework, and privacy are the only things girls fight about in flats," she said knowledgeably.

"Find out exactly what your rent covers, make sure there aren't any hidden rates to be paid later, ask how they work the food—does everyone have their own shelf in the fridge, or do they take it in turns buying basics? If you are all going to have a week each in charge of the food, get a list of what people buy and how much they spend. Stupid to have you buying gorgeous fresh-ground coffee or expensive tea, when they only get instant and tea bags."

"And what should I ask about housework?" Pat wondered.

"Do they have a Hoover, if so who uses it and when? It would be awful if they were all manic house cleaners, washing down paintwork every day. And examine the place carefully, they might be so careless that the place is full of mice and rats."

Privacy meant that Pat was to inquire what arrangements they had about the sitting room:

Did people book it if they were going to ask anyone in, or did everyone eat, play, watch telly together, or did people entertain in their own bedrooms?

So, armed with all this intelligence, she dialled the "Third Girl wanted, lovely flat, near park, own room, friendly atmosphere" advertisement. Auntie Delia would have snorted at the ad, and said that they sounded like a bunch of dikes to her. Pat still couldn't believe that Auntie Delia didn't snort and say outrageous things anymore.

The girl who answered the phone sounded a little breathless.

"I can't really talk now, the boss is like a devil today, he says I shouldn't have given this number. Can I have your number and I'll phone you back later when he leaves the office? It's a super flat, we wouldn't want to leave it in a million years, it's just that Nadia went off to Washington and we can't afford it just for two."

Pat didn't like the sound of it. It seemed a bit fast and trendy. She didn't like people who said "super" in that upward inflection, she didn't like the thought of people suddenly dashing off to Washington, it was too racy. And she thought the name Nadia was affected. Still, she might use them as a rehearsal. There was no law saying you had to take the first flat you saw.

The breathless girl rang back ten minutes later. "He's gone out for an hour," she confided. "So I'm going to make use of it, ringing all the people back. I thought I'd start with you because you work in a bank, you might get us all an overdraft."

Pat took this little pleasantry poorly, but still you had to practice flat-getting somewhere, and she arranged to call at eight o'clock. She made a list of questions, and she promised herself that she would take everything in, so that she would go better equipped to the next and more serious interview.

It was an old building, and there were a lot of stairs but no lift. Perhaps they all became permanently breathless from climbing those stairs. Feeling foolish to be feeling nervous, Pat rang the bell. It had a strange echoing chime, not a buzz. It would have, thought Pat. Nadias, and Washingtons, and Supers, naturally they'd have to have a bell that pealed rather than one which buzzed.

Joy wasn't at all breathless now that she was home. She wore a long housecoat, and she smelled of some very, very expensive perfume. She was welcoming, she remembered Pat's name, she apologized for the stairs but said that you got used to them after a month or so. There were eighty-three steps, counting the flat bits between floors, and they did encourage you not to be forgetful about things like keys.

Pat stared around the hall. It was literally covered in pictures and ornaments, and there were rugs on the walls as well. At one end there were a couple of flower baskets hanging and at the other a carved hall stand full of dried flowers.

"It's far too nice to sit inside," said Joy, and for a wild moment Pat thought that they would have to go down all the stairs again before she had even seen the flat.

"Come into Marigold's room, and we'll have a drink on the balcony."

Marigold! thought Pat. Yes, it would have to be Marigold.

A big room, like one of those film sets for an

56

Anna Neagle movie, with little writing desks, and a piano with photographs on top. There were flowers here, too, and looped lacey curtains leading out to a balcony. There in a wheelchair sat Marigold. The most beautiful woman that Pat had ever seen. She had eyes so blue that they didn't really seem to be part of a human body. She could have played any number of parts as a ravishing visitor from Mars. She had so much curly hair, long, shiny, and curly, that it looked like a wig for a heroine, but you knew it wasn't a wig. She smiled at Pat as if all her life she had been waiting to meet her.

"I wish Joy would tell people I live in a wheel-chair," she said, waving at Pat to get her to sit down. She poured some white wine into a beautiful cut-crystal glass and handed it to her. "I honestly think it's so unfair to let people climb all those stairs and then face them with what they think will be a nursing job instead of a home."

"Well I don't, I never, you mustn't . . ." stammered Pat.

"Rubbish," said Joy casually. "If I said you were in a wheelchair nobody would ever come at all. Anyone who has come wants to move in, so I'm right and you're wrong."

"Have you had many applicants?" asked Pat.

"Five, no six, including the lady with the cats," said Joy.

Pat's list had gone out of her head, and she had no intention of taking it from her handbag. They sat and talked about flowers, and how wonderful that in a city the size of London people still had a respect for their parks, and rarely stole plants or cut blooms for themselves from the common display. They talked on about the patchwork quilt that Marigold had made, how difficult it was to spot woodworm in some furniture, and how a dishonest dealer could treat it with something temporary and then it all came out only when you had the thing bought and installed. They had more wine, and said how nice it was to have an oasis like a balcony in a city of ten million or whatever it was, and wondered how did people live who didn't have a view over a park.

"We must have a little supper," Marigold said. "Pat must be starving."

No protests were heeded, a quick move of her wrist, and the wheelchair was moving through the pots and shrubs of the balcony, the flowers and little writing bureaux of the bedroom, the bric-a-brac of the hall, and they were in a big pine kitchen. Barely had Joy laid the table for three before Marigold had made and cooked a cheese soufflé, a salad had already been prepared, and there was garlic bread, baking slowly in the oven. Pat felt guilty but hungry, and strangely happy. It was the first evening meal anywhere that seemed like home since they had taken Auntie Delia away.

She felt it would be crass to ask how much did people pay and who bought the groceries, and what kind of cleaning would the third girl be expected to do. Neither Marigold nor Joy seemed to think such things should be discussed, so they talked about plays they had seen, or in Marigold's case books she had read, and it was all as if they were just three friends having a nice dinner at home instead of people trying to organize a business deal.

At eleven o'clock Pat realized by the deep

chiming of a clock that she had been there three hours. She would have to make a move. Never had she felt socially so ill at ease. She wondered what she should say to bring the visit to an end and the subject of why she was there at all into the open. She knew quite a lot about them. Marigold had polio and never left the flat. Joy worked in a solicitor's office as a clerk, but next year was going to go into apprenticeship there and become a solicitor too. Marigold seemed to have some money of her own, and did the housework and the cooking. They had met some years ago when Marigold had put an ad in the paper. Marigold had found the flat.

Nadia was mentioned, a little. There were references to Nadia's room and Nadia's clock, which was the big one that chimed, and some chat about the time they had made the curry for Nadia's dinner party and everyone had gone on fire from it.

Resolutely Pat stood up and said that her little hotel closed at midnight and she had better get back, as they didn't have a night porter.

"Well, when shall we expect you?" asked Marigold.

Pat, who hadn't even been shown her room, hadn't been informed about how much rent, what kind of life-style was to be expected, was stunned.

"What about the five other people, and the lady with the cats?" she asked desperately.

"Oh no," said Marigold.

"No indeed," said Joy.

"Well, can I think about it?" Pat asked, trying to buy time. "I don't know whether I could afford to live here, and you mightn't like my friends, and we haven't really sorted anything out."

Marigold looked like an old trusted friend who has suddenly and unexpectedly been rebuffed.

"Of course you must decide for yourself, and perhaps you have somewhere else in mind. We are terrible, Joy, not to give Pat details of rent and things. We're simply hopeless."

"The rent is £20, and we usually spend about £10 a week each on food, and flowers and wine," said Joy.

That was expensive, but not for what you got. You got a magnificent home, you got lovely meals, you got two very bright nice women to live with.

Pat heard her own voice saying, "Fine. Yes, if you think I'd fit in here with you, that's fine. Can I come at the weekend?"

That night she wondered what she had done. Next morning she wondered whether she had been insane.

"I don't know," said tough little Terry. "If the food's as good as all that, if the one in the wheelchair does all the work, if the place is like something out of *Home and Garden*, I think you're laughing. If you don't like it you can always move out."

"I didn't even look at my bedroom," said Pat with a wail.

"They'll hardly give you a coal bin hole," said Terry practically.

Joy rang her breathlessly that day.

"It's super that you're coming. Marigold's so pleased. She asked me to tell you that there's plenty of room in your bed-sitting room for anything you want to bring, so don't worry about space. Any pictures or furniture you like."

Pat wondered why Marigold didn't ring

herself. She was at home, she didn't have to avoid a spying boss. Pat also wondered whether this was a polite way of telling her that there were four walls and nothing else in her room.

On Saturday she arrived with two students who ran a flat-moving service. They carried up her little tables, her rocking chair, and her suitcases. They had cluttered up her hotel bedroom ridiculously, and she wondered whether there would be any more room for them where she was going. As they all puffed up the eighty-three steps, Pat felt very foolish indeed.

Joy let them in, with little cries of excitement. They paraded through the bedecked hall to a huge sunny room, which had recesses for cupboards, a big bed, and a washbasin. Compared to the rest of the flat, it looked like an empty warehouse.

Joy fussed along behind them. "Marigold said we should empty it so that you wouldn't feel restricted. But there's lots of furniture available. There are curtains and shelves for these"—she waved at the recesses. "Marigold thought you might want your own things."

Pat paid the students, and sat down in the warehouse. Even her rocking chair looked lost. When she unpacked it wouldn't be much better. Auntie Delia's things would look lovely here. All those monstrous vases, even that beaded curtain. Maybe she should send for them. They were all in the little house in Leicester. They would be hers when Auntie Delia died. Strictly speaking they were hers already, since she had rented the house out just to get money to pay for her poor aunt in the nursing home. The rent covered the fees. The tenants didn't like all the overcrowding from the furniture but Pat had insisted the house should remain untouched since Auntie Delia *could* get better one day and *might* come home. She felt slightly disloyal thinking about taking Auntie Delia's treasures, but surely she couldn't live in a barn like this while Auntie Delia lived in a world of her own, and the tenants lived in a house that they thought vastly overstuffed with things they didn't like.

It was morning coffee time, so she gathered from the smell of fresh coffee coming from the kitchen. She was right, they assembled on the balcony, and had coffee from lovely china cups.

"I'll be sending to Leicester for my real furniture this week," she said.

"We'll be dying to see it," said Marigold, her china-blue eyes lighting up with excitement.

"And I must give you some money and everything," blurted out Pat. "I'm not much good at this you know, not having shared a flat before."

"Oh, Joy will look after that," said Marigold. "She's so good with money, working in that office where there's a lot of accountancy. She should have been a solicitor from the start you know, it's so silly to have waited until she's twenty-seven before starting her indentures."

"I'd never have done it at all if it weren't for you," said Joy gratefully. "I'd still be working on there and taking my money each week."

"It would have been pointless," said Marigold. Her blue eyes looked out over the park, where people who weren't in wheelchairs jumped and played and ran about.

Pat sighed happily. It was so peaceful here and she had the whole week-end before facing the bank again. Nobody ever told you how easy it was to find a flat.

"Would you like me to do any shopping or anything?" she asked helpfully.

"Joy does that on Friday nights, we're very well organized," smiled Marigold. "We have a small deep freeze as well. It helps a great deal."

While the rest of London sweated and fussed and shopped and dragged themselves through traffic jams or in crowded trains to the seaside, Joy and Marigold and Pat sat peacefully reading, listening to music, or chatting. By Monday Pat felt she had been on a rest cure. She and Joy had done a lot of the washing up, and preparing of things, rougher jobs like peeling potatoes and cutting up meat, and taking out rubbish.

Joy was friendly and eager to do everything, Marigold was gentle, serene, and calm. Pat began to think that she couldn't have found two more perfect flatmates.

On Sunday night she telephoned the people in Leicester and asked them to arrange to have seventeen pieces of furniture, some huge, some tiny, collected and delivered to London.

Nobody had telephoned the flat, nobody had gone out. Pat wondered what happened if you invited a friend in for supper. Would they all eat as a foursome? She saw no other way.

She gave Joy £80, and asked what to do about the tenner for food.

"I'll spend £20 this week, and you spend it next week," said Joy cheerfully.

Pat wondered where Marigold's tenner came into it but said nothing. Why upset things? Things are not always so peaceful in life, it's silly to question just for the sake of questioning.

On Tuesday she rang Joy at work to say that she was going to the theatre so would not be home for dinner.

"Oh." Joy sounded upset.

"But that's all right, isn't it?" asked Pat. "Marigold won't start to cook until we get home anyway, so it's not a question of letting her know in advance. I'd ring her at home but I . . . well, I just thought I'd ring you."

"Oh yes, it's better to ring me," said Joy. "No, no problems. I'll pop home at lunchtime and tell her, it's not far. Don't worry."

It all seemed very odd to Pat, but she put it out of her mind.

On Thursday her furniture arrived. Marigold was delighted with it. She whirled around in the wheelchair, stroking this and patting that.

"Lovely inlay," she said.

"We must strip this down," she said.

"What a magnificent curtain. Wouldn't it look lovely on the balcony?" she said.

So of course Pat, flattered and pleased, hung Auntie Delia's bead curtain up on the balcony, where indeed it looked lovely.

That night she asked if they ever heard from Nadia how she was enjoying Washington.

"No, we've not heard," said Marigold.

"Nadia doesn't write many letters," said Joy.

"What did she do, I mean what job had she?" asked Pat. Her slight jealousy of Nadia had disappeared, now she had only curiosity.

"She worked in an antique shop," said Joy.

"Managed an antique shop," said Marigold.

"Well, she worked there first," laughed Joy. "But Marigold told her she knew much more than anyone in it, and gave her confidence, so she ended up managing it for Mr. Solomons."

"She knew twice as much as Mr. Solomons from the start," said Marigold.

"Anyway Mr. Solomons fancied her enormously, so that it didn't hurt," said Joy with a giggle.

"Did she fancy him?" asked Pat with interest.

"Not until Marigold told her to have some intelligence and fancy him," giggled Joy again.

"Oh," said Pat.

Marigold seemed to think some clarification was called for.

"It always strikes me as silly to go to bed with half-drunk people, who forget it, or who feel embarrassed by it, or who do it so often that it's meaningless, and then refuse to go to bed with someone like Mr. Solomons who would appreciate it, would remember it with affection, and would advance Nadia because of it. It just seems a foolish sort of thing to have a principle about."

Put that way, thought Pat, it was unanswerable.

"But she left him all the same?" she probed.

"Oh no, she didn't leave Mr. Solomons," said Joy laughing. "Mr. Solomons left her. He had a heart attack and went to live in the country, so she managed his place for him, and took a share in the profits."

"And had a very nice cut and first refusal on everything they stocked," said Marigold, stroking the little mahogany cabinet beside her, almost sensuously.

"So why Washington?" asked Pat.

"She's running a little antique shop in Georgetown now," said Marigold distantly. "Very different kind of stuff, I'm sure."

"She got sort of unsettled, and took the first job she heard of," said Joy artlessly.

"Some silly business with a chap who used to restore paintings, very silly really," said Marigold. And the conversation about Nadia stopped there. It was as clear a break as if "End of Episode One" had been written in fire in the air.

Out of sheer curiosity, Pat stopped in Solomons' antique shop. There was no elderly owner type about, so she supposed that the good proprietor's heart could not yet have recovered from Nadia's exertions.

She asked how much they would give her for Aunt Delia's inlaid cabinet if she were to sell it. She described it very carefully.

"About five hundred pounds," said the young man. "Depends on what condition it's in, of course, but not less I'd say."

That was odd. Marigold had said it was pretty but without value. Marigold said she should take great care of it because it might be worth fifty pounds. Imagine Marigold not knowing how much it was worth. A flaw in the lovely, graceful, all-knowing Marigold. A flaw no less.

"Is Nadia still here?" she asked on impulse.

"No, why, you a friend of hers?" the man asked.

"No," said Pat. "I just know people who know her."

"Oh, she left here a few weeks ago. Kevin would know where she is." He pointed out a young and very attractive bearded bending figure, who was examining the frame of a picture.

"It doesn't matter really," said Pat hastily,

66

thinking this might be the silly young man of Marigold's description.

"Hey, Kevin, this lady's a friend of Nad's."

Kevin stood up. He was very handsome in a definitely shabby, ungroomed way. Pat could see that his nails, his unwashed hair, wouldn't have fitted into the elegant furniture back in the flat.

"I was just looking around, and I remembered that this is where the girl who lived in the flat where I've just moved in used to work . . ." said Pat apologetically.

"Have you moved in there?" asked Kevin flatly.

"Yes, a few days ago."

"Have you moved all your stuff in?" he asked.

"Well yes, yes I have," Pat's voice trailed away. She felt unreasonably frightened.

"Did she tell you it's worth buttons, peanuts?"

"No," said Pat defensively. "Marigold said it's very nice furniture and I must take care of it. Why, anyway?"

"Will you tell her you've been in here?" he asked very unemotionally.

"I might, I might not. Why do you ask?" said Pat. She was definitely frightened now, which was ridiculous. She also knew that she would never admit to Marigold that she had nosed around Nadia's old place of employment and nosed out Nadia's silly young man.

"I don't think you will," he said. "Nadia never told her anything towards the end, she was absolutely terrified of her. So was I. It's her eyes, they're not human."

"They're just too blue," said Pat. "She can't help that."

67

"No, but she can help a lot of things. Do you know that she hasn't polio at all?"

"I don't believe you," said Pat, feeling her legs getting weak.

"No, she hasn't, that's why none of them ring her at home. She goes out, you know, when everyone's at work."

"Don't be ridiculous."

"No, I saw her several times running down the stairs, and taking a taxi. I took a photograph of her once to prove it to Nadia, but she said it was trick photography."

"But she's paralysed," said Pat.

"So she says. It's nice being paralysed if you get everyone else to do all the work, pay all the bills, and live in fear of you."

"Don't you think that someone would have to be mad to pretend to have polio, just to get out of carrying out the rubbish?"

"Marigold is mad, very mad," he said.

Pat sat down on a reproduction sofa.

"Didn't you guess?" he asked.

"I don't believe it," said Pat.

"Nadia doesn't to this day," said Kevin.

"Is that why she went to Washington?" asked Pat.

"She's not in Washington, she's back in my flat. In Clapham," he said. "She told them she was going to the States, that was the only reason that Marigold let her go."

"You mean she had no job, and just lives in your flat because she's afraid of Marigold?" Pat said. "I don't believe a word of it."

"Go down there and see," he said. "She'll be sitting there complaining about the noise, and saying how little light there is, and how cramped the place seems to be. She doesn't even bother to get dressed properly, she hangs about all day complaining. That's what Marigold has done to her."

"Does she want to be back in the flat?"

"She wants it so much I think she's becoming as mad as Marigold. 'It was so peaceful. We were so gracious. We had such lovely music, not the neighbours' trannies.' That's all she says, day in, day out."

"Why did she leave it if she liked it so much?" asked Pat, almost afraid to hear the answer. Everything Nadia said about the flat was so true, there might be some truth in Kevin's whole terrible tale.

"She left it because I told her that she had given all her lovely furniture to this woman, that she had turned herself into a prostitute for her, that she had cut off her whole life for her, that she was working to support her. I told her to examine all these statements and if she thought they were true to move out. So she did and they were and she moved. But not without tissues of lies of course about Washington, which that nice silly Joy believed but Marigold saw through at once. Marigold didn't mind anyway, she had loads of stuff, hundreds of pounds' worth, from Nad over the years, and she'll always get other slaves."

"But Joy's normal."

"She used to be, when she had a bit of a life of her own, and boyfriends, and big plates of spaghetti with the girls from work. She should have been married years ago and have three nice fat children by now, instead of trying to become

69

a solicitor and earn more money for that Marigold."

"You're very bitter about her."

"I'm bleeding obsessed with her, that's what I am. She's ruined Nadia totally, she's turned Joy into a zombie, there was another one there, too, I can't remember her name, but she had to go out to bloody Africa as a missionary or something to get over it all. Having left some very nice lamps and some very good old cut glass thank you."

Pat's heart missed something of its regular movement. She remembered admiring the lamps, and Marigold had said they were from a dear friend who went to Africa and didn't need them.

It was the end of her lunch hour. She walked out without saying anything. She knew where to find him if she needed to know any more. He would take her home to meet Nadia if she wanted confirmation of it all. She was a free, grown-up woman, nobody could keep her there against her will.

On the way back to the bank she passed an expensive flower shop. It had unusual little potted plants. One of them was very, very blue. It had a long name but Marigold would know it anyway. It would look lovely on the balcony table. It would be so peaceful there this evening after work. It was like a dreamworld really. It would be such a misery trying to get everything out of the flat now that she had just got it in. Anyway, why should she? Kevin was just a silly young man. Jealous obviously because Nadia had been so happy in the flat. Anyone would be happy in that flat, it was so very, very peaceful, you didn't need anyone else or anything else in the world.

70

Lancaster Gate

It was funny the way things turned out. If she hadn't made that huge scene, and cried, and nearly choked herself crying, and admitted all kinds of weaknesses, she wouldn't be here now. She would be back in the flat, cleaning the cooker, polishing the furniture, ironing his shirts, so that he would think it was wonderful to have all these home comforts and value her more.

She would have gone to the cinema maybe, but maybe not. Films were so full of other people's relationships, and she kept identifying, and saying "If I behaved more like her, would he value me more?" or wondering why some screen woman could be so calm when everything was collapsing around her. Lisa could never be calm. She could pretend at calmness very successfully, but deep down it was churn, churn, churn. Sometimes she was surprised that he couldn't hear her heart sort of hitting against her bones, she could hear it thudding as well as feel it from inside, she could actually hear the wuff wuff sound it made. But fortunately he never managed to hear it, and she could always fool him into thinking she was relaxed and at ease. Sometimes the nights that had started with her heart thudding very seriously had turned out to be their best nights, because she acted out the calm role so well. Lisa had often thought how extraordinarily easy it was to fool someone you loved and who loved you.

Or who sort of loved you. But no, no, don't

start that, don't start analysing, worrying, your heart will begin the booming thing again, and you've got nothing to boom about. Here in London, staying in a big posh hotel, signing the room-service dockets with his name, putting the Mrs. bit in casually as if you had been doing it for years and it was now second nature. She wondered how long it took married people to forget their single names. Brides were always giggling about it. She supposed it would take about three weeks, about the same time as it took you to remember each January that the year had changed and that you must write a different date.

And it was what they called a glorious day on the weather forecast, very flowery indeed for the Met Office, but that was the word the man had used, and she had run to the window to see if he was right, and he was. There were railings across the road and people were putting up pictures, and postcards, and souvenirs, to sell to the passing tourists. And they seemed to be shouting to each other and laughing. They must know each other from meeting every week-end here, and they didn't sound like rivals or enemies. They didn't look as if they'd mind if a passing tourist bought from one rather than another. They were unpacking little canvas stools as well, and some of them had flasks. They were old and young. Lisa thought it was a funny kind of life. She wouldn't be able for it, her old anxiety would show. People wouldn't buy from her because she would have an anxious face wanting them to buy, and the more they passed her by because of her anxious face the more anxious it would become. But then that was the same kind of vicious circle that everyone kept getting caught in. It was like the whole problem with Him. If she felt unsure of him and thought that he was losing interest in her, she became strained and worried and not the carefree girl he had once fancied, and so he *did* start to lose interest, and because she could see this happening she became more strained and worried, and he lost more interest.

But stop, stop. Not today, today is glorious. It has been defined as such by the weatherman on the radio, than who there must be surely no saner, soberer judge. And today you don't need to act at being relaxed, you are. He's there in the bathroom shaving, he's happy, he's glad you're here. You've made love half an hour ago, he liked it, he's humming to himself. You make him happy or happier than he'd be if you weren't here. You're fine really. Remember that. He didn't have to take you with him to London for the conference, now did he? He couldn't have been planning something else, something awful like meeting someone else, if he took you so readily.

Lisa smiled happily, thinking of how readily he had agreed to take her with him. She hadn't meant to ask at all. She had packed his case yesterday morning . . . was it only yesterday? Friday, it must have been. She had been polishing his shoes.

"You don't need to do that," he had said, a bit embarrassed.

"I was doing my own," she had lied.

"They're suede, funny face," he had said, laughing.

What was it? It couldn't have been funny face, he called her that a lot, it was meaningless as an endearment, it wasn't even special. He called his daughter funny face on the phone . . . often. He called his secretary funny face. Once she had been holding for him on the phone, and she could hear his voice clearly as he crossed the office. "Get me a cup of coffee, funny face," he had said. "I've got a bugger of a day." It was probably because he knew she wore suede shoes. Idiotic, it couldn't have been that. Put baldly it was really madness. What was it then? Why did two tears fall down onto the shining leather shoes in her hand? She could have hit herself with rage. It wasn't as if she knew it was going to happen. You always sort of know when you're going to cry but not this time. It was automatic, as if someone had tinkered about with her tear ducts when she wasn't looking. And once started there was no stopping. She dropped the shoes and said a hundred times that she was sorry, she didn't know what was wrong. She tried to laugh through this appalling shower of tears, and that made her worse. She would sort of catch her breath and cough, and then it would get worse, and there were actual whoops coming out of her at one stage.

He was astounded. He thought he was to blame.

"What did I say, what have I done?" he had said over and over. "You knew I was going away today, you *knew*," he had repeated. He felt cornered, he felt she was blaming him. She couldn't even stop this terrible heaving to assure him that of course she knew, and that today wasn't any worse than any other day. He looked very wounded.

"The conference starts on Monday. I want to get into top form for it, I don't want to arrive exhausted. I want to be there and rested, and to have made my own tour of the hotel. I don't want to be thought of as your typical northern hick who arrives all impressed by everything. It's important, Lisa. You said you understood."

The use of her name maybe. She stopped for a moment. She actually had breath to speak. But instead of saying what she meant to, something like of *course* she understood, she heard her own voice betraying her, ratting on her. She actually said, "*Why* do you have to go away? We could have had this weekend together, just the two of us. Nobody would have known we were here, it would have been lovely."

When the words were said she decided that she had now lost everything, that the whole hard uphill race had been lost. She didn't know to whom she had lost, but she had lost. He couldn't stand people who begged, people who made demands. He had told her that was why he had left his wife, why the great love of his life (which had not been his marriage) had ended, because these women made demands. They wanted more of him than he could give, they saw something wonderful in a forced intimacy, they thought that the phrase "just the two of us" was safe and reassuring. He thought it was threatening and claustrophobic.

And because Lisa had thought that she had lost him, she abandoned herself to the tide. It was a great luxury, like getting into a warm bath when you're tired and cold. She had said all the unsayable things, the whines, the moans, the loneliness, how hard it had all been on her. How she had given him, if not the best years, then all the fun hours of her life, and for what? Nobody could know they lived together. Nobody could see them out together. It was clandestine and anxious-making, and leading nowhere, and she, Lisa, who was free, was abandoning every other man, every other chance of happiness, and for what? For someone who didn't give two damns about her. Well all right, it was all right. She kept repeating the words "all right" as if they were a magic charm. She had no idea what she meant by them, but they were safer and less final than saying something even more hackneyed like "it's all over."

He hadn't seemed relieved that it was all over or all right or whatever she meant; he hadn't seemed distressed, either. He looked interested, like he would have been interested in a farmer telling him about spraying crops, or a news vendor explaining what margin of profit there was in selling papers. He sounded as if he might like to hear more.

"Come with me then," he said.

He had never taken her anywhere before, it was too dangerous. He had always said that in his position he couldn't afford anyone to point at him about anything. Times were too tricky, things were too rough. He couldn't mean it now, he was just saying it to placate her, he knew she'd refuse for his sake. It was another ploy, another bluff. He had once explained to her why he won so much at poker. She had realized even then that the same rules that he used at the card table he used everywhere.

As suddenly as he had asked her she accepted.

"Fine," she said. "I will. Where shall I meet you?"

No backtracking, no well-perhaps-not-this-time. He was on as well, that was one of the rules of the game. If you offer, you must follow through.

"Nowhere near the office, too likely to be seen. Take a bus to the big petrol station on the London road. I'll meet you there at . . . ten past four."

"Right," she said. He kissed her and said it would be great, he'd like showing her London.

"You hardly know it any better than I do," she said.

No tears, no joy, no excitement, no gratitude. He looked at her approvingly. It was almost as if he thought she had gained a few housepoints. She had faked grief, she had got him to take her to London. Well done, Lisa. He said jauntily that he wouldn't wait a minute after a quarter past four, and she said equally lightly that that was fine, and he left, suitcase in his hand, and she heard the car starting as he went off to work and to talk to the office funny face.

Lisa had felt light-headed, like the time she once went out in a speedboat, and nothing had been real. She sat down to steady herself. She must make a list. Obviously she wouldn't go to work. So what excuse this time? She didn't know how long she'd stay with him in London. The conference lasted four days, Monday to Thursday. She'd have to invent something that would take a week. Quick, she'd have to tele-phone in the next few minutes and alert the Head's secretary before assembly began and someone started looking for her. A death. Exactly, a death in London. Better than flu, a woman's disease, or a heavy cold. She dialled, she spoke, she waved her hands around in the air as she told the weary Miss Weston, the Head's tame dog, that an aunt, her nearest relative, was dying. She even got a bit sad about it as she filled in the form and details of this mythical aunt. No, there simply was nobody else, nobody at all, she had to go. She'd ring from London next week to tell them what was happening. She knew how terrible it would be trying to find a substitute at this late stage, but she had heard only just now, this minute, and she was going to London this afternoon. "At ten past four," she said meaninglessly but to make it more real in her own mind. Miss Weston said she would tell the Head, and implied that the job of telling the Head was far worse than saying good-bye to a favorite aunt. Miss Weston was never very good with small chat anyway.

Now, on with the list. Lisa had to get a smart case, she only had an old grip, not suitable at all, and what else? Take money out of the bank, get her hair done, ring her brother to make sure he didn't call her at school. He hadn't telephoned her for four months, but there was always the chance. Her brother was in his usual bad humour.

"You got me away from my scrambled eggs, they'll be all hard. Oh all right. No, of course I wouldn't telephone you, why should I? Oh very well. I don't know what you think you're doing. Have you read about the unemployment in this country? Where do you think you're going to get another job if you're fired? Sometimes I think you've no sense of responsibility. No, of course I won't say anything to anybody, but Lisa, I wish you'd tell me what you're up to. I was saying to Angela the other night that you are so secretive and you just ring me out of the blue to say the oddest kind of things. No, why the hell should I wish you a good time? I'm not able to run out on everything and everybody and dash off to London on some whim. Good-bye now, good-bye."

No other friends to alert really. Funny after all the years of living in the same town. But she'd see Maggie at lunch and she'd tell her, and they'd have a bit of a giggle, and then Maggie would say, "Make sure he pays for you, I think he's mean," and Lisa would defend him to the hilt, he wasn't mean, he was careful with money, and that's how he got where he was and had all the things he had. She admired him for it.

It was a rush but it was a great day. There had been a few valleys. Maggie said she had heard that his wife was expecting another baby. Lisa said that it couldn't be true, he hadn't even seen his wife for six months. Maggie said it took nine months to produce a baby and this one was nearly ready to be produced. Lisa said it was all ridiculous, he'd have told her, and Maggie said sure, and anybody would tell you it didn't have to be *his* baby just because it was hers, and Lisa brightened. She darkened a bit at the bank when she tried to take out £60 from her deposit account and the clerk told her she had only £50 in it. She was sure there was over £200, but of course things like avocados were more expensive than the things she ate when she lived alone, and she did buy lots of little things for the flat.

She bought him a Johnny Cash cassette that they could play in the car, the kind of music he liked. It was a new one, they assured her. She was there at three-thirty and by four o'clock she knew every car accessory that they make these days. She bought a chamois so that the assistant wouldn't think she was loitering with intent. At five past four she got a horrible feeling that he might have been joking. She really should have rung him to make sure he meant it, but that would have looked humble and she didn't want that. Suppose she saw his car flying past. Suppose just suppose he did stop there for petrol and saw her, and hadn't meant to take her. That wouldn't be merely humble, it would be pathetic. Lisa shook herself, physically, like a dog trying to get rid of drops of rain, but she was trying to get rid of these hauntings and fancies. She seemed to have them these days the way people got mosquito bites, or dandruff. And then she saw him pulling in and looking around for her.

And the four hours, well it had been like a dream sequence in a movie. Or rather, like one of those sequences where they show you people making a long journey across America, and they cut from shots of the car on one motorway to another, lights from petrol stations and hotels flash on and off, signposts to cities pass by— and they were in London, and they hadn't talked much, just sat beside each other listening to both sides of the Johnny Cash over and over, and Lisa never asked where they'd be staying or how they'd hide from all the people from his company who were bound to be at the hotel, or what day she was going to be sent home. She didn't want to break the magic.

And when they came to London he looked a bit helpless because he didn't know which way to go, and he turned right once when there was no right turn and a taximan shouted at him, and Lisa was secretly delighted because he looked vulnerable then, and like a little boy, and she wanted to hug him to take the shame away, but she made no move, and finally after an hour of going backward and forward he found the hotel and suddenly he was his old self again. Because the world of hotels is pretty much the same everywhere, it's just London traffic that can throw you.

She had wondered what to do about a wedding ring. He had never bought her any kind of ring, and she hadn't liked to get one this morning when she was shopping . . . well, in case he thought she was being small-townish about it all. Perhaps people didn't wear rings when checking in, perhaps it was more sophisticated not to. She had worn gloves anyway, it seemed a good way of avoiding doing the wrong thing.

The foyer was huge and impersonal, but full of people and shops, and newspaper kiosks and theatre booking stands. It was very different from the hotel that she and Bill had stayed in when Mother was ill, and had suddenly been taken into hospital in London. That time they stayed in a small hotel near the station, and the woman who ran it asked them for the money in advance, and Bill had said they would have to sleep in the same room to save paying for two. And the woman who ran the hotel had turned out to be nice and kind when she discovered that their mother was dying, and had made tea for Lisa, and had told her how her own mother had died.

And it was different from the hotel that they had all stayed in when Mother and Father and Bill and herself had come to London for a week one October as a treat. That had been owned by a friend of father's, a North Countryman, and Father said they wouldn't be robbed there like they would everywhere else. And it had been a vaguely unsatisfactory holiday for no reason that any of them ever understood and none of them ever dared say. Just a lot less than they all had hoped for probably.

But here in Lancaster Gate it was a different world and a different life, and he looked pleased that she was there and that was all that mattered. She smiled at him as the porter took their cases. She had bought one very like his, and got a cosy warm feeling in the lift because the cases looked like matching luggage, the kind of thing they might have been given as a wedding present if they had been a normal couple.

And he must have ordered a room with a double bed especially because she saw from the brochure she had been looking at in the lobby that most of the rooms had twin beds. And he gave her a kiss when the porter had gone, and said, "There's nothing like a life of sin. Let's ring for a gin and tonic and let's go to bed."

And they did, and then they went out to a restaurant where the Italian waiter asked them if they were married and Lisa said "No" very quickly so that he wouldn't think she was trying to pretend in any way (except to the hotel) that she *was* his wife, and the waiter said he thought not, they looked too happy and too much in love. And Lisa's heart, which hadn't pounded or thudded since that morning, went into a little cotton-wool ball of happiness.

So it was indeed funny the way things turned out, she thought again. Instead of losing out by behaving like a weak-wife type, clinging, dependent, she was being patted on the back and taken on a nice happy trip to London. There was a knock at the door and she leaped off the bed to answer it, thinking it was breakfast. It wasn't, it was a bowl of fruit and some flowers with a "Compliments" card. She gave the boy twenty pence and hoped that it was enough. He came out of the bathroom, all clean and young-looking, a towel around his waist. He was as excited as a child and nearly as excited as she was.

"Who's it from, who's it from?" she begged.

He tried to look casual. "I always arrange little surprises like this for you," he said, teasing her, and they opened the card.

It was from the president of the company, an American gesture, he said, to make the employees feel they are part of a happy family, to make them pull harder because they think they are being looked after. He was very pleased, even though he wouldn't show it.

"Must have taken a secretary a long time to write out all these personal cards," he said, not wishing her to think that he thought the president had written it.

"Still," said Lisa. "They did go to the trouble."

She reached out for the card, and her heart became a big ball of putty and sank down in her body. It was addressed to "Mr. and Mrs." and hoped that they would both enjoy their stay.

"Is it . . . is it to tell you that they *know* you've brought a woman with you?" she asked fearfully.

He looked unconcerned. Not at all, the secretary had probably found out from the hotel which delegates had checked in with their wives and put Mr. and Mrs. on those cards. Just administration. He was putting on the cuff links she had given him and he gave her a kiss on the nose.

She felt that the day was a bit less glorious and immediately felt very angry with herself for feeling that way. What had happened? Nothing. She was a cheat and a tramp, and a mistress, and illegally registered in the hotel as the "Mrs." she wasn't. But that was all rubbish. The first night she had gone to bed with him she had rid her mind of all those labels, they didn't count in anybody's mind except the fevered minds of a long-gone generation. Why was a silly card upsetting her?

The breakfast arrived and they sat by the window reading the two newspapers that had been sent up as well. She touched his hand when she poured him more coffee. He smiled, and she hoped in a beaten sort of way that it was going to be fairly glorious anyway.

"What shall we do?" he said.

"I'd like to look at the pictures and things they're hanging up on the railings down there. Maybe I might buy a couple of things."

"It's bound to be rubbish," he said, not disagreeably, but as one who knew about such things.

"All the same, it would be nice to stroll around and then maybe go for a walk in the park," she said.

"Perhaps we should move farther away from the hotel," he said. He was right, of course. It would have been idiocy to have hidden it for seventeen months back home, where such things were hard to hide, and then blow it in a city of ten million people, just by parading around in front of people who were bound to know him, and to know that she oughtn't to be there. Lisa agreed quickly.

"We can go anywhere else," he said helpfully.

"We could get the underground to St. Paul's and have a look at that," she said eagerly, to show that she didn't mind being a second-best woman, a person who had to be hidden rather than paraded.

"Yes, we could do that," he said.

"Or walk up to Oxford Street maybe, and look at the shops."

"They'll be a bit crowded, Saturday morning," he said.

She felt the familiar terror, the well-known realization that she was losing his interest came flooding over her. You counter that with brilliant acting, she told herself smartly. You don't give in, you don't allow yourself to look beaten or sulky. You act.

"Listen, my love, I'm doing all the suggesting, I don't mind *what* we do. It's a glorious day, even the man on the wireless said so. I'll do whatever you'd like, or anyway I'll discuss it."

She smiled the bright birdlike smile that she felt must look so phoney. She always thought she must look like a model in an advertisement on telly who has suddenly been told she must act.

But no, as always, he responded as he would have done to a normal remark.

"Well, I'll tell you what I'd *like* to do," he said.

"Yes?" Mask set, eyebrows raised, mouth in inquiring smile.

"It sounds a bit odd but, well, I've arranged to have one of these executive health checkups. You know, we were talking about them. They have them on Saturday mornings. Do everything—heart, blood pressure, X rays, blood tests, the lot. It makes more sense than spending hours and days at home.

"They have them on Saturdays so that executives can go without telling anyone at work what they're up to. When I thought I was going to be

85

here by myself, I booked one for today, and sent a deposit. I could cancel it but you . . . you know, it seems a pity. It would set my mind at rest."

The fluttering fear that was never too far from her heart came back and buzzed at her, it even got into her eyes.

"Stop looking worried, funny face," he said, laughing. "Nothing happens to me, it's because I do things like this that I'm so healthy. They won't find anything wrong. It's just wise to have it done at forty-five, that's all."

She was ten years younger and a hundred times slower in every way, in thinking, in walking, in making up her mind, in knowing what to say.

"Are you sure you don't have any pains or anything?" she faltered.

He was sure, and he was quite willing to cancel it. It was just that they didn't have anything like this at home, and you know that once you went for any kind of checkup back there, everyone knew about it, and they all had you buried before you came out of the doctor's surgery. Still, it did seem a pity to waste the nice morning, and she had been saying only yesterday that they didn't have much time together, just the two of them. Perhaps he would ring and cancel it.

She knew she was being manipulated when she insisted that he go. She knew he used the phrase "just the two of us" in heavy inverted commas. She knew that he had never intended to back out of it for a minute. Anyway she thought it was a good idea for him to have the checkup. So it was on with the act.

No, nonsense, she would be very happy to stroll around herself. She'd meet him afterwards. She'd go down and look at those pictures that he didn't want to see. It was ideal really, they could each do what they wanted, and then meet for lunch.

He didn't know whether it would be over by lunchtime. But she thought that this was the point, that the checkup took only a couple of hours. Yes, well he hoped so but maybe they had better not make a firm arrangement for lunch just in case.

Oh act, act. Fine, that suited her too. After she had looked at the paintings on the railings, she'd have a quick look at Oxford Street, and then take the tube to St. Paul's. She hadn't been there since she was a child, she'd love to see it again. Don't cling, don't cling, you mustn't appear dependent. Choose some very late time and he'll suggest earlier. He'll like you for saying you can manage alone, you'll like it if he says he wants you earlier. Don't ruin it, don't balls up the glorious day.

"Why don't we say six o'clock here!" Bright, light tone, utterly nonclinging, utterly ridiculous as a suggestion. His examination couldn't possibly take from eleven in the morning until six at night.

"That sounds about right," he said, and the day went dark, but the voice stayed bright, and there were no giveaway signs as she bounced cheerfully out the door.

The lobby looked less glittering and glamorous and Londonish. It looked big and full of people who trusted other people or didn't give a damn about other people. She looked at the house phones on the wall. Should she ring up and just say "Love you"? They did that to each other, or they used to a lot in the beginning. No, it was silly, there was nothing to be gained and it might irritate him. Why risk it?

87

She wound her way across the road, jumping this way and that to avoid the traffic, because it looked too far to walk to the pedestrian crossing, and anyway she was anxious to get to the other side. It reminded her of Paris, and all those thousands of water colours of Notre-Dame, all of them exactly the same and all of them different prices, or so it seemed.

There was a young man with very red hair and a very white face looking at her.

"Scarf, lady?" he asked hopefully.

"I want to look at everything before I buy," she said happily.

"Surprising more of you Northerners aren't killed if that's the way you cross roads up there," he said good-naturedly.

He meant it nicely. It was to keep her chatting, she knew that. She also thought that he fancied the look of her, which was nice. She felt it was so long now since anyone had fancied her that she wouldn't know how to react. But somehow his marking her out as a Northerner annoyed her, she was irritated, even though she knew it was said in friendship. Did she sound provincial, did she look provincial, crossing the road like that?

Suddenly she thought with a violence that made her nearly keel over, that there was a great possibility that he thought she was provincial too. That could be the reason why he wasn't prepared to make any public announcement of their being together. Not announcement, she didn't really want as much as that, she wanted . . . a bit of openness. It was bloody obvious now that she thought of it. Living with someone, having it off with someone, having an affair, all this was accepted now . . . by everyone.

She stood there, not even seeing the blur of Towers of London, Trafalgar Squares, and Beefeaters that waved like flags from the scarf rack. She could only see herself years ago at suppertime, listening to her mother talking about people who gave themselves airs. Her mother had wanted Lisa always to remember that she came from good stock. They could hold their heads up with any of them, they were as good as anyone for miles around, they had nothing hidden away that could never be dragged out. Lisa and Bill never knew what brought on these kinds of statements, they had never even known what she was talking about. Suddenly Lisa knew. It was the reassurance game, it was trying to say "it's all right."

Lisa felt like shouting it out aloud this very moment. She had an urge to tell the boy with the red hair that her father had been a local government official, that her mother had been a nurse, that her mother's father had owned a chemist's shop. She wanted to say it in a voice so clear and loud that he would hear it, before he left for his checkup, so that he would realize how lucky he was to have gotten a girl from such good stock who was so willing to play along in a shabby game with him. That it was against her training, her background, her . . . well her kind of people. She wanted him to know, without having to spell it out, that she was better than he was, better in the way that older people valued things, that she had come from respectable people. His father had worked in the potteries, that much she knew and only that.

Of course he had married into money, and why shouldn't he, a bright boy like him? Any family would have been delighted to have him as a son-in-law. Would her own family have liked him? Yes, her father would have admired him, her mother would have been a bit boringly embarrassing about stock, but she would have accepted him. However, she'd have liked him to know, if only there were some way of telling him indirectly, that her family wouldn't have fallen over themselves in gratitude . . . that he'd have had to make an effort to be accepted.

Lisa's head cleared and she looked at the boy again.

"I don't feel very well," she said, feeling she owed him some explanation of why she was standing there looking at him wildly.

"Do you want to sit down, darling?" he asked kindly, and pushed out a stool for her. He looked a bit worried and even embarrassed. His customer had turned out to be a nut case. That's what he must be thinking, Lisa told herself miserably.

He gave her a cup of very sweet coffee from his little orange flask. Over the rim of the cup she looked up at the hotel. Was there any chance that he would be looking out the window and would see her sitting down, drinking coffee there? Would he be worried, would he rush down to know if she felt faint? What would she say if he did? But as the hot sweet coffee went down inside her chest, Lisa had another feeling too. No, he wouldn't be looking out the window, straining for a view of her crossing the road. *She* did that kind of thing, he didn't. She was the one who would look hopefully out the window of the flat at home to see him turning the corner in the evenings. If she was the late one home, he was always reading or looking at television. He never stood at windows. He wouldn't be looking down.

"I feel much better, thank you ever so much," she said to the red-haired boy.

"You still look a bit shaky, love," he said.

"Could I sit here for a little bit?" asked Lisa, more to please him really than because she wanted to. She thought he would like to feel he was doing her a service. She was right, he was delighted. He moved the stool back against the railings and lit her a cigarette while he talked to two Americans and sold them a wall hanging with Big Ben on it.

"When they get home they'll probably have forgotten what city Big Ben is in," he said. He didn't think much of Americans, he told her. Scandinavians were educated people, Americans weren't. He asked her if she was going to be in London for long.

"My husband is going to Harley Street for a checkup today," she said cosily. "It may depend on what he's told. But I think we'll be here a week."

She wondered whether she was going mad, actually mad, at the age of thirty-five. It did happen to people, they started telling the most fantastic, unreal tales and nobody noticed for a while, then they had to go and have treatment.

"Harley Street today, a Saturday?" said the red-haired boy cheerfully. "Meeting some bird more likely. You won't find any doctors in Harley Street today. You'd better keep an eye on your old man, my darling, he's with some blonde."

He smiled a big cockney grin, full of quickness and good humour. He liked most people he met, this boy did. He didn't particularly fancy her probably, he was like this with old dears of a hundred and with fellows as well.

"It's possible," she said. "Quite possible."

The red-haired boy looked alarmed. She must look as if she were going mad again; he must be regretting his little pleasantry.

"He'd be mad if he was," he said. "Lovely woman like you, no blonde could be any better. No, he'd need his head examined he would, if he told you he was going to a doctor and went off to hold hands in a park with a blonde."

His face had a kind of transparency about it. It was watery somehow, with pale eyes set far apart from each other. It was a very simple face. It wouldn't disguise things, and look differently to the way it was feeling. It wasn't the kind of face that could smile and tell you that its health needed a checkup if it wasn't true. That face could never become troubled and talk about its marriage having been a sad sort of thing, better not spoken of, if in fact his wife was pregnant and he was planning to try and get the marriage revved up again.

"Are you married?" she asked him.

"No, darling, never met a lady that was worthy of me," he said.

"Neither am I," she said.

She didn't care what he thought. She tried not to look at the flicker of puzzlement and irritation that came over his white, transparent face. It was because of his face that she had decided to tell him the truth, even though it would have been better in the short encounter between them if she hadn't.

She got up, folded the stool together, and placed it very precisely beside the railings.

"I really do feel a lot better, thank you. I might come back and buy something from you later on," she said.

"You do that, my darling," he said, relieved that she was going. She felt that even here she had stayed too long, talked too much, revealed a dependence. Was she ever going to be able to stop?

There was an opening into the park and she walked in. The grass was yellowish, there hadn't been any rain for a long time. A series of glorious days probably. She looked at the people. No delegates to the conference, nobody from back home had arrived yet; there was no danger of being seen by anyone. And even though he was careful about his health, it was funny that he hadn't said anything about the checkup before. And why had they got a "Mr. and Mrs." card with the fruit and flowers? He must have said all along that he was bringing his wife with him. And the room had already had a double bed in it, before he had planned for her to accompany him. And what kind of fool did he think she was to believe he was having an executive checkup all bloody day? Or did he care what she thought? Was it just a case of it being more comfortable to have an undemanding fool of a woman who paid her own way and wasn't any extra trouble than not to have one, or to leave her at home sulking?

She strolled around idly, noticing that everyone in the park seemed to be with other people. There were groups of girls, and there were families, and there were a lot of pregnant women walking with that proud waddle they develop, hands folded oddly over the bulk in front, managing to look

93

frail as well as huge, so that husbands had protective arms around shoulders.

And she wondered, did he have his real wife in London for the week-end, and was he in fact going to go back to her, and was it she who was pregnant or someone else? Maggie would say anything to get her nice friend Lisa out of this thing. Or did he have some other girl, who also had to be fobbed off with lies and hurried telephone calls? She knew how real his excuses could sound. She wondered whether any other woman in the whole world would have gone to live with a man who was not divorced and who went home every six months to see his daughter, but apparently didn't talk to his wife except about business matters.

She wondered if it was worth going back to the hotel to pick up the case. She thought not, really. It had cost £12 and that was a pity, but what was £12 compared to other things she had spent? She had her handbag with her and her money, there weren't many clothes at the hotel. She hadn't brought much with her in order not to appear too eager, not to look as if she was assuming that she was staying for the whole week.

She didn't make any plans about what was his and what was hers in the flat. She'd sort that out tomorrow or the day after when she got back, and she'd take what she felt like taking. She wouldn't take lots out of viciousness, or too little out of martyrdom.

She didn't even start fussing and worrying about what stations the trains went from and how to get there, or what times they were at, and how much they cost. She didn't even know whether she would go in to work on Monday and say her aunt hadn't died in London after all. It was strange, but she didn't even seem to be imagining how he would react when he came back at six o'clock and she didn't turn up. Would he contact the police? Would it embarrass him with the hotel and with everybody? Would he think she was dead? It didn't matter.

She always thought that things ended suddenly, that people had a big row, or they parted with clenched teeth and noble smiles like they did in old movies. And she stood still beside a seat which had a lot of old people sitting on it, and she took some deep breaths one after another as if she was testing to see how her heart was feeling, whether it was thudding, or if it was surrounded by that awful, horrible, empty feeling of fear like it so often was, when she thought he was angry or bored with her. And funnily it didn't seem to be in a bad state at all.

She wished she had someone to tell, someone who would congratulate her, someone who would be interested. If Mother was alive . . . no, of course she couldn't have told Mother about it, what was she dreaming about? Mother had been interested certainly, but you didn't tell Mother about having affairs, that wasn't something people from our stock did, people who were busy holding their heads up with the best of them. And Father, he might have liked the story if it had been about someone else. He used to listen to her tales about other people, and say, "Fancy, aren't folk strange?" Maggie would treat it lightly, and probably come out with new stories about him, things she hadn't liked to tell Lisa at the time. And there was nobody in the staff room she could tell, and Bill, well Bill and Angela would just have one of their worried conversations about her. She really had very few friends.

And that was the one cloud on her new freedom, she realized. That's what she'd miss, having him for a friend. In a few ways and some of the time, he had at least been a friend.

Marble Arch

These days she felt that the flower sellers, the men with piles of things that had fallen off lorries, the policemen, and the road sweepers were her friends. She felt they were all part of some kind of club, the only remaining English people in a sea of foreigners. It was a racist kind of thought perhaps, she said to herself, because if you started noticing how many people there were who smelled of garlic, or who wore face veils, or head-dresses, then the next step might be to wish they weren't there. It would be better not to notice differences at all, to think that everything which walked on two feet was a fellow human.

Anyway she had no right to be anything but grateful to all the tourists. She reminded herself of this as an Arab thrust a piece of paper at her with an address down the Edgware Road on it, and she pointed him in the right direction. He was going to a chemist's shop, she noticed. She wondered whether it was for a prescription or to buy boxes of soaps and talcums. Without the Arabs her own business would have folded long ago. She sold handmade handbags in a shop within a shop. They were quite expensive. Young

Londoners didn't have the money young Kuwaitis did.

Sophie unlocked her little shop and started to hang up the bags. She then got a stool and sat out in the morning sunlight waiting for customers. It was much more expensive to have a street frontage, but it trebled business. She was glad she had such a good head for business. She really needed it because nobody around her seemed to understand the first principles of earning a living. She frowned with the beginnings of a headache, and moved out of the sun. It had been a very late night.

It hadn't been night when she finally got to bed, it had been four o'clock in the morning. Eddie had brushed the hair out of his eyes and half raised himself on an elbow as she left, but he was now back in a deep innocent sleep again and here she was sitting with a headache, trying to trap the tourists who came to Marble Arch, trying to keep awake and make a living for Eddie and herself.

She never thought of herself as earning a living for both of them. That wasn't the way the words or the ideas fell together. Only sometimes, when she had a headache or when they had talked long and without direction during the night, did she think wistfully how nice it would be if he was the one who got up in the mornings, and she was the one who could raise herself on an elbow and say "Good-bye, love, take it easy." But that wasn't really considering an alternative, it was only thinking about things that would never be, like the way you sometimes imagined what it would be like to be a sea gull when you saw one swooping backwards and forwards over a harbour.

Sophie thought a bit about last night's discussion. It hadn't been any different from the ones that had gone before, just longer. Eddie's dark brown eyes and their long black lashes looked dull with the pain of the world. They had lost all the flash and brilliance they had when he wasn't talking about the cruelty of the world. Dead they sat on his face as he spoke on bitterly about the producers who were pansies, the agents who were fairies, the script editors who promised the moon, the misguided advice of friends who said, "Well, why don't you just *go* to Framlingham or Fraserburgh or some ridiculous place and see what happens?"

Eddie wasn't going to just go anywhere. At thirty-seven he was too old now to just go to a stupid group of overexcited students or experimentalists and help them out with their productions. He had been in acting too long, learned too much, was too professional to give in, to sell the past. What had all these years been for if he was going to give in now? What would his love for Sophie mean if he was to allow that painted Jeffrey to feel him up and take him to that queers' pub as a possession, just in order that he could get a part? No, life was cruel, and rotten, and the good people always lost out, and it was a plot, and you couldn't fight the system hoping to win, but at least you could try.

Sophie had never seen life as being cruel and rotten before she met Eddie, but she had always seen it as fairly difficult and tiring. She thought if you worked hard you made money, and then you had leisure time and you enjoyed that. If you were very lucky indeed you worked at something that wasn't awful, and then you enjoyed both work and leisure. She thought it must be very strange and sad to work in a world where there seemed to be steaming clouds of sexual desire and frustration, mostly homosexual, and that this was governing who got jobs and who played where and who succeeded or who failed.

It was so different to her own world. She had managed to leave the very dull, very depressing place where they had trained her how to sell cosmetics so well that she firmly believed she could sell lip gloss to men with beards. She had always wanted to be in business for herself but with no capital it looked impossible. Her father hadn't wanted her to leave the cosmetic people. He thought she should thank her lucky stars day and night for the good luck she had got in life. Her father had never had much luck, there were more weeks when he collected money from welfare than from an employer. Her mother had worked regularly and quietly in a restaurant. She said that her one ambition was that Sophie should never have a job which meant walking and standing, and dealing with dirty plates and diffi-cult customers. She was happy when Sophie was selling nice, fresh, good-smelling oils and paints for people's faces. She was worried when she seemed to become a person of no account sitting in a little stall shouting her wares to the public.

Sophie sighed, thinking how little everyone around her knew about business. If she had been her father,she would have kept a steady job; if she had been her mother, she would have demanded to be a cashier in that restaurant, where she could have sat in a little glass box near the door, rather than get varicose veins by walking and standing; if she were Eddie, she would take any acting job anywhere if she wanted to act, or more probably she would decide that if acting didn't want her among its ranks, she would take some other job and act in her spare time. Really she had made very little impression on anyone, with her own businesslike attitudes. Nobody realized that it wasn't easy to be organized and disciplined, and to make money. It took a lot of time, and worry, and ate into all those hours you could be sitting around and enjoying yourself. Nobody ever got drawn into her little belief that people might be here on earth to work hard. Nobody but Peggy. Peggy was her one success.

Peggy had been a mess, and Sophie thought she would always be one, but she was so warm and friendly that you looked through all this bamboo curtain of rubbish and saw a lovely, big, responsive soul inside. Peggy had been to the same school, had done the same useless meaningless course in "business administration." Well, hardly done it, Peggy had barely attended a class there. She had been in chip shops and coffee shops, and places with plastic tabletops where people ate ice creams and drank fizzy drinks instead of learning business administration or delivering bundles of dresses from the wholesale house to the retail, which was what they were being paid for.

Peggy had a year of liberty, then came the storm. Her mother couldn't understand why she wasn't fitted for a wonderful job, some high business post. Gradually the tales of the chip shops emerged, and Peggy left home under the darkest cloud you could find, a cloud of ingratitude.

Sophie had seen her from time to time. Usually she came to borrow a few pounds. More often than not Sophie got them back. Sometimes she came to grumble. This man had let her down, that man hadn't told her he was married, the other man had been perfectly nice for a fortnight and then it turned out that all he wanted was to beat her and for her to beat him. She worked in Woollies for a while and was sacked for stealing. She thought that this was unfair. Sophie thought it was also pretty unfair to steal from Woollies, and Peggy only grudgingly agreed.

She worked for a while in one of the coffee shops of her youth. Sophie always had coffee there just to have a chat. Sometimes she thought it mightn't be such a good idea. Peggy looked weary, and dirty, and beaten, she seemed to resent Sophie's smart looks, essential for her trade, and her smart little car, essential for bringing her trade from door to door.

But still Peggy didn't have anyone else, and when she was arrested the first time and charged with being drunk and disorderly, Sophie was the one she sent for. She sent for Sophie when she was in hospital, too, suffering, they told her, from malnutrition. Sophie came when she was charged with soliciting, and when she was finally sent to prison on her third charge, it was Sophie who waited for her three weeks later in the little car and drove her back home.

When Peggy immediately retrieved a bottle of barley wine that she had hidden in the hallway of the depressing house where she lived, Sophie decided she had had enough. Quite enough. There they were sitting in this filthy room, and she was refusing a glass of cloudy, muddy-looking drink with the excuse that it was a bit early in the day. Her old friend Peggy had become a prostitute, a thief, and a near-alcoholic.

The years of dragging herself up and away and onwards were looking useless, if she could be dragged down again so quickly by Peggy. She lost her temper, and said all this and more.

"I'm not just dumping you because I've become all up-in-the-air," she shouted eventually. "Stop telling me that I have ideas above myself. "I've no ideas for God's sake, I just work bloody hard, and it isn't easy and everyone around me seems afraid of work or . . . or sneers at it and at me. So now I'm telling you I'm sick of it, sick, sick, sick. I have no more pity for you. I haven't any more words, any more 'Poor things' to say to you. You can go whatever bloody way you like, I don't care if I never hear about you again, because every time I hear from you you want something, money, help, someone to take you home from gaol. If you don't want something at the beginning, you end up wanting something. You drain me, and make me feel weak and feel nothing. So to hell with you Peggy, to hell with you, I'm sick of you."

And then it was Sophie not Peggy who cried. Peggy was amazed. Not upset, just amazed.

The great cool Sophie was sitting there crying, the calm Sophie had shouted. The mask had slipped. Peggy was transfixed. Instead of the list of excuses, explanations, and life's miseries that normally fell out unasked for, she heard herself say quite calmly:

"What would you like me to do?"

"I'd like you to look after yourself for a change and not rely on me to look after you. I'd like you to do something quite extraordinary for you, that's go out and earn a bloody living like most people in the world."

Sophie gathered up her bag and her car keys and banged out of the dirty room in the depressing house, and went off and sold cream that took lines from under your eyes to women who ran small dress shops. In and out of her car she got, dragging display literature, explaining that people who bought dresses would like to have unlined faces to wear with them. She went on and on until the last late-closing shop had closed, then returned to her flat and worked on reports until midnight and went to sleep.

Next day Peggy was at her door. A tidier Peggy, not drunk, not hung over, not pleading.

"Can I come with you on your rounds?" she asked simply.

Sophie was tired. "Yes, if you don't talk," she said, and the day was much like any other, except for the vaguely comforting feeling of Peggy sitting silently beside her. They hardly spoke a word to each other until lunchtime. Then Sophie offered her a drink.

"I'll have a coffee," said Peggy.

During the coffee Peggy had asked intelligent questions about the kind of stores, shops, and boutiques they had been visiting. She wanted to know how much credit they got. Since Peggy couldn't have had a pound note to her name, Sophie wondered at the drift of the conversation. Surely Peggy couldn't see herself as a shop owner, even if she were going to pull herself together? But anything was better than the kind of thing Peggy normally talked about, so Sophie answered her sensibly. Sophie was also relieved that no malice seemed to be directed towards her for yesterday's outburst.

Peggy came silently in the car with Sophie for about a week, except for the day she had to go and see a probation officer or social worker. She didn't have any tales to tell about these visits, no theories about how women in such jobs were sadists. Sophie began to feel quite optimistic about her, but didn't want to rock any boat by saying it was a useless way to spend your days, sitting in someone else's car. Perhaps Peggy was just desperately lonely, she thought.

Then Peggy came up with her suggestion. She wondered, would these women in the shops buy handmade bags?

Sophie's first thought was that Peggy was planning to steal the bags, but no, she said, she had learned a bit of leather work once, and it turned out she was quite good at it. Would Sophie like to come and see some of it that evening?

The dirty and untidy bedroom was still untidy, but not with clothes, makeup, and empty barley wine bottles. This time it was with bits of leather and cord. Sophie stood transfixed.

Because the bags in all sorts of shapes and sizes were beautiful.

Some of them were soft pinks and blues, others were bold blacks and whites. They were made on a patchwork system, because Peggy had only enough money for scraps, she said. She looked shyly at Sophie, and blushed with pleasure at the evident delight and surprise she saw.

"I was wondering, could I earn a living selling them?" asked Peggy as timidly as a child. Sophie's heart was so full of pride and delight and resolution that she hardly trusted herself to speak. This must be the way teachers feel, or nurses when their patients get better, she thought; and they sat down and made plans for Peggy's new career.

Things moved very quickly after that; the only problem was that Peggy couldn't keep up with the demand. One boutique took a dozen, and rang up three days later for three dozen more. Sophie spent a whole Sunday with Peggy working out what they should do. If she were to get someone else to help her, they would have to halve the money. They had already seen the huge markup that shopkeepers put on the bags. It was time to define them as "luxury items," as "specialist work." They got labels made with "handcrafted by Peggy Anderson" on them, and they charged three times the price. They got it. And Peggy was in business.

So great was the business that Sophie decided she would abandon cosmetics for it, and that is why she was sitting in her little stall near Marble Arch. Not all the bags were Peggy's, no one person could keep up with that demand. But she sold six of Peggy's a week, and she paid Peggy ten pounds a bag, everyone was happy.

Now that Sophie had time off from the endless reports, and shop calls, and fights about commission that had made up her working life, she was able to have a social life. This was something she hadn't seen much of in the hard years of the cosmetic world. But it wasn't hard to find. There was George, silly, dull, kind George who wanted to marry her six weeks after he met her, and who took her to tennis parties and to drink outside Hooray Henry bars, where everyone talked about the last or the next tennis party, and what car everyone else was driving.

And then there was Michael, who was kind and dull too. And Fred, who was far from dull, but also very selfish and made no bones about telling her that he would like a wife doing something a little more classy than working as a hawker on Oxford Street. And suddenly one night there was Eddie. At the theatre on a summer evening, when Fred had gone to get the drinks and they had started talking about the play, Eddie had asked if she was an actress, and on impulse she had told him exactly where her little shop was, hoping he would call there. He did, and they drifted into friendship, and an affair that became a real love affair, and then it seemed only right that Eddie should live with her, and now she couldn't live without Eddie.

It was for Eddie that she got up early in the mornings because bills were bigger for two. It was for Eddie that she begged Peggy to make more bags, since the Peggy Andersons were the sure-fire sellers. It was for Eddie that she closed the shop for an hour and went off to the Berwick Street market to buy each night's dinner.

People told her that she had become nicer since she met Eddie. Her tired mother, whose veins were like knots of rope nowadays, and her sad-eyed father, both said she was more cheerful these days, but they put it down to her feckless life among the traders rather than to any love or warmth that had been added. They still thought her foolish to have thrown up her chances of real money.

Peggy said she looked marvellous, better than the days when she used to wear all the makeup she was selling. Love was great, said Peggy gloomily, for those lucky enough to find it. But

Peggy didn't seem to like Eddie. She thought he was lazy and that he took too much from Sophie.

"I don't trust him," she had said once. "He's one of the takers. I should know, I used to be one. He'll take all you can give, and then one day he'll decide you are nagging, or not enough fun, or not sexy enough, and he'll go and take from someone else."

Sophie had just laughed. "Nothing worse than a reformed drunk for telling you the evils of having a glass of sherry."

Peggy simply shrugged. "Don't say I didn't warn you," she said, and went back to her leather cutting. She worked now about ten hours a day. Whenever Sophie called, she was either bent over minute pieces of leather or she was out. Looking for pieces from her various outlets, she said, or having a walk to clear her head. Sophie was amazed that she could change lifestyles so simply but Peggy said that she mustn't be naive. Occasionally she visited Mr. Shipton in the afternoons, he had a couch in his office, and Mr. Shipton was very nice about giving Peggy pieces of leather and suede from his factory, so Peggy was very nice to him from time to time on his office couch.

Sophie found that sad and a bit disgusting, but Peggy said rubbish, it was glorious compared to picking people up in the streets, and how else could she afford all the material, so Sophie tried to put it out of her mind.

But today her mind was troubled as she sat and smiled at the tourists and made the odd sale. She felt very restless and anxious for something to change. It wasn't just the heat and the headache, it was as if she had been getting ready for this feeling. Systematically she ticked off all the good things about the way she lived. She had Eddie, beautiful tender Eddie, with his big dark eyes that made her feel weak just thinking about them, like girls were meant to go weak at the knees over pop stars. Eddie was so moody and marvellous that you never knew what to expect when you got home in the evenings. But that's what made the evenings when he had bought her a huge bunch of lilac, and was waiting in his black dressing gown to take her straight to bed . . . so magic. It quite paid for the other evenings when he wasn't in, and came in sulkily slamming the door, because yet another fairy casting director had wanted his body, not his acting.

The only time they talked about the future was about Eddie's future. There had been that time he nearly got a part in a show going to the States, and Sophie had become so excited and said she must get Peggy working overtime to make enough bags so that she could sell them there. Eddie had been firm that she mustn't leave her place in Marble Arch, and that it would only be a couple of months' separation. She had loved him for being so solicitous about her work.

At school they used to have a teacher who always made them "count their blessings." Sophie remembered that it had been a hard thing to do in those days when she wanted to look like a model, and live in a house with a swimming pool. Nowadays it wasn't really all that much easier. Blessings should be accepted, not counted. So she had Eddie, so she had her health, apart from the odd bad headache. So she had a way of earning a living that she enjoyed. At the age of twenty-seven she was in business for herself, few other women could boast that. Even if Peggy became unreliable again, she still had plenty of other people who made bags. What could be wrong with her?

A couple stopped and picked up one of Peggy's bags. They examined the label and gave funny little cries of recognition.

"That's the girl we met at the theatre yesterday," said the woman. "Peggy Anderson, she said she made bags, these are lovely."

"Do you know Peggy?" asked Sophie with interest. Peggy never mentioned anyone at all except the awful man whom she met on the couch now and then.

"Yes," said the man, who seemed a nice chatty kind of fellow, but to Sophie's practised eye, a chatty fellow who would be nice to meet and who would buy nothing. "We went to this lunchtime play yesterday, and got talking to a girl in the wine bar, she was waiting for her fellow to turn up. Very good-looking girl, lovely red hair."

"They are awfully dear," said the woman sadly. "But they are lovely. Are there any others of hers a bit cheaper?"

"What was the play?" asked Sophie suddenly, knowing somehow that they were going to say *The Table Lighter*, a silly little play which Eddie had seen yesterday. He had said it was a silly little play because he hadn't got a part in it. He had also said he had gone to it with Garry, a friend of his who was an agent, a useless agent. Peggy must have gone with Eddie, she didn't know anyone else, but why had neither of them mentioned it?

"It was *The Table Lighter*," said the woman. "This Peggy says she usually goes out at lunchtime, it takes her mind off work, and her chap is an actor, very good-looking fellow. He was late because he had been seeing someone about a job, I think."

"It's a small world," said the man.

"It is indeed," agreed the woman.

"Oh very small," said Sophie. "Did they seem very close, Peggy and this actor? I just ask because I used to be rather worried about her, you know, she didn't seem to have much social life . . . I was wondering whether this might be something, well, you know, serious. . . ."

Her heart was pounding, and she felt strangely outside herself as she asked the question. How great it was to be so cool and calm and not to panic when the world was falling down. This is what she must have been expecting all morning.

"I don't think so, do you?" said the woman to her husband. "Not a real thing going, they just seemed to be great friends laughing and joking without a care in the world. It's incredible to think that he's an actor and she's a leather worker like this. They didn't seem to have a care in the world."

The nice man put the bag down. Twenty pounds was too much even for the work of someone he had met.

"That's right, I felt that too, sort of carefree. But then you know there are people who can be like that, and something sort of looks after them. It's like as if there were a big smiling God who says, 'Go on, Peggy and Eddie, amuse yourselves, I'll look after you.'"

They couldn't know as they looked at the steely green eyes of the little girl in the bag shop that they were looking into the face of a big smiling God who didn't know how to stop smiling.

Bond Street

The light was very bright when Margaret came out of the station. Everything seemed to dazzle her. Even the daffodils on sale in big baskets seemed too harsh a yellow. People's spring clothes seemed too loud, and the buses must have been resprayed recently. Surely they were never so aggressively red before? Or was it because there were so many of them in Oxford Street?

She was a little tired, she often felt tired before she began a shopping spree, it was tension she supposed. Nobody liked shopping, places were too crowded, assistants not at all helpful, so many foreigners who didn't even attempt to speak English properly. Shopping was hardly some-thing you did for fun. But then Margaret did shopping slightly differently from most people. She didn't actually pay for the goods she brought home. Her tensions and frustrations came not from trying to catch the eye of a shop assistant, but from avoiding it.

She made a list, like any conventional shopper would do. She took a shopping bag, she always carried enough money to pay for these listed items, but rarely if ever broke into it. She paused and window-shopped. She had coffee when her feet were tired, she got into little chats with other resting shoppers. In the evening she would go home again, sighing a little on the underground until someone would stand and give her a seat. Margaret had shopped in London like this once a month for nine years. Never in those nine years had she come into contact with a store detective, a security man, or anyone remotely suspicious of her.

Blinking slightly in the sunlight, she looked at her list.

Red towels.

Knives.

Tights.

Remnants.

Pendant.

Giant cup.

Table lighter.

Jacket.

A lot of them could be "bought" in Selfridges, but she wanted a jacket from Marks, and she had seen a nice table lighter in a small souvenir-type shop on her last visit. She might go down to Liberty's for the remnants. She made sure that her wallet with the £84 in it was safely zipped into the pocket inside her coat. You couldn't be too careful these days, with teams of pick-pockets coming to London from abroad. She straightened her shoulders and went off to buy towels.

She had painted the bathroom last week. Harry had been delighted with it. He said it looked really cheerful with all that white and the window frame red. He was going to buy a nice cheerful red and white bath mat, he promised.

"And I'll get some red towels when I'm doing my shopping," Margaret had said.

"Aren't towels a bit dear?" Harry had wondered with a frown coming over his big kind face.

"Not if you shop around, they would be if you bought the first good ones you saw," said Margaret.

"I don't know what I'd do without you, you're a great little shopper," Harry had beamed, and Margaret felt safe when she saw his frown disappear. She felt very frightened when Harry worried, he looked so old.

The towels were easy. You pick up a big one, a middle-size one, and two small ones, you take them out under the light to examine them properly, so that you have separated them from the big piles where they are stacked. Then moving slowly, and concentrating on them carefully, looking neither left nor right, you move farther and farther away from their original place. Put down your shopping bag and examine the corners of the towels to see that they are properly finished, drop the smaller ones into the bag on the ground, never looking around, that's the secret, then in a businesslike way fold the big one into a small manageable size and put it in on top of the others, walking with the bag held out in front of you toward the desk where it says PAY HERE. Anyone watching you would think you are taking the items to pay for them, people at PAY HERE never watch anything at all. You then ask the PAY HERE people where curtains are, and if, suppose, by some terrible chance you are stopped ... then you say, "I went straight to the Pay place, and I got so absorbed in the curtains that I simply forgot."

Margaret didn't know what would happen if she were caught. She assumed she would be able to talk herself out of it if there were only one item in her bag, which was why she worked on the time-consuming principle of taking only one thing, and then checking it in as a parcel or in a left-luggage locker. *That's* what made shopping so tiring for her, all the endless walking backward and forward to luggage lockers, but it seemed only sensible. The day she was lazy was certainly the day she would be caught.

No problem either with the knives. Nice steak knives with wooden handles, Harry would love these. She would say she had found them in the attic, that they were a present for an anniversary, a present which must have got tidied away. They would laugh together over their good fortune in having found them.

The tights were a luxury for herself. She still had good legs and she hated the kind of stockings that looked cheap and hairy. Every month she collected four or five pairs of nice sheer tights, sometimes in what they called "the new fashion shades." She never mentioned these to Harry. He would occasionally say, "You've got better legs than half these women on the television," and she would smile happily.

The remnants were for dressmaking. She wasn't very good at it, but anyone could sew a pillowcase or a cushion cover, and it made Harry feel happy and comfortable, looking over at his wife sewing away contentedly while they watched television. She took enough to make a tablecloth too. That would only need a hem around it and Harry would never look at the edges, just at the nice bright colour on the table at breakfast, and he might say, "Imagine, you made that cloth yourself. I don't know how other fellows manage with their wives, I really don't."

The pendant was a present for their son, Jerry,

who was away in the North at university. It would be his birthday next week. Jerry was a worry to her, he often looked at her very hard without saying anything.

"What are you thinking about?" she'd ask.

"Nothing, Mum," came the invariable reply, but she felt that he was staring at her, and pitying her somehow and worrying about her. She didn't like that at all.

Once she had sent him a cashmere sweater for his birthday and he had rung up not so much to thank her as to protest.

"They cost a fortune, Mum, however did you afford it? They cost half what Dad earns in a week."

Margaret realized she had gone too far.

"I bought it in an Oxfam shop," she said, pretending to confess to a little economy, but her heart was pounding with fear.

"But it's new, it's all wrapped up in cellophane," argued Jerry.

"Someone gave it away, a present they didn't want."

"They must have been mad," grumbled Jerry, still suspicious. From then on, it had to be gifts that nobody could put a real price on. The pendant would have cost about £7 had she paid for it, but she hadn't of course because she had asked the nice young man to show her some earrings and put the pendant in her pocket as he went to get an earring tray.

She and Harry had seen a television play the other night where the husband had his tea out of a huge china cup. Harry had smiled and said wasn't it lovely.

"I've seen those in the shops," said Margaret. "Would you like one?"

"No, it's only silly, they cost a fortune and maybe my tea would get cold in it. It just looked nice, that's all."

Margaret said she had a half-memory of seeing them in a sale where they cost about fifty pence.

"Oh well then," Harry had said and went back to looking at the television.

The one Margaret took would have cost her seven pounds fifty pence, but when she was showing it to Harry tonight she would leave out the seven pounds. She thought it was a great deal of money to pay for one cup and saucer. Sometimes she felt aggrieved if the items she took were very expensive. She liked the best, but she liked things to be good value.

The table lighter was a present for Harry's brother and his wife, who were having a twenty-fifth anniversary party next week. Harry's brother Martin never approved of Margaret, something Harry wouldn't and couldn't see in a million years. The families met rarely. A cursory visit around Christmas-time, another in the summer. Martin's wife never had a cigarette out of her mouth, she never wore stockings, her hair was a mess, she had a loud laugh. Margaret was glad not to see too much of her. But she was always charming when they came to the house, and laughed insincere little peals when Martin said to his brother, "Well, she has you rightly tamed, Harry, never thought I'd see the day when you'd be out planting vegetables and filling window boxes."

"Harry's marvellous at gardening, he grows a

116

great deal of what we eat," Margaret would say loyally.

"That's how you must be able to afford this place," Martin had once said, looking around at lamps, ornaments, vases, and linen tray cloths, all carried home from Margaret's monthly shopping trips.

"I don't know how you afford this style, I really don't."

Martin had been far from helpful over that bad business years ago. Far from standing up for her and trying to keep up a good name for them, he had encouraged Harry in all that silliness.

"Never thought you had it in you," he laughed coarsely when Margaret had called a family conference to deal with the situation. "A young lassie, too, well that beats everything." Martin's sluttish wife had let the cigarette ash fall down her stained cardigan with excitement. Old Harry, and a young girl from the factory, and a baby on the way. Excitements like that didn't come very often.

Margaret wondered whether the table lighter was too good for them. After all they would have humiliated her, set her adrift if they had had their way. Why should she get them anything? But still, it was all part of the scheme, the plan, the whole elaborate complicated business that made her victory assured. She had to be the perfect sister-in-law as well as the perfect wife. Only a perfect sister-in-law, herself a nonsmoker, would be so thoughtful as to give something like a table lighter. So quietly it went into the bag. Later she would get a really cheap box for it, they would assume it had cost a couple of quid instead of

117

twenty. They would be surprised it worked so well. Part of Margaret's good taste.

It would be a dull evening at their anniversary. Their children were loud, too, and drank beer from cans. The lazy wife would make a small attempt at food, but it might only be sandwiches and trifle. There would be a lot of drink of course. And sometime in the evening Martin would nudge Harry and ask him were there any more little girls that he could pass on to his old brother, and Harry would look sheepish and silly and hope that Margaret hadn't heard.

Martin would love Margaret to have her come-uppance even at this late stage. He couldn't believe how well she had managed that business years ago. Looking back on it, Margaret herself often wondered how she had been able to cope with it.

There was Harry, all shuffling and foolish, and not able to look at anyone. There was this girl, small, fat, very fat now that she was five months pregnant. There was her father, a bit older than Harry, and even more shuffling, and everyone shouting about money, and rights and duties, and doing the proper thing, and not letting anyone get away with anything. Until Margaret had spoken.

"The only decision we have to make is this," she had said. "If Harry accepts that he is the father of this child, then he must marry the lady as soon as possible and give the child a name and a home. I will take our son and this house, and whatever it costs for both of us to live here. Harry must provide for two families, he will have no access to my home. I'm sure, with overtime, he'll earn enough to keep us all."

Her voice sounded so calm that everyone

118

stopped shouting and listened. Martin and his wife had been invited especially to give more support, but they sat open-mouthed through it all.

"If Harry thinks that he is only one of several people who might be the baby's father, then he should give the lady some money towards the upkeep of the child—a small lump sum, to thank her for his pleasure, and to acknowledge some limited degree of responsibility."

The room was silent.

"And what about you, Margaret?" asked Harry. "What will you do?"

"If you leave our home, and go with this lady to some room, I will never see you, nor allow you to see Jerry as long as I live. If you fail in your payments, I will get a court order against you. I have to look after *my* child, just as this lady has to look after hers. If you decide that you cannot be the sole person to be named as father, and you pay this lady a sum of money, to be agreed between you and her and her father, then when everybody has gone, I will make your supper as usual, and I will live here with you, never mentioning this whole incident again, unless you want to."

"You'd forgive me?" stumbled Harry.

"It's not a question of forgiving, there's nothing to forgive, it's the bargain we made when we got married. I give you a comfortable home, and you give me your presence and loyalty, and support me. There's nothing unusual about it at all."

And she had gone out into the kitchen to put some flowers in water, while their voices came from the sitting room, and then they all left.

Nobody came in to say good-bye or to tell her what had happened.

There had been no sound from the sitting room, and she didn't know whether Harry had left with them. The five minutes were like five hours, the clock ticked, and the water tank burbled, loudly, menacingly. But she wouldn't run in to see was he there, had he stayed, had she won.

She tore the stems of the flowers to little green rags as she waited. She knew this was some kind of test. It was too long, he must have gone. If she had lost, what would she do with the house? There was no point in scraping and saving to make it nice, just for a ten-year-old boy and herself. If she had won, she would really keep her promise, she would make it a wonderful home for him, for them. Even if she had to steal, she thought, she wouldn't backtrack on her word.

Then the door of the kitchen opened, and Harry, red-eyed, came in.

"I'm giving her £50," he said.

"That seems very fair," said Margaret.

She never asked why, or whether had loved the girl, or whether she was a marvellous lay, or how and when they had met. She kept her bargain, and the next time she had gone to Oxford Street, she started bringing home little treats for Harry and herself. Her reward was his guilty devoted smile, his belief that he had married a Wonderwoman and nearly lost her through his own stupidity. That made her feel very good.

There was only the jacket left now; everything else, including her coat, was in the left-luggage office. She had a scarf and a brooch in her handbag. That was how she had got the jacket four years ago, the nice lilac one, that Harry had said made her look so young. This time she wanted black velvet.

She took one from the rail, and with one movement removed the price tag, throwing it behind the radiator, and pinned her own brooch on the lapel. The jacket was on her in a flash, with her scarf knotted under its collar. In seconds she had taken a different jacket out to hold it up to the light.

"It's nice," she said to the salesgirl.

"Nice cheerful red," said the girl.

"And they wear very well," said Margaret. "I've had this one for quite a while, I was wondering should I get it in another colour."

"It's a good idea to buy a couple if they suit you," said the girl.

"But," said Margaret, "I think it's a bit extravagant of me really. I'll just go and do the rest of the shopping and if I've anything left over I'll come back later."

"That's a good idea," said the girl politely.

And she walked out into the afternoon sunlight to collect all the shopping from the left-luggage and go home to Harry.

Oxford Circus

My heart sank when Frankie got a job in the BBC. Up to now all the disasters in her life had been reasonably contained among her ever-dwindling circle of friends. But if she were in reach of a microphone she might easily broadcast them to the nation. They might even become national incidents. Because Frankie was rarely out of trouble. I think it was only because I was such a boss that I was a friend of hers at all. I liked the self-importance of rescuing her. I liked her undying gratitude and useless promises to be more careful the next time.

Clive didn't like Frankie, which was unusual because Clive liked almost everyone. He said she was brainless. Yet she had a far better degree than any of us. He said she liked getting into trouble, but he hadn't seen the tears pouring down her face as she sat in the police station wrongly accused of starting a fight in a restaurant and causing a breach of the peace. Frankie hadn't started the fight, she had tried to stop somebody else's. Clive said she was vain. That couldn't be right either. Would somebody who was vain turn up at a dinner party in filthy painting clothes because she had become so involved in doing up a neighbour's child's playroom that she had forgotten to look at her watch and just ran out to catch a taxi the way she was?

Frankie had recently disentangled herself from a particularly horrible man who owned a restaurant and a bad temper and who had beaten Frankie very badly on three separate occasions. The day she said she was leaving him, he had taken some of her best clothes and burned them in his incinerator.

She had taken nothing from the horrible man except a few bruises and a series of misunderstood memories. That was another fault of Frankie's, she never learned from anything. If she were to fall down and pass out six nights in succession because she had drunk too much, she never considered for one moment that there was an element of cause and effect. She just regarded each falling-down as a terrible happening to be deeply regretted. There would be other restaurant owners who would throw all her clothes into the incinerator. I just hoped there wouldn't be many of them in the BBC.

"I want a reduction in the licence fee," was all Clive said when I told him that Frankie was going to work at Broadcasting House. "The thought of that woman's voice coming at me from the radio is enough to make me take sick leave."

Clive can be very silly once he has a bee in his bonnet about something, so I took no notice except to say that she would be doing research, not actually speaking on the air.

"That's a mercy," said Clive. "But the number of apologies for whatever she has researched for some unfortunates will be legion."

For once we were having a quiet night at home, and I had cooked a dinner. Usually neither of us have much time, what with Clive giving evening classes and me taking them. For once we decided not to study but to stick photos into an album, and we had them all out on the floor when the doorbell rang. In London that's unusual. We hadn't invited anyone, and nobody selling Bibles or double glazing would ever climb the stairs to our flat, however great the commission in this world or the next.

It was Frankie.

"I'm not going to stay a minute, I'll leave the door open so that I won't even be tempted," she said, blocking the door open with her handbag and creating such a draught that all the photos blew out of their little piles.

123

"Close the bloody door," said Clive, and I knew the evening was ruined.

"I just wanted to borrow one sweater, and one skirt. Until lunchtime tomorrow only. To go to work in, the job starts tomorrow you see, and because Bernard burned all my things I've got nothing to wear except this dress, which I don't think would be suitable for the Beeb."

It was a lovely dress, cut to the navel, with rhinestones all around the bit of bosom it had. It would be unusual in the BBC but might just hasten on the disaster that was bound to befall Frankie. I said cheerfully that I would go and see what I could find.

Frankie sat on the floor, falling out of her rhinestones and oohing and aahing at the pictures.

"My God, didn't we all look foul at your wedding?" she shouted, and even through the bedroom door I could feel Clive bristling.

Then:

"Clive, that's not you. I don't believe it. With all the curls and the little toy horse sitting on a stool. It's beautiful." She positively gurgled over the picture. I had begged him once with tears in my eyes not to throw it out, and had won only by such a small margin that I had always kept it hidden in the bottom of the drawer. I took it out to gurgle a bit myself over, privately.

I rushed out of the bedroom carrying my only good skirt and a new blouse which I had not yet worn.

"Would these do?" I said hurriedly.

Frankie was so far into the photos now that nothing would have got her out of them.

"Look at that picture of you and me and Gerry!" she exclaimed happily. "Do you remember that night you went out with him and I had to pretend to your mother that you stayed with me? It was awful, I kept getting so confused about what I was meant to have been doing, or what we were meant to have been doing, that I'm sure I gave the game away."

Oh she had, she had, then and now, but that was Frankie, so innocent, and hopeless. Always.

"I believe you have joined the BBC," said Clive in a heavy overdone effort to save me embarrassment. It was as if he had flashed a notice saying let us change this unsavoury subject of my wife's past. I hated him for it.

Even Frankie must have sensed some tension, because she sort of gathered up her limbs, and breathed a few dizzy remarks about hoping she'd cope with her first day as a new girl, and snatched my clothes and ran.

Clive had put away the photos. The one of him with curls he had torn into eight pieces, and thrown into the basket. He said he had remembered he had a lot of study to catch up on. I went to bed in a sulk, couldn't sleep, so got up and did the ironing. Clive said I was behaving like a martyr, that I was only ironing to make him feel guilty. No, I said, harassed working wives love ironing, it keeps them sane, they use it as therapy in mental hospitals, everyone knows that. He said I was becoming as childish as my friend Frankie, and even more immature. I said his shirts were now a size too small for him, or a half size anyway, why else would all the top buttons be loose?

Oh it was a lovely evening.

Frankie rang me at work, nobody except Frankie ever rings me at work. The principal hates it, and he's right, you can hear the whole form screaming while you're out of the classroom. I've told Frankie this again and again, but she never remembers. She wanted to meet me at six o'clock to give me back my clothes.

"I don't need them at once," I said, furious to have brought the principal's wrath down on me again for nothing.

"But I want you to have a little drink, just two little drinks in the BBC Club," she said beseechingly.

There was no time to chat. I could hear a noise like a tank division coming from my classroom. Anyway I'd always wanted to go into the BBC Club, that's what did it.

"Yes," I shouted. "Where is it?"

"Get off at Oxford Circus, and walk in a straight line," she said. "I'll have your clothes in a nice plastic bag ready for you."

I hoped that she'd remember to get some replacements for herself. I could only too easily see her sitting there in her bra and pants drinking a pink gin.

The real reason I gave in so easily was that I wanted to avoid meeting Clive. We had parted in a mutual sulk that morning and I didn't look forward to apologizing or waiting for him to. It would do him good not to see me waiting there anyway. We usually had a beer and a sandwich from the fridge at about six, before he went out to teach a lot of foolish self-advancing housewives all about economics, and before I went to learn Italian. I was doing a degree in Italian so that I could teach it in a school where the children were older, and more appreciative, and didn't scream like deprived railway engines.

Two little drinks at six o'clock, and the chance

of seeing some personalities . . . it was a great idea.

The BBC Club was huge, and had two separate entrances, each with a porter's desk where you had to show an identity card before being let in.

"Perhaps your friend has signed you in," said a porter kindly, examining the visitors' book. My friend hadn't. There was no passport to personalities for me at all. I felt very sad.

I waited on a chair, feeling foolish, for about half an hour until Frankie arrived, breathless. She was desperately sorry but she'd been to the shops, it was late closing, and she'd got herself something to wear instead of my skirt and blouse.

She had indeed. It was an outfit of skin-tight black velvet pants and a sort of a big red handkerchief tied under her bosom. It looked great, but it didn't look like the kind of thing she could wear the next day at work. I had grave doubts whether it was even the kind of thing she should wear in this club.

We were about to sweep in when the porter asked for her card.

"But I work in BBC," said Frankie proudly.

"I'm afraid you have to be a member of the club though," he said kindly.

Frankie was like a toddler whose ice cream had been snatched away. I thought she was going to cry.

"We can go to a pub," I said.

"I don't want to go to a pub, I want to go in here, it's where all the BBC people go," said Frankie in a five-year-old voice.

At that moment a couple of men were waiting for the porter to finish so that they could go in, and they were amused by Frankie's predicament.

They asked her what programme she worked on, and good-naturedly signed us both in, looking at Frankie's outfit appreciatively.

We were in. It was a big room, hot and smoke filled, and crowded with people. I couldn't see anyone I had ever seen on television, and I wasn't near enough to people to hear any famous voices from radio either. I was a bit disappointed.

Frankie had wriggled up to the bar and gotten us drinks. There was nowhere to sit, nowhere to lean even, so we stood in the middle of a crowded room, like people at a party where we knew no one. I didn't like it at all.

"I have a purpose in coming here," hissed Frankie, looking left and right in case anyone was listening.

"Oh my God," I said.

"No, listen, you're always getting frightened over nothing. I think you don't go out enough, you and Clive. I mean poring over old baby pictures every night, it's not natural."

"We won't be doing that again for a while," I said darkly.

Frankie didn't notice any nuance in my tone. She was far more interested in her purpose.

"I'm here for a special reason," she said again. Anyone who knew Frankie even slightly could see that trouble lay ahead. I who had known her since school felt weighed down with doom.

"You see there's this guy, my boss on the programme. He's absolutely great, very dynamic, people just do anything he says, and he was saying today that he thought I was getting on very well for someone who had just come in. I really did, you know. I used my initiative and brought many more files than they asked for, and we found a whole new line to go on . . ."

"Go on about the guy," I said resignedly.

"Well, he said that what I needed was someone to sort of talk me into the programme, let me know the feel of the place, what they were at, where they were going, and what they wanted to do. And he said that I should try to live and breathe the programme constantly, thinking up new ideas, new ways of dealing with them, that's what makes a programme great he says. Martin says."

"So?" I said.

"So I thought I should start doing it straight-away," beamed Frankie.

"Are we going to look for people from the programme and start living it and breathing it?" I asked in disbelief.

"No . . . not exactly. You see the one to tell me is this boss man, Martin. He really IS the programme. I thought I'd meet him here and get to know him, off duty."

"But if you're going to meet him, why am I here?" I said, hurt.

The two little drinks didn't seem such a good idea now I thought Frankie was going to dash off and leave me at any moment with over half an hour to kill before going to my Italian class.

But that wasn't it, there was more.

"No, he's much too important for me just to turn up here and strike up a chat with him about the programme. That would be very forward. It's more complicated than that."

I sighed.

"Some of the others were telling me that he has this utter dragon of a wife, a real Tartar

129

woman, who won't let him out of her sight. She works in the Beeb, too, but in another department and she won't let him have any fun. She comes in here every night and stares across the room at him with awful eyes; then at seven o'clock she marches him home for dinner like a schoolboy."

I automatically looked at the clock as if to count the minutes before this ritual took place.

"You've only got a half an hour," I said jokingly.

Frankie was utterly serious.

"I know, that's why I have to find her. I must strike up a friendship with her as soon as possible, so that she'll realize she has nothing to worry about, that I'm not after her husband. If she and I became friends then it would all be fine."

I looked at Frankie, in her flame-coloured top and her tight, tight pants, her hair falling over her face like someone who had just got out of bed and was waiting, slightly tousled, for the next lover. I didn't think her mission was going to be possible. But there's no use explaining some things to Frankie so I offered to get another drink and plunged into a sea of bodies around the bar.

When I came back Frankie was gone, or I thought she was, but she had only gone out to make a phone call.

"I have to identify her first," she said. At that moment someone was paged over the loud-speaker.

"That's her," giggled Frankie.

"Where?" I scanned the room.

"We'll see. I went out to a public phone box and rang here asking to speak to her. We'll just have to see who goes out."

Like schoolchildren, we watched the door.

Eventually a small blonde disappeared through it.

"That couldn't be his wife, not monsterish enough," said Frankie firmly.

"Did they tell you he hasn't slept with her for years, but he can't leave her because of the children or her health?" I asked sourly. I was feeling very annoyed with this childishness, and hated being part of it. I also wondered whether Clive was worried about me. Maybe I should have rung him.

The small blonde came back, shrugging her shoulders at her friends. "Nobody there apparently," she said. "The phone was dead."

"It is her," said Frankie in amazement.

"Now, Frankie," I begged. "Don't go up to that woman and start one of your explanations, you know how people misunderstand your way of talking. It's always happening if you think about it. Why do you have to do it today? Let it go for a day or two. Please, Frankie?"

It was, of course, useless. I hadn't even finished speaking when Frankie had bounded over to the blonde's side.

I was too embarrassed to do anything except stare into my drink, and wish I were a million miles away, or about three miles away, at home with Clive, the row over, forgiven, forgotten, the two of us sitting there listening to records, laughing over it all, and making great plans about how we would see the world eventually. It all seemed so safe, and so much what I wanted compared to standing in this awful place with terrible things going on a few feet away.

I hardly dared look over for fear of what was happening. The small blond woman was hauntingly familiar. Was she on a telly programme? Was she a film star? How did I know her face so well? Frankie had said something about her being a producer, you don't see producers' faces.

I knew it, I knew it, I was summoned over and introduced. Everyone seemed to be quite happy and relaxed, they always do with Frankie . . . initially.

"Is it your first day in the BBC too?" asked the blonde kindly.

"No, I'm not here, I mean I'm only here because Frankie asked me to have a drink with her after work. I'm just going off to my Italian lesson," I said, wondering why did I always sound like someone who had never learned English but was trying to pick it up as I went along.

"I'm a teacher actually, in a dreary old school, nothing bright and glittery like this," I said, wondering why I said it. I preferred the school a million times with its familiarity and chalk and noise to this strange place where you might be standing next to a newsreader and anything could happen.

The blonde seemed nice. Frankie had obviously told her some cock-and-bull story about being lonely and nervous in her job and wanting to get to know colleagues in the corporation. This had endeared her to all of them. They said that it was only too rare that people admitted to knowing nobody, most people went around and knew nobody for ages because of this English trait of reticence.

One of the men bought us a drink, we were part of a group.

Frankie was making a great effort to convince

the blonde that she was a serious, steady person interested only in her job.

"I'm not at all like my teacher friend, always flitting around," she said. I didn't think anyone could have believed her. There was I in a jumper and skirt, while Frankie looked as if she was about to do a gypsy dance, and strip in the middle of it. They couldn't have believed her, could they? But it was important for Frankie's purpose that they did, so I went along with it.

"Yes, Frankie is always trying to get me to settle down. I couldn't give two pins for my work, just the holidays and the hours are all I could care about. Frankie likes to live and breathe her job, she puts in endless hours of overtime, silly I call it."

Frankie smiled, the blonde frowned at me.

"You shouldn't stay in teaching, if you don't like it, it's bad for you and the children. I really do think it's a vocation, half my family are teachers, and the other half used to be. Those of us that didn't do it well got out," she said.

Inside I agreed with her, but I had to go on, no use in being converted too easily. I'd never see this woman again, and she wouldn't judge Frankie by her hopeless, feckless friend, surely. I'd better make myself a really bad case, whom Frankie was trying to reform.

"Oh I don't know, it's a job the same as any other. Worse paid than a lot, but then you can always read the paper when the kids are doing a test, and our Head is a bit soft about things like doctors' certs. If I want to earn a few quid, real money I mean, in some other job, I just don't turn up for a few days. I get paid just the same."

Never in my life had I done anything of the

sort. One teacher had once, and we were all appalled and shocked. The principal was a kind man who thought I was a bit flighty sometimes, but only because I did play with the children so much, even after school. His only real grievance was that my classes were too exuberant.

"I'm always trying to make her grow up, to tell her the joys of living and breathing her work," said Frankie in a goody-goody voice.

"Is it seven?" said the blonde. "Damn it, I was having a lot of fun. Martin will be around in front of the building in his car, I must run." She gave Frankie a warm good-bye, and wished her well, hoped to see her again. Barely glancing at me, she said she hoped I'd find a happier job soon.

"I'm really sorry to run," she said to the others. "It's just that we have to be home to change, we're going out tonight. My brother's having a little dinner."

It was only as I saw her side-face on that I realized why she was so familiar. She was like a twin of my principal. My nice kind idealistic headmaster, who had, now that I remembered it, a sister who used to be a teacher but who was now a senior producer in the BBC.

Tottenham Court Road

A lot of the books seemed to be about lesbians, which wasn't what she waned, however uninhibited and daring they might be according to the jacket descriptions, and then there were a sizeable number for gay men, with pictures of very beautiful muscled men on the covers, but this again wouldn't be any help. In horrified fascination she saw the section where Alsatian dogs and horses seemed to be people's partners, and about five shelves where people weren't naked at all but clad from head to toe in black leather and brandishing whips.

What she wanted and couldn't find was a book that would tell her how to be an enormous success as a woman in bed with a man. They didn't have any books for twenty-nine-year-old virgins. Such things weren't meant to exist . . . they were an embarrassment to society.

Oh the world was full of books telling twelve-year-olds not to be afraid of menstruation, and telling eight-year-olds about little eggs growing inside mummy's tummy, and assuring seventeen-year-olds that they would go neither blind nor mad from masturbation but that it wasn't as good as a healthy, meaningful, one-to-one sexual relationship. Julia was worn out reading helpful letters to people who complained of being frigid, advising them to relax and to be loving and to specify what they wanted. Who would tell her what she should want, and how to do it at her age without making an utter fool of herself? Twelve, even ten, years ago, she could have put herself at the mercy of her seducer, virginity would have been an honor then, something to be treated with respect and awe and tenderness. Nowadays she couldn't possibly tell any would-be seducer that this had never happened before. If it weren't so sad, it would be laughable.

There were no men in raincoats in the shop, no sinister figures with moustaches and sunglasses salivating over pictures in filthy books. In fact

Julia found it very hard to find a book to salivate over herself. They all seemed to be wrapped in cellophane. She wondered how you knew what to buy. There was no way she was going to ask for assistance either from that man who looked as if he should have been a head gardener in a stately home or from the tired, aging woman at the cash desk. She would have to hope that the blurbs, and the overwritten sentences about the material being uncensored, and straight from Scandinavia, would put her on the right trail.

The worst bit was over really, the walking into the shop and settling down with the browsers. She wore a head scarf, which she normally didn't do, in some mad wish to look different, to put on a different personality for this reckless, sinful venture. She had given herself two hours to look for the right book, or maybe books. She had five pounds in her handbag. If it worked it would be an investment well made, and perhaps there was an additional gain, in courage. She would never have believed herself capable of setting off deliberately and examining the outside of pornographic bookshops. She had finally settled on the one which looked as if it had the biggest selection. Really, you could get used to anything, Julia decided. She had now stopped worrying about what the other people in the shop thought about her, and was no longer afraid that they were all going to jump on her and rape her because she had shown herself mad for it by going into a sex shop anyway.

She moved unhappily from the Oral Love section to a small specialist area called Domination. Mainly women in thigh-high boots with evil smiles, and men cowering behind sofas.

Disconsolately she leafed through one of the magazines which was open—they had to leave something for you to browse through in that kind of shops—and saw sadly that it was Party Games, and that you would need coloring pencils to work out whose limb belonged to whom.

It was very depressing not to be able to find what she wanted when she had got herself as far as this. Julia had thought that the hard part would be making the decision to find the shop, and going in, and perhaps even understanding the terminology of the book without anyone to practise with, like you could with yoga or wrestling. She didn't know that her specific requirement would be uncatered for. And it wasn't as if it was easy to know where to go either. She had thought that Soho was the right area to hunt, but fortunately she had been able to ask people at work in a jokey way where they bought sexy magazines, and a knowing guy had said anywhere on Charing Cross Road, in the small places. Much better than Soho, because not priced for tourists. "Get out at Tottenham Court Road tube station, and you'll be fine then, Julia," he had said, and the others in the travel agency had laughed. Because you just didn't associate Julia with poking around in a porn shop. She looked too clean and wholesome and well brought up.

But they probably assumed that she had at least some kind of sex life, Julia thought in a troubled way. She didn't talk about having one, true, but then neither did anyone else. They were fairly sophisticated there, or even distant about things like that. Katy was married, and Daphne was divorced, and Lorna wasn't married but seemed to have a regular chap called Clive who was mentioned casually in dispatches. They probably thought that Julia met people at weekends, and maybe went to bed with them. If they knew she didn't, and hadn't, they would have been mildly embarrassed and sorry for her rather than shocked. It was that kind of office.

But her two friends Milly and Paula would have been shocked, and horrified. They were heavily into going to bed with people. Milly regularly with the same, very unavailable man, whom she said she didn't love, but was irresistibly drawn to, and Paula with somebody new and hopeful-sounding every couple of weeks. Julia invented the odd holiday sexual happening, and would feel very trapped when Paula would ask, "But was he good? I mean, you know, did he *satisfy* you?" Julia would say that some had and some hadn't and this kept Paula happy, and reflective about the differing abilities of men in this field.

Everyone plays games, even with friends, and Julia felt that she would have been breaking all the rules of the game if she had suddenly confessed that she had not known the experience and would they please tell her what it was like from start to finish. Paula and Milly would assume that she was having an early menopause, an unexpected nervous breakdown, or had developed unhealthy voyeuristic tendencies that she wanted to indulge. They would never actually believe that such a thing could be true.

And really it was only too easy. Julia had been adamant about not going to bed with Joe, her first and long-lasting boyfriend. She was full of the kind of thought that said in letters of fire that you lost them if you gave in to them. She had this firm belief that if she and Joe made love outside marriage he would never trust her again, and that he would assume she would be lifting her skirts for all and sundry. She didn't know from where she got this expression "lifting her skirts," it was coarse and unlikely and had nothing to do with love. She must have heard her aunt use it about some serving girl. Her aunt was like that.

Joe had gone to university and found a nice girl there. When he told Julia that their unofficial engagement had now better be forgotten, Julia had asked in a pained way, "Does she . . . er . . . sleep with you?" and Joe had laughed lightly and said that there wasn't much chance of actually sleeping with someone at university but they did make love of course.

So Julia, who was now twenty, decided that there must be other standards than her own, but for the next five years the only people who offered her the initiation rights were drunken people, or people who had been stood up or let down by some other girl, and who were using her as a substitute. And suddenly the years were passing, and she never knew what it was like to have the earth move, or to hear wild cries of ecstasy mingling with her own, and she felt frowningly that this was bad news. . . . Still, there had been so much else to think about, borrowing the money, setting up a different kind of travel agency to anyone else's in a different kind of partnership, going abroad three times a year to investigate things like they all did, and there was getting a flat and doing it up, and keeping her aunt and her father happy by visiting them regularly with lots of cheery stories and bright dismissals of all their ills and complaints. And there was going to the theatre, and meeting Paula and Milly in each other's flats for great meals with lots of wine, and really it was hard to know how the years went by without going to bed with people.

But now it was important. Julia had met a very nice man indeed. He was in publishing and she had met him one evening last year when she was touring the nightclubs of a foreign resort with a notebook, writing down details of atmosphere for next season's brochure. Michael had been sitting in one of the clubs and had seen what she was doing. He offered her a bit of advice about excluding it, because the drinks were too dear and the floor show was too touristy. Together they roamed several other clubs and at the end of along night he suggested she come back to his room for a drink. Julia was about to agree when she suddenly realized with a horrible shock that she literally didn't know how to do it. There she was, twenty-eight years old, and she didn't know whether she was meant to lie down on the bed naked and wait for him to do everything, or if she should undress him, or if she should move up and down when it was happening or round and round, and it was all very well to say that she'd learn in time, but who could learn in two minutes what they should have been learning over the last ten years?

Lightly she said no, and refused for the rest of the week also, on the grounds that she didn't go in for holiday things. This sounded, she hoped, as if she went in for real-life things very seriously, and Michael seemed to think that this was reasonable enough. He didn't live in London, but he came to see her for half a dozen week-ends, and for three of those she pretended she had someone staying in the flat and couldn't ask him to stay. Then twice she said she had too much work to do, and didn't want to ask him back. Finally, the last time, she had asked him to the flat for a meal, and when she was getting the usual excuses ready he had held her hand very gently.

"We get on well together," he had said.

"Sure, very well," she admitted, almost grudgingly.

"Then why do you close me out?" he asked. He had been so gentle and understanding that if she had said at that very moment what was worrying her she knew it would have been all right. Why couldn't she? Because she felt foolish. She felt that she was grown-up and intelligent in every way except this. She couldn't bear the vulnerability, it would show. She was even afraid that the whole thing might be messy and might hurt her. Because she was such an ancient virgin, it might be impossible to pierce her virginity. Think how appalling that would be.

She had bought time.

"The next time you come to London you can stay here for the whole week-end," she said. "I'd like that. It's just that, well, I'm not ready for it now, and I don't think people who are grown-up and equal should have to make excuses to each other, do you?"

He had agreed, and they had talked of other things, and he had his hand on her neck as they talked, and occasionally he kissed her and told her she was very dear to him. And deep down she thought that it would be possible to lose her virginity before he came back in a few weeks, and it would all be fine from then on.

It's harder than you think to find somebody to

sleep with you, in a limited time, and for a limited time and with no strings, and with no buildup. Julia went to a party and behaved outrageously with a businessman who was in London for a few days, having what he said was a whale of a time. She even managed to get him home to her flat. Staring at herself in the bathroom mirror, she wondered whether it could ever have been so terrible for anyone as it was going to be for her. He was very silly and he kept laughing at his own jokes, and he was rather drunk. His idea of romance was to plunge his hand unexpectedly and painfully down the front of her dress. But Julia thought, brushing her gritted teeth in order to be nice and inoffensive for the beautiful act, it was better to learn on someone awful.

When she went back to the sitting room he was asleep on the sofa, and no amount of cooing or even shouting could revive him. Eventually she took off his shoes, threw a rug over him, and went to bed in a rage. Next morning she had to make him breakfast, assure him that his wife wouldn't be hurt in any way, and kind of hint that it had all been rather wonderful. She went to the office in a rage also.

In the next ten days she got two more men back to her flat. One was a friend of Lorna's and Clive's who told her eighteen times about his wife having upped and left with a teenager. She promised him consolation and a shoulder, even a whole body, to cry on. First though, there was the story of the wife, over and over, what he had done wrong, what he hadn't done wrong, how he couldn't blame her, how he'd like to throttle her, how he hoped she'd be happy, how he hoped she'd rot in hell. When it was bedtime and Julia got herself into and out of the state of self-pity and self-disgust about making love to such an unlovable man, he said that he would like to lie beside her all night, but that they couldn't make love as he hadn't been able to do that for a long time now. It was quite normal. Apparently the doctor had told him that thousands of men had the same problem.

The other possible bedmate had been a really loud vulgar friend of Paula's who showed a marginal interest in Julia one night in a pub. Immediately she returned his interest a hundredfold. Since he had been making passes at her unsuccessfully for a couple of years, he was delighted. On the way home he told her what a splendid stud he was, that he wished one could get references for that sort of thing, that he loved women, big women, little women, young women, all women. Julia was nearly in a state of collapse by the time the taxi turned into her street.

"Do you like virgins?" she inquired hopefully.

He did, he loved them, he was very good with them. He hadn't had one for ages now, but he did like virgins.

It was halfway through the drink before deflowering that Julia remembered an article she had read the previous Sunday about venereal disease. It would be just her luck to wait twenty-nine years and then do it for the first time with someone who was riddled with syphilis, and then pass it on the next week to the only man she had ever really wanted. Suddenly she went all funny and said that she couldn't go to bed with him because she thought she had sprained her back. The remark sounded even more stupid than she could have believed possible.

"Let me do all the work," he had said.

Julia had no idea what he was talking about, but was sure she would catch some disease if she allowed herself to find out. She shooed him out into the night, and decided it would have to be a bookshop.

She had told the girls in the travel agency that she was going to the Family Planning Association, so she would take a long lunch hour. She had in fact been on the Pill for a month so that she was now protected. All she needed was someone, anyone, who would tell her how not to make an utter fool of herself and drive Michael away next Friday night. It was Tuesday now, for God's sake, she really didn't have any time to lose. She had suffered so many humiliations already, it didn't seem too much to ask the man who looked like a head gardener for some advice.

"I wonder if you could tell me, do they publish any books, sort of manuals of instruction really, on how to make love . . . in an ordinary sort of way?"

"I beg your pardon?" said the gardener, and for one wild moment Julia wondered whether he in fact worked in some other shop, and she had done something unpardonable. No, of course he worked here, she had seen him directing people towards the shelves of their choice.

"Well, I was looking for something . . . to give to my niece," she said triumphantly. "She's . . . er, getting married soon, and I don't think she knows exactly what will be expected of her."

The gardener looked concerned on behalf of the niece but didn't see how he could help.

"Couldn't you tell her yourself, madam?" he asked politely, but puzzled.

"Oh I have, I have," Julia said. "But only basic things really, and she wants to be sort of tigerish, if you know what I mean. She feels she's going to lose out by not knowing the techniques that a man expects. She wants more than just clinical information, it's the response she's keen to learn really."

"I don't expect her husband will want anybody to teach her that except himself," said the gardener, a trifle hypocritically and pompously Julia thought. What was he doing running a porn shop if these were his views? Oh well, I've got as far as this, she thought in despair, I might as well wade on.

"You see she's in an unfortunate position. This chap she's marrying, he's been around a lot, and my . . . niece more or less pretended that she had, too, so she's going to feel very foolish when he discovers that she hasn't. I said I'd try and find a book that would tell her what to do."

The gardener still looked mystified by it all. Oh why couldn't he understand, why couldn't he just say that there was such a book and sell it to her?"

"But I don't see what she can learn from a book, madam," he droned on, trying to be helpful. "If I might suggest something, you'd be better off spending the money on a couple of bottles of wine, and sitting down with her and giving her the benefit of your own experience. If it's hard to talk about things like that, a drink often helps. She'd thank you much more for that than for just a book."

Julia was now desperate, and desperate people say desperate things.

"I *can't* tell her anything," she hissed in a low voice. "I don't know anything. I'm a nun."

"*A nun?*" bayed the gardener in horror.

"Well yes, we don't wear nuns' clothes these days, we work out in the world. You see, it all changed after that council in Rome, you hardly ever see nuns as nuns so to speak these days. Half the people walking around might be nuns."

She wasn't even a Catholic, she knew only the vaguest things about nuns, but she was banking that a man who ran a porn shop might know less.

She was wrong.

"Well I never," he said. "My sister is a nun too. But she wears dark clothes, and a short veil like a scarf since Vatican Two." He looked stunned at Julia's poncho cape and green trousers, at her sunglasses pushed back over the top of her scarf, and at her long, painted fingernails.

"I suppose that you sisters must be getting more and more worldly all the time," he said with deference.

"Well, it's so we'll look more normal at work," Julia explained. "Not to frighten off the other people, and make them think we are too holy or anything."

"And do you teach, Sister, or do you work in a hospital?" he asked with awe.

"A travel agency," said Julia before she could help herself.

"Why do nuns do that?" he asked with interest.

"It's mainly to help send people out on the missions," Julia replied, beginning to sweat, but thinking that in fact it mightn't be a bad sideline for their own agency. If she ever survived this ordeal she would suggest it to the others.

"So now you see why I need that book for . . . my niece," she went on briskly, and hoping to give the air of a worldly, businesslike nun.

"Well, I really don't like to suggest anything, Sister," he said fearfully.

"Nonsense," Julia said. "You must learn to accept us as we are, women working in the world, like other women. It's just that we've given up sex . . . or never taken it up," she finished lamely.

"Perhaps a bigger store might have one of these books on preparing for marriage . . . by a woman doctor," he said, trying to get out of it.

"I've been through those, nothing tigerish enough for my niece," said Julia.

"Tigerish." He thought for a while. "We're out of tigerish books, Sister," he said firmly.

"What would you suggest?" she begged.

"I don't think the fellow's going to mind at all, he'll like showing her around, if you'll forgive the expression."

"But she's quite old, my niece. I mean she's in her mid-twenties, he'll expect her to know tigerish things."

"Oh no, he won't, Sister. I'd go off and set her mind at rest about that. I mean it's not as if she was nearly thirty or something, he won't expect anything."

Julia walked sadly out of the shop. The man who looked like a gardener rushed and opened the door for her.

"It was a pleasure to meet you, Sister," he said. "I hope we'll have the pleasure of seeing you here

again . . . but perhaps not, of course. I'm sorry.
And I'm sorry for suggesting all that stuff about
the bottles of wine and the bit of chat. I mean I
wasn't to know you were a nun, Sister."

On the way back to Tottenham Court Road
tube station she saw an off-licence. The gardener
was probably right, maybe two bottles of wine
would work better than a book. Maybe she could
pretend to get drunk on Friday and see what
happened, maybe she could make Michael a little
bit drunk and watch what he did.

For the first time since the whole terrible
problem had begun to obsess her, Julia saw a ray
of hope. Perhaps it mightn't be as awful as she
thought it was going to be. He was hardly going
to get out of bed, put on all his clothes, and say,
"You have deceived me." It was laughable, really,
and that was another thing. She and Michael did
laugh together about a lot of things, they might
even be able to laugh one day about the thought
of a nun in cape and trousers running a travel
agency for missionaries and visiting porn shops
in her lunch hour.

Well, it was either believe that or ask the good-
looking Italian boy who was struggling with his
map trying to find Oxford Street whether he'd
like to rent a hotel room for the afternoon with
her. And, really, Julia thought that for a twenty-
nine-year-old virgin she had coped with quite
enough that day.

Holborn

Rita sat down to make a list of all the things she need to do. Now that she had been such a fool as to agree to the whole ridiculous idea, she might as well try and get through it as painlessly as possible.

She wrote LIST at the top of a piece of paper and stared at it in rage. Why had she agreed to meet them? Normally she was so quick and firm at getting out of things she didn't want to do, but his voice had disarmed her.

Ken had rung up last night and said he was in London, he and his new wife, they were still on their honeymoon, wouldn't it be nice if they and Rita and . . . er . . . Jeremy, was it, could get together for a civilized meal? It wasn't Jeremy, it was Jeffrey, he must have known. She knew that his wife was called Daisy, people didn't forget names, he must have done it on purpose.

She said hold a minute and she'd see if Jeffrey had planned anything. It was meant to be her excuse, she was going to come back to the phone and tell some lie.

"Right, of course," Ken had said pleasantly. "I hope he hasn't. It's our first time in London, and we'd love a bit of advice from a native."

Jeffrey had said why not, it would be nice to meet them, he'd love to give them a bit of advice, he'd tell them about boat trips to Greenwich and he'd mark their card. He was full of enthusiasm. The fact that she had spent a whole year living

149

with Ken didn't seem to disturb him in the least. What was past was past; they had both agreed that it was silly to brood.

She had come back to the phone and said it would be fine, where should they meet? Ken didn't know London at all, so he said he'd make his way to wherever she said. He wondered if they could make it straight after work or early evening anyway, because they'd want an early night.

"You haven't changed," giggled Rita, with a small pang of jealousy that he still wanted to be between the sheets with his bird well before midnight.

"Oh, it's not that," Ken said casually. "It's just that we . . . well, Daisy gets tired easily. She's rather frail you know, we don't like too many late nights."

So Daisy had turned out to be frail, had she? Marvellous, bloody marvellous, thought Rita. She was cunning to be frail, old Daisy. It meant she didn't have to go on all those wearying walks with Ken that Rita had endured, climbing hard sides of hills instead of easy ones, packing endless pairs of woollen socks for week-ends because you never knew when the next bout of walking fever would come on. How wise to be frail. Rita went back to her list-making.

Hair, she wrote. Yes, she'd take time off at lunch, an extra half an hour, and get her hair done, silly to try a totally new style in case it didn't work, but she did need a cut and conditioning treatment sometime, so why not today? She decided that as soon as the hairdresser's opened she would ring round and get a lunchtime appointment.

She had another cup of coffee to celebrate that decision being made. Jeffrey was still asleep. Most of the world was still asleep. It was only 6 A.M., but Rita couldn't sleep.

Clothes, she wrote. They had arranged to meet at Holborn station of all places; it was the only possible meeting point she could think of that was near Jeffrey's work, her work, and that Ken would be able to find. Ken really did sound bewildered by the size of London, not at all like the confident man she had known in Wales. Yes, clothes. She would wear her new skirt, the long patchwork one, and she would get a very simple sweater to go with it, in a matching colour, green maybe, or dark brown. She needed a new sweater anyway, it wasn't a question of buying anything especially for the occasion, that would be idiotic. What did she want to impress Ken for now? All that business was long over. She had ended it, she had left and come to London, she wasn't hoping he'd still fancy her. No, she needed a new sweater. Why not get it today? The shops in the Strand opened at nine o'clock, and she needn't be at work until half-past.

Photos, she wrote. She had a small pocket album of pictures of their wedding last year, it would be nice to show them to Ken. He would be interested, he would even recognize some of the people, her sister, her friends from Cardiff. And anyway, Rita thought, I look great in those pictures. After three months on a diet, naturally I look great. Why not let the frail Daisy have a look at me when I was two stone less than I am now? If they were still on their honeymoon, they wouldn't have wedding pictures yet, so she could be one up.

Handbag. Her own was a bit tattered, it didn't really go with the patchwork skirt, it didn't go with anything. She definitely needed one. At least twice last week she had been on the point of buying one. It had nothing to do with the fact that Daisy would probably have a frail little trousseau handbag with her either. No, she must get a handbag today.

She would borrow Lilly's cape. Lilly had a lovely black cape of fine wool with braid on the edge, which would be ideal over the outfit she was planning to wear. She must telephone Lilly at 8:30 A.M., before she left home, so that she could bring it to work with her. She had borrowed the cape twice already for parties and had lent Lilly her pendant in return. It was a gold pendant that Ken had given her. She still hadn't decided whether she would wear it tonight. Probably not.

It was still too early to talk to people, Rita grumbled to herself. She wished that people woke up sooner. Not that she could say much to Jeffrey, he would be busy getting out his guidebooks to London, and his list of pubs that served Real Ale. He was so very confident of her, it would never cross his mind that she was excited about seeing Ken again, and that she was sleepless with worrying about how to present herself in a good light. Jeffrey would laugh tolerantly and say how like a woman. Jeffrey had a good comforting line in clichés when he wanted. Rita often thought he used them like warriors used armour to avoid having to meet any real thoughts head-on. Jeffrey was always pretty predictable.

Now that's one thing Ken wasn't. He was tiresomely unpredictable, you never knew what was going to happen. She hadn't liked it at the time and she didn't like it now, but that was the real reason she had got up so early. For all his protestations about having an early night, Ken might easily be persuaded to come back to the flat for just one drink. Jeffrey loved people to come back and so normally did she, but if Ken was going to see her home she wanted to look at it with an eagle eye herself first.

Coffee cup in hand, Rita walked through the sitting room. Ken would laugh at the coffee table, not out loud but he would laugh. They used to use the word "coffee table" as an adjective to describe things and people they didn't like.

But what *did* you put things on, Rita complained to herself in irritation, if you didn't have a table of some sort? She just wished it didn't look so much like the kind of thing that held posh magazines and books nobody read. Well, she could cover it in things, ashtrays, knitting even. But God, how she and Ken had laughed at people who spent their time knitting. She hadn't known then that it was quite a peaceful thing to do while you watched television or listened to records. No, it might be pushing it to leave out her knitting, even though she was halfway through another great sweater for herself, and they only took her a week these days.

When she lived with Ken they had stripped down furniture and thought that the modern reproduction stuff was so ugly that it made you want to cry. She had no stripped-down pine in her sitting room now; in fact, quite a few little desks and corner cupboards of the type they used to laugh at. Rita shook herself and reasoned that she could hardly refurnish the whole flat before 10 P.M. that night for a man who might not even see it, and for one whom she no longer loved. Yes, she knew that she didn't love him, but she wanted to think that he still loved and admired her. Having it both ways certainly, why not? A lot of people had things both ways.

Jeffrey, for example, had things both ways. He had his freedom to go racing, she never interfered with that, and he had his home to come back to. He had her as a kind of modern practical stepmother to his two sons who came to tea every Saturday. She never bothered doing the place up for them, she never wanted to impress them with tales that they could tell their mother when they got home. Funny that she never put on any show for these two silent big-eyed children so that they could observe and note and tell their strange, silent, big-eyed mother, Jeffrey's first and foolishly ill-considered wife.

In fact she had met Heather on a few occasions and talked to her exactly like she would have talked to a client in the beauty salon. She regarded Heather as somebody you made conversation with, it didn't grow naturally. A lot of the women she beautified were like that, they wanted nothing about you, nothing about them, but lots of cheery stuff on the weather, the price of shoes, the traffic jam, and the wisdom of taking a holiday early in the season. Rita was very good at it. Heather had been easy.

So perhaps Ken and the dreaded Daisy would be easy too. But she could never in a million years talk like that to Ken, she used to imitate salon chat to him when they were living together, and sometimes he and she would make up a joke salon conversation with each other . . . the kind of one where both sides were eager to find some harmless incontroversial middle ground to speak about. If Ken caught a hint of that in her conversation tonight . . . an accidental little suspicion of it . . . she would die. Yes, she couldn't bear him to think she had gone over to the other side, to the enemy.

It was time to ring Lilly. Lilly grumbled and said it was raining and she was going to be taking her dry cleaning anyway, but of course agreed. "I love a bit of excitement over people's past," said Lilly. "You've always been so uneventful, happy, safe, married, never trying to pick up clients' husbands like we have. I'm glad there's a bit of drama here."

Drama indeed! It could hardly be described as that. Much more a middle-class acquisitive wish to show off, Rita thought sadly, as she woke Jeffrey and handed him a cup of tea because of some feeling that she was being disloyal to him by all this concentration on Ken. Jeffrey was pleased and touched, he looked very boyish and tousled sitting up in bed, drinking his tea as if it had been the most generous gift anyone had ever given him. Somehow this irritated Rita, and she said she was late and ran out of the flat.

She spent half an hour and almost a whole week's salary in a department store before she went into the salon. The sweater was far too dear and so were the handbag and the earrings that she felt she needed as well. They were all items she would have defined as luxury and out of her reach. She felt a low gloom come down on her after the initial exhilaration. A lot of eyebrow plucking, contour massaging, skin peeling and salon chat went into earning that much money. She tried to tell herself that she needed a couple of nice things, but she felt guilty. The kind of people who bought handbags and sweaters at that price were usually debs or wives of tycoons. There would be problems at the end of the month when they came to do the hire-purchase repayments, but perhaps she could borrow something before then.

Lilly handed over the cape. They sympathized with each other again and again about working in the only beauty salon in London that didn't incorporate a hairdresser's, and the day's work began. Between clients they had a giggle about how funny it would be if the dreadful Daisy came in to have a face-lift or something, and how Lilly would deliberately sabotage her.

Since she was already so much in debt Rita thought that it would be a pity to spoil the whole appearance by forgoing the hairdo, so that took care of the best part of a tenner and a half hour over her lunch hour. The afternoon seemed very long. Lilly wanted to know all about Daisy, but Rita didn't know very much apart from her newly discovered frailty. She had been a nurse in the hospital where Ken ended up after one of his falls from a cliff, and had met Ken shortly after Rita left Wales. Rita had heard surprisingly little about her from the couple of friends she still had in Cardiff. She was said to be "very sensible" and "very good for Ken," two remarks which Rita always assumed were in the nature of mild insults.

"Well, whatever she's like, she can't look as well as you do tonight," said Lilly loyally and admiringly, when the salon finally closed and Rita dressed herself up.

"I don't really care," Rita said. "But I'd like

156

him to have a bit of a pang about me. It's only natural, isn't it?"

Lilly agreed it was totally the right attitude, and asked if she could sort of pass by the station, too, so that she could have a look at them all meeting.

Rita didn't want that at all. It seemed too stagey. "That's not fair," complained Lilly. "I've lent you my cape, I've been excited about it all day. I want to have a look. I won't say a word, I won't pretend I know you."

"Jeffrey will recognize you," said Rita.

"No, I'll keep my head down. Oh go on, you can't stop me anyway. It's a public street, everyone has a right to be there."

Very reluctantly Rita agreed, and they set off about thirty yards apart from each other.

It was a mild evening, and the lights of the shop were competing with the sunset as the girls walked towards the station. On evenings like this Rita felt that she had made London her own, she lost the impersonal side of it. It was like any big town, you had your own little quarters, the place where you lived, the place where you worked, the place where you shopped. It was a matter of breaking down a huge city and making it manageable.

Lilly was ahead. She stopped to buy a newspaper, and looked up the cinema times. This was her ruse, her cover for why she was hanging about. Rita saw Jeffrey there, looking at his watch. This irritated her, too, because he was early, at least five minutes early, and there he was already fussing about the time. She could see no sign of Ken and his frail bride.

Just as she reached Jeffrey, who began to make

delighted sounds at the way she looked, she saw Lilly talking to a woman with a walking stick. They seemed to be greeting each other as old friends. Rita squinted. No, she didn't know the woman, and by her appearance she was hardly a client from the salon. You had to have a certain kind of chic and a certain kind of money before you could come in and have your face slapped by Rita or Lilly. Then, with a shock that nearly knocked her down, she saw that the woman was introducing Lilly to Ken. There he was, all smiles and grins and eager handshakes, the kind of over-eagerness that meant he was shy. My God, that woman couldn't be Daisy. She was years older than everyone, she could be Ken's mother. There had to be a mistake. Daisy was around the corner, this was some dreadful old woman who knew everyone, Ken, Lilly, half of London perhaps. Wave after wave of sickness passed over Rita, she actually thought she was going to faint. Jeffrey was talking away:

". . . really smashing, and you bought earrings too. They do suit you. Love, you look like a magazine cover, that's what you look like."

"That's Ken," Rita rapped out, pointing.

"And he's talking to Lilly," beamed Jeffrey. "Isn't that a coincidence?"

He started moving over in great bounds with his hand held out and Rita followed on legs that seemed too weak to carry her. She kept well away from the edge of the pavement, the slightest stumble she felt might push her out under the traffic.

"Ken!" she said. "And Lilly! Now who says London isn't a village?"

"This is Daisy, Rita," said Ken in the voice of

a child coming home from school with his first prize.

Rita looked at her. She was forty, she couldn't have been a day less. She had stringy hair pushed behind her ears, and she leaned on a stick, She had a great big smile, like someone's elderly and kindly invalid aunt.

"You're just the way I imagined," beamed Daisy, and with her free hand clutched Rita's shoulder and gave her a sort of clumsy hug. She gave Jeffrey a hug too. Jeffrey looked as if all his birthdays had come at once. A little world of good-natured nice people had all gathered together, he was as happy as a king.

Lilly was like someone with shell shock.

"Rita told me that she was meeting friends tonight, but . . . well, isn't it absolutely extraordinary?"

"How do you know each other?" snapped Rita in a bark. She was just recovering from the hug. She hated women who embraced you, and particularly women who embraced you from the awkward position of leaning on a stick.

"Peggy's an old . . . Peggy's a family friend . . ." stammered Lilly.

"I used to nurse with Lilly's mother," said Daisy. "And when Lilly was a child I used to come to the house and scrounge Sunday lunch. Your mother was so good to us, Lilly. We young nurses never had a penny in those days and there was always a huge meal there. It was really like home."

Ken couldn't go to bed with this woman, Ken couldn't be on honeymoon with her. She wasn't frail, she was a cripple. What had he been thinking of? He must have had some kind of nervous breakdown. Why was she called Peggy and Daisy, and why was she standing there leaning on her stick in her shabby jacket and skirt smiling all around her and looking so horribly *old*?

"Let's all go and sit down," said Jeffrey happily. "There's a pub near here or we can go straight to the restaurant. Lilly, you'll come with us. Shall I get a taxi?" He was so excited by it all that Rita could have hit him hard with her new handbag.

"Oh no, I can't, I have to, I mean I'm going," said Lilly, who, to give her some credit, thought Rita, looked wretched about it all. She didn't want to come and witness the shambles of an evening that it was going to be.

"Nonsense," said everyone at once including Rita, and suddenly there was a taxi and the five of them were in it, four of them chattering like birds in a box, Rita trying to calm down her mind, which seemed to be trying to get out of her forehead.

Why had nobody mentioned to her, even in passing, that this Daisy was an old woman? Very sensible, very good for Ken, what did they mean? Ken was fifteen years younger than she, at least. That might have merited a brief remark when Daisy's name came up. Rita looked at her. She was laughing and saying how exciting it was to be in London, and that she had already seen a man who read the television news, and an actor, and thought she had seen a woman MP, but Ken said it wasn't her after all.

"Why does Lilly call you Peggy?" asked Rita suddenly.

Daisy had an explanation for that too. Daisy had been her family name, like a nickname. When she was younger and worried about what people thought of her, she thought it was a silly name to have. So in the hospital she had pretended she was called Peggy. She had two identities now, one from the people she knew from those four years in the training hospital, who still called her Peggy, and her real name, which she had taken up again when she got a bit of sense and decided not to upset her parents any more than she need by rejecting the name they had given her.

They got to the restaurant. Everyone fussed about Daisy. The taximan helped her out of the cab.

"Did you have a fall, my girl?" he asked her kindly.

Girl! Rita nearly laughed aloud.

"No, it's arthritis," said Daisy. "It's normally not nearly as bad as this. I feel such a fool with the stick, I'm always tripping people up with it. Most of the time I don't need it at all, it's just this week it's bad. I couldn't have timed it better, a wedding and a honeymoon and a stick, wouldn't you know?" The taximan was delighted with her. So was the waiter in the restaurant. He found her a chair with arms to sit on. Quite naturally, as if she had been the one who invited them all there, Daisy started arranging where they should sit.

"Rita, sit there by Ken, you have so much to say to him after all these years, and I'll take Jeffrey and Lilly here to tell me all about London."

There was no fuss. They were seated. Rita raised her eyes to Ken.

"It's great to see you," she lied straight at him.

"You look lovely, like a model," he said truthfully, straight back at her.

161

"I feel overdressed and stupid," she said, with honesty and feeling.

"You were always lovely to look at," he said. "But I think you've got even better-looking." His voice had a simple quality about it, like the way he used to say that mountains were beautiful, or that some piece of wood they had been scraping and stripping all week-end looked perfect. Just objective, happy admiration.

"Jeffrey's in insurance, isn't he?" said Ken after Rita had just stared at her plate for a bit.

"Oh, yes, he's with a company but he does a bit of free lancing as well."

"Perhaps we could get a bit of advice from him. We've got a small house. Do you remember Rodney Row? It's one of those."

They used to laugh at Rodney Row and say they were doll's houses for doll people.

"I'm sure he'd be glad to give you any tips," she said. "Jeffrey loves helping people he knows, and not just to make a commission, you know."

"Oh no I wouldn't think that, but of course we'd be very happy to do anything through him if it would help. I mean if there was any value to him out of it," said Ken.

"I don't think he'd like to make money out of friends."

"No, perhaps it's better not to mix work and pleasure," said Ken agreeably, looking at the menu.

Pleasure. Pleasure. Had she remembered it all wrong? Was it she, not Ken, who was going mad? Perhaps he had always been the man who was destined to marry some aging nurse with a walking stick? Those wild months of freedom and abandon, and being sure with each other because

162

together it was easy to reject other people's pretensions and nonsenses . . . had all that been real, or was it just in her head?

The others were laughing loudly. Daisy had said something endearing to the waiter, and he had brought her a rose. She put it behind her ear, in the middle of that lank greasy hair, and smiled a big smile with a lot of yellow teeth.

"Isn't this all great, Ken?" she laughed at him down the table.

Rita wouldn't let it go, there had to be something. There must have been something there, she couldn't have got it all so wrong, her memories of what they had. If they had nothing it would be like some kind of surgery, something would have been taken out of her.

"Look at those four over there," she said, desperately indicating a table where two middle-aged couples sat eating and making occasional little forays of conversation. "Looks like a real salon-talk setup, don't you think?"

Oh please, please, let him fall back into it, let us both start like we did in the old days. He might say "One thing about the Italians is they know how to cook food" and she would say "Isn't it funny the way all Italian restaurants seem to be run by families?" and he would say "And they always seem to be so good-humoured, it must be coming from all that sun" and together they would laugh about how people could and did talk in clichés from birth to death. Please, please, let him remember salon talk.

Ken looked obediently at the four eaters.

"They don't seem to be having a good time, is that what you mean?" he asked.

"Yes," said Rita flatly.

"I often think that people in restaurants must look over at other tables and envy them," he said. "They must wish they were part of a good scene like this." He beamed down the table at Lilly and Daisy and Jeffrey and raised his glass to his travesty of a wife, and Rita wondered with a sharp pain whether she was going to be wrong about everything else as well. Had she never got anything right?

Chancery Lane

Dear Mr. Lewis,

I'm sure you will think this very, very odd and you will spend the rest of your life refusing to talk to strange women at parties in case something of the sort should happen again. We met very briefly at the Barrys' last week. You mentioned you were a barrister and I mentioned the Lord knows what because I was up to my eyebrows in gin. I was the one who was wearing a blue dress and what started out as a feather boa, but sort of moulted during the night. Anyway, your only mistake was to let me know where you worked, and my mistakes that night were legion.

I know nobody else at all in the legal world and I wonder if you could tell me where to look. In books people open the Yellow Pages and suddenly find exactly the right kind of lawyer for themselves, but I've been looking in the windows of various solicitors' offices and they don't seem to be the kind of thing I want. They're full of files and girls typing. You seemed to have a lot of style that night, and you might know where to direct me.

I want to sue somebody for a breach of promise. I want to take him for everything he's got. I want a great deal of publicity and attention drawn to the case and photographs of me leaving the court to appear in the newspapers. What I would really like is to see all the letters involved published in the papers, and I want to be helped through the crowds by policemen.

But what I don't know is how to begin. Do I serve something on him, or send him a writ or a notice to prosecute? I feel sure the whole thing will gather its own momentum once it starts. It's the beginning bit that has me worried. If you could write back as soon as possible and tell me where to start, I should be forever grateful.

I feel it would be unprofessional to offer you a fee for this service, but since it's a matter of using your knowledge and experience for my benefit, I should be very happy to offer you some of mine in return. You may remember that I am a tap-dancing teacher (I probably gave several exhibitions to the whole room that night). So, if ever you want a lesson, I'd be delighted to give you one.

Yours sincerely,
Jilly Twilly

Dear Tom,

Thanks belatedly for a wonderful party last week. I don't know what you put in those drinks but it took me days to get over it all. I enjoyed meeting all your friends. There was a woman with the impossible name of Jilly Twilly, I think, but perhaps I got it wrong. She wore a blue dress and a feather boa of sorts. I seem to have taken her cigarette lighter by mistake, and I was wondering if you could let me have her address so that I could return it. She seemed a lively sort of girl, have you known her long?

Once more, thanks for a great party.

John Lewis

Dear John,

Glad you enjoyed the party. Yes, I gather her name is Jilly Twilly, unlikely as it sounds. I don't know her at all. She came with that banker guy, who is a friend of Freddy's, so he might know. Pretty spectacular dance she did, wasn't it? The women were all a bit sour about it, but I thought she was great.

Greetings to all in chambers.

Tom

Dear Ms. Twilly,

Thank you for your letter. Unfortunately you have approached the wrong person. Barristers are in fact briefed by solicitors in cases of this kind. So what you must do if you have a legal problem is to consult your family solicitor. If this firm does not

166

handle the kind of litigation you have in mind, perhaps he may recommend a firm who will be able to help you.

I enjoyed meeting you at the party, and do indeed remember you very well. You seemed a very cheerful and happy person, and I might point out that these breach-of-promise actions are rarely satisfactory. They are never pleasant things for anyone, and I cannot believe that you would actually crave the attendant publicity.

I urge you to be circumspect about this for your own sake, but please do not regard this as legal advice, which it certainly is not.

I wish you success in whatever you are about to do, but with the reservation that I think you are unwise to be about to do it at all.

Kind wishes,

John Lewis

Dear Mr. Lewis,

Thank you very much for your letter, I knew I could rely on you to help me, and despite all those stuffy phrases you used I can see you will act for me. I understand completely that you have to write things like that for your files. Now, this is the bones of the story. Charlie, who is the villain of the whole scene and probably of many other scenes as well, is a very wealthy and stuffy banker, and he asked me to marry him several times. I gave it some thought and though I knew there would be problems, I said yes. He bought me an engagement ring and we were going to get married next June.

Because you are my lawyer and can't divulge anything I tell you, I will tell you privately that I had a lot of doubts about it all. But I'm not getting any younger, I haven't been in so many shows recently, and I teach dancing when I'm not in shows. I thought it would be fairly peaceful to get married and not to worry about paying the rent and all that.

So Charlie and I made a bargain. I was to behave nicely in front of his friends, and he was to behave unstuffily in front of mine. It worked fine, a bit gruesome at some of those bank things. Merchant bankers en masse are horrific and Charlie did his best with my friends. I wasn't going to let him down in his career and he wasn't going to interfere in mine. If I got a dancing part, so long as I wasn't naked, I could take it.

And it was all fine until Tom Barry's party, and when I woke up Charlie wasn't there, he had left a note and taken my engagement ring, the rat. He said . . . oh well, I'll make a photostat of the note, we'll probably need it as evidence. I'll also write out his address and you could get things going from your end.

I suppose it will be all right to pay you from the proceeds. I don't have any spare cash just now.

Warm wishes,

Jilly Twilly

Photostat of note:

Jilly,

Now I've finally had enough. Your behavior tonight is something that I would like obliterated from my mind. I do not want to see you again. I've kept my part of the bargain, you have failed utterly in yours.

Perhaps it is as well we discovered this before we were married. I am too angry to thank you for the undoubtedly good parts of our relationship because I cannot recall any of them.

I have reclaimed my ring. You may keep the watch.

Charles

Dear Ms. Twilly,

You have utterly misunderstood my letter. I really cannot act for you in any way in your projected action against Mr. Benson. As an acquaintance, may I take the liberty of reminding you once again of how unwise you would be to start any such proceedings? You are an attractive young woman, you seem from my short meeting with you to be well able to handle a life which does not contain Mr. Benson. My serious and considered advice to you, not as a lawyer but as a fellow guest at a party, is to forget it all and continue to live your own life without bitterness. And certainly without contemplating a litigation that is unlikely to bring you any satisfaction whatsoever.

Yours sincerely,
John Lewis

Dear, John,

Stop telling me what to do with my life, it *is* my life. If I want to sue I'll sue. Please have the papers ready or I will have to sue you for malpractice. You have wasted quite a lot of time already. I am enclosing a copy of the letter where Charlie mentions my marrying him. It will probably be exhibit A at the trial.

Kind wishes and hurry up,

Jilly

Darling Jilly,

You must know that the bank can't put any money into the ridiculous venture you suggest. I didn't come to America to meet show-biz people and interest them in your little troupe of dancers. I know that it must be disheartening for you not to get any backing, but in six months' time we will be married and you won't need to bother your pretty little feet about a career. I love you, Jilly, but I wish you wouldn't keep telephoning the bank here on reverse charges because I am here only for a conference and it looks bad to get several calls a day, all about something which we haven't the slightest intention of doing.

Look after yourself if you can,

Charles

Dear Ms. Twilly,

These chambers will have no further correspondence with you about any legal matters whatsoever. Kindly go through the

correct channels, and approach a solicitor
who will if necessary brief counsel for you.

> Yours faithfully,
> John Lewis

Dear John,

What have I done? Why is this kind of
thing always happening to me? I thought
we got on so well that night at Tom Barry's
party. Did I tell you by the way that
Charlie was quite wrong? Tom Barry was
not one of his friends, he was a mutual
new friend that we had met with Freddy who
was one of Charlie's friends. So I didn't
break any bargain by behaving badly.

I just thought that the publicity of a big
breach-of-promise case might give me
some chance of being noticed. People would
hear of me, I'd get more jobs. You see
without Charlie or my ring or anything I
have so little money, and I was only trying
to claw at life with both hands.

It's fine for you, you are a wealthy, settled
barrister. What would you do if you were
a fast-fading, poor little dancer betrayed by
everyone? I'm nearly twenty-six, my best
years of dancing are probably over.

It was my one chance of hitting back at
life, I thought I should grab it. Anyway,
I'm sorry, I seem to have upset you. Good-
bye.

> Jilly

Dear Jilly,

My letter may have seemed harsh. I do
indeed see what you mean about grabbing

at life, and I admire your pluck, believe me I do. What you need is not so much a court action, it's much more a good friend to advise you about your career and to cheer you up. I don't think you should get involved with anyone like Charlie, your worlds are too different. I only vaguely remember him from the party at Tom Barry's but I think he was a little buttoned up.

You need somebody younger than Charlie Benson.

Perhaps you and I might meet for a meal one evening and discuss it all, totally as friends and in no way in a client-lawyer relationship. If you would like this please let me know.

Cordially,

John

Dear Monica,

I'm afraid I won't be able to make the week-end after all. Rather an important case has come up and I can't leave London just now. I know you will be disappointed, still we did agree that I should do everything possible to advance my career, so that is what I'm doing. I hope the week-end goes awfully well, looking forward to seeing you soon.

love
John

John,

I was sorry about the week-end. Daddy and Mummy were sorry you were kept in

London. Daddy kept saying that all work and no play . . . you know the way Daddy does.

I came to London last Tuesday. You weren't in chambers and you weren't in your flat, even though I phoned you there lots of times up to midnight. Maybe Daddy is right and although we all want to advance your career, perhaps it is a question of all work and no play.

Love anyway darling,

Monica

Dear Darling John,

How can I thank you for the lovely, lovely week-end. I always wanted to go to Paris and it really cheered me up. It was such a relief to be able to talk to someone so understanding. I'm afraid you must have spent a fortune but I did enjoy myself.

See you next week-end,

love Jilly

Dear Monica,

I must say I thought your phone call to the office today was hysterical and ill-timed. I was in consultation and it was very embarrassing to have to discuss my private life in front of others. I do not know where and why you have got this absurd notion that we had an understanding about getting married. From my side certainly we have no such thing. I always regarded you as a good friend, and will continue to do so unless prevented by another phone call like today's.

You may check your letters from me to
see whether any such "understanding"
was mentioned. I think you will find that
nowhere do I mention marriage. I find
this an embarrassing topic so will now close.

John

Dear Tom,

I appreciate your intentions in writing to
me with what you consider a justifiable
warning. I realize you did this from no
purposes of self-interest.

Still, I have to thank you for your intention
and tell you that your remarks were not
well received. Ms. Twilly and I are to be
married shortly, and I regard your information that she has had seven breach-of-
promise actions settled out of court as
utterly preposterous. In fact I know for a
certainty that the lady is quite incapable
of beginning a breach-of-promise action, so
your friend's sources cannot be as accurate as he or you may think.

Under other circumstances I would have
invited you to our wedding but, as things
are, I think I can thank you for having had
the party where I was fortunate enough
to meet my future bride and wish you well
in the future.

Sincerely,
John
Lewis

Seven Sisters

It was very odd that they should live in Seven Sisters, Pat thought for the hundredth time. It seemed too much of a coincidence that anyone who was giving a wife-swapping party, with uninhibited fun and carefree swinging for sophisticated couples, should just happen to live in a place with the group name of Seven Sisters. She had said so to Stuart as well.

"They have to live somewhere," he said unhelpfully.

Pat had studied the *A to Z*.

"I don't really see why they call it Seven Sisters, it's more Hornsey really," she complained.

"If they'd called it Hornsey you'd probably say that that was even more suggestive," said Stuart mildly.

For two weeks before the party Pat lived on a high level of anxiety. She examined her new set of underwear with a worried frown. It was red and black, the black bits were lace and, in one instance, a rosette. Again and again she tried them on in the bathroom and examined herself critically in the mirror. She looked so very white, and the dark colours made her look almost dead. She wondered whether this would fire all the men with lust, whether they would be driven insane by the combination of dead white skin, red silk and black lace, or whether one of the women would take her aside and advise her to use a fake tan lotion. The awful thing was that there was

175

no one to ask. Even if she were to write to this appalling magazine where Stuart had first seen the article about wife swapping and had replied to one of the box numbers, she still wouldn't get a reply in time.

Over and over she rehearsed what she would say: "Hallo, *lovely* of you to ask us . . . what a super house." No, she couldn't tell this terrifying harlot who owned the house in Seven Sisters that it was lovely of her to have invited Pat and Stuart, since Pat and Stuart had in their corrupt and pleasure-seeking way told the Seven Sisters lot that they wanted to come and take off their clothes and go to bed with a load of strangers. The more she reminded herself that this is what they had arranged to do, the more faint and foolish she felt.

Even though she tried to put it from her mind, she wondered if there would be time for any conversation before they got down to action. Would she find herself stark naked in a corner talking to some other naked housewife about the children's drama group or the new supermarket? Would Stuart stand naked laughing with new people about the tomatoes they grew in their allotment?

That was the kind of thing that happened at the ordinary parties they went to . . . tame little evenings where people kept their clothes on, and didn't mate with each other, and discussed how expensive the season tickets on the train had become, and how hard it was to find a doctor who could spend two minutes listening to you. Tame evenings, dull evenings. Getting in a rut, becoming old before their time, suburban even though they hadn't yet reached their middle-class suburbia, no excitement, nothing very different, nothing that made them gasp.

Two children, the national average, Stuart working in a bank . . .

God Almighty! . . . Suppose some of the bank's clients were at the party! It wasn't so ridiculous. People don't live beside their banks, some of them could easily live off the Seven Sisters Road. Had Stuart thought of that? She had better tell him, they could call it all off. It would be foolish to imperil his whole career. . . . No. He must have thought of it and rejected it. He was utterly set on going to this party now. He would only think she was groping around for some excuse.

. . . nice little flat, no garden unfortunately, but then they went to the allotment at weekends. Children very strong and happy, love their school. Debbie in the school play again this term, and Danny hoping to be picked for the third team. Lots of friends at school always running in and out of the neighbours' houses, too, and playing in the adventure playground at the end of the road. Not an earth-shaking life, but a happy one . . . even the school principal had said the other day . . .

Sweet God! . . . Suppose the school ever got to hear of this! How utterly shaming for Debbie and Danny to be branded the children of perverts, sexual freaks. They might even be asked to leave lest their family shame might taint the other children. Relax. How could the school hear of it, unless other parents, or indeed some of the staff, were there being uninhibited and swinging in sophisticated adult fun? . . . Yes, of course, if anyone was there, a conspiracy of silence would have to be maintained.

. . . anyway the school principal had said that he had enormous admiration for the parents of today, since they made so many sacrifices for their children and were so supportive and aware of all their needs. But he felt sure that this effort was repaid in a thousand ways by the fact that they lived in a peaceful community, far away from the wars and tensions and differences that rend other countries.

Stuart had said that people who went to these parties were normal, ordinary, good, respectable citizens like everyone else. He said that all they were doing was trying to push forward the frontiers of pleasure. They were trying to add to the delights of normal sexual love between a married couple . . . and be less selfish about it . . . by offering to share that love with other married couples. He had read, and he believed that there was a lot of truth in it, that this kind of generosity, this giving of your rights in your partner to other friends, was an act of love in itself. And, even more important in these treacherous days, it completely bypassed the need to be "unfaithful" to the other partner—there would be no forbidden lovers, or illicit affairs. It would all be out in the open. It would be healthy and good.

Stuart talked about it with the enthusiasm he had when he first talked about his allotment. His eyes had that gleam that they once had when he had planned a life of self-sufficiency. The rest of London might starve, might poison itself with nuclear fallout, but Stuart and Pat and Debbie and Danny would grow what they needed for survival on their little allotment, and, a-ha, who'd laugh then? Pat had asked mildly how Stuart would protect his runner beans and cabbages against twelve million starving Londoners if they were the only family which had managed to be self-sufficient. Stuart had said it was a technicality.

The Saturday and Sunday gardening continued, it had lost its first flush of real excitement, but nowadays it brought them a gentle pleasure. Perhaps this would happen with wife swapping, too, Pat thought. Soon the heady excitement and flush of enthusiasm would pass, and they would settle into a weekly wife swap happily and resignedly travelling to Seven Sisters, or Barking, or Rickmansworth, or Biggin Hill.

Stuart seemed so alarmingly calm about it all. This as much as anything disturbed Pat. She had asked him, did he think he should get new Jockey shorts.

"No, love, I've plenty up in the wardrobe," he had said, mystified.

"For the *party*," she had hissed.

"Why should I need new Jockey shorts?" he had asked, as puzzled as if she had said he should buy a new transistor radio. "I have nine pairs upstairs. I tell you, I have plenty."

As the event drew nearer Pat worried more about Stuart. Did he have no nerves, no feelings, that he could take it all so calmly . . . the fact that he had written to a box number and a woman with a voice like a circular saw had telephoned?

She had never given too much thought to their sex life. It had always seemed very pleasant and adequate, and she certainly didn't regard herself as frigid, not in the sense of the women's magazine articles on the topic. She couldn't remember saying that she had a headache, or that she didn't feel it. There was, she supposed, a sort of sameness about it. But then, for heaven's sake, some things *are* the same. The taste of a bar of chocolate or a gin and lime is always the same. The sound of Beethoven's Fifth or Johnny Mathis is always the same. Why this great urge for something different?

Pat was hurt and puzzled. She had read about women who discovered that their meek and conventional husbands actually liked bondage or violent pornography . . . so perhaps she should feel relieved that Stuart had suggested only nice old middleclass wife swapping. Still, Pat felt aggrieved. If she was prepared to live for the rest of their days with their life as it was now, saving for the house, going on a trailer holiday once a year, and making love comfortably in the darkness and privacy of their own room twice a week, then it was somehow ungrateful of Stuart not to feel the same about it.

Pat had an appointment with the hairdresser on the afternoon of the Terrible Day.

"Going somewhere nice?" asked the hairdresser in her bright, routine way.

"Err . . . yes," said Pat.

"Oh, to a function is it?" asked the hairdresser.

"Um. No, no. Not a function. Private house. Old friends, and new friends. A party. An ordinary party," Pat screamed defensively.

The hairdresser shrugged.

"Very nice, I'm sure," she said huffily.

The baby-sitter arrived on time. Pat had hoped that she might ring and say she couldn't come. That would mean the end of this ludicrous outing across London to copulate with strangers. The only tingles of excitement she felt were the ones

180

which ran through her brain asking her if she were certifiably insane.

Debbie and Danny barely looked up from the television.

"Good night, Mum. Good night, Dad. Come in and see us when you get back."

Pat's eyes filled with tears.

"Stuart love . . ." she began.

"Good night, you lot," Stuart said firmly.

She had assumed that they would take the car and was startled when Stuart said that it was much simpler than driving to take the tube.

"Only one change," he said. And to Pat the words seemed sinister and fraught with meaning. She wondered if he was saying that they would only swap with one couple when they got there. She felt nausea rise in her throat. Suppose it was like a dance in the tennis club years ago, when nobody asked you to dance and you ended up grateful for some awful person who eventually did suggest a shuffle around the floor. Could this happen tonight? Suppose some appalling, foul couple rejected by everyone else nodded encouragingly at them? Would they have to say yes? Did the house rules say that there was no opting out?

"Yes, but wouldn't it be nice to have the car coming home?" she asked.

"Mightn't feel like driving on the way back," said Stuart succinctly.

Worn out with pleasure? Exhausted? Asleep on some strange other wife's bosom? Going home with someone else? Staying with the awful woman in Seven Sisters? What could he mean, he mightn't feel like driving? The whole nightmare was now quite frightening. Why had she ever agreed to this wicked and silly thing? Why had Stuart ever suggested it?

The tube came immediately, as trains always do when you are going to the dentist or a wife-swapping party. The stations flashed by. Stuart read the back of someone else's evening paper. Pat examined her face three times in her compact mirror.

"You look fine," Stuart said to her when she got the compact out a fourth time.

"I suppose you're right. Anyway, it's not my face they'll be looking at," she said resignedly.

"What? Oh. Oh yes," said Stuart, smiling supportively, and going back to reading the late football results.

"Do you think we'll take off our clothes immediately?" Pat asked wretchedly as they walked out of the station and towards the house.

"I don't know, I expect it depends on whether they have central heating," Stuart said matter-of-factly.

Pat looked at him as if he were a total stranger.

"Did she give you any indication of how many people were going to be there?" Pat asked shrilly after another minute of walking. "I mean, they're not very big houses. They can hardly have dozens."

"No, she said just a few friends," said Stuart. "A few friends, she didn't say how many."

"But we're not friends, we're sort of intruding on them in a way, aren't we?" she begged. There were tears in her eyes. They were only one corner away from the house now. Right-turn that and they were in the road and there was no going back.

Stuart looked at her, moved by the tears he could hear in her voice.

"It'll be lovely, Pat dear. You'll love it. You're always a bit nervous at times like this."

She looked at him, her eyes flashing.

"What do you mean at times like this? What 'times like this' have there been before? When have we done anything remotely like this. It's the only time like this . . ." To her horror, she burst into tears.

Stuart looked very distressed. He tried to touch her, to put his arm around her, but Pat pushed him away.

"No, stop saying it's all right, and that I'll love it. I'll hate it. I'm not going. That's final."

"Well, why didn't you say this before? Why did you wait until we're nearly there?" Stuart asked, his innocent, round face looking both foolish and puzzled at the same time. "I can't understand why you didn't say to me that you thought it wasn't on, then we'd never have set it all up. I thought you wanted to come too."

Pat gave a snort into her tissues.

"You *said* it sounded an adventurous thing . . ." he said.

Pat coughed loudly.

"You *said* we'd try it once and if we didn't like it we'd have got it out of our system," he went on.

Pat blew her nose.

"Why, love? Why have you changed your mind now? Just tell me. We'll do whatever you want to. We won't go if you really hate the idea. Just tell me."

Pat looked at him through her red eyes. His face was indeed very round and innocent. She

183

wondered that she had never noticed that before. He was simply another disappointed young bank clerk. Another man in a dead-end job, with an average wife, a few drinks on a Saturday, two nice but time-consuming and money-swallowing children, a car that needed a lot of money spent on it, or else needed to be replaced. They had a loan of a trailer each year, but he would never feel the sands of the West Indies or the Seychelles between his toes.

She began to speak and then stopped. She must be very careful now. It was as if he had been a negative, and now somebody had shown her the developed print. She could see all the frustrations, the hours of commuting, the thickening of his waist. Those things were far from the James Bond or Wild West books he read for a half hour before he went to sleep each night.

A surge of understanding went out from her. He just needed some excitement, something out of the ordinary, some proof that he wasn't a mouse, that he was going to do something daring in his life before he grew old and retired and walked with a stick and crumpled and died.

Quite calmly she looked at him and said:

"I'm jealous. That's it. That's the truth."

"You're what?" he said.

"I don't want them to have you, to see you. I don't want those girls to . . . you know, make free with you. I'd be very jealous. I love you. I don't want them loving you."

"But, Pat," he said desperately. "We've been through all this; it's got nothing to do with love. It's got to do with swapping. It's got to do with excitement, and frontiers . . . and not doing the same things always . . . till the end of our days."

She had been right. She resolved that she would do everything her feeble imagination and some sex manuals could dream up if only they got home unscathed from Seven Sisters.

"You're too great," she said hesitantly. They didn't use flowery endearments, they never paid each other extravagant compliments. It was hard to begin on a street in the middle of the evening in North London on the way to a wife-swapping orgy. But people have to begin somewhere.

"You're too . . . important. Too precious, and exciting. I love it when we . . . er . . . screw. I don't want other women to share it. It's my . . . er, pleasure."

"Do you love it?" he asked innocently.

"Oh I do." She closed her eyes, a sigh of genuine pleasure that she might in fact be going to win escaped her, and it sounded like genuine desire.

"I didn't think you minded all that much one way or another," he said.

"If you knew how I do," she said. And then firmly: "But I wouldn't feel at all the same if you let all these women crawl over you . . ."

She paused. It was a calculated risk. In fact she had given little thought to Stuart's part in the whole sorry business, she had been obsessed with her own role. But she thought that to say this would have been to confirm Stuart in thinking that he had married parochial, puritan riffraff and that his excitement would be between the covers of books for the rest of his days.

"I often . . . er . . . get panicky in case some of the women who come into the bank might . . . er, proposition you," she said.

Stuart looked at her.

"There's no need to worry like that. That's kind of paranoid that jealousy," he said soothingly. "I've always been faithful to you. Even this business tonight is *with* you."

"I don't want to share you with them," she said. "I'm not going to. They've got lousy old husbands, awful fellows. I've got you. Why should I be so generous?"

He paused. He looked up the road, he looked down the road. Her eyes never left his face. Down the road won.

"Suppose we got a couple of kebabs . . ."

"And a bottle of wine."

As they turned to go back to the station, a middle-aged couple stopped in a car to ask them where the Road was.

Pat asked them what number they wanted.

As she had suspected, it was number 17.

"Have fun," she said as she gave them directions, and she and Stuart dissolved in laughter.

"They were a bit old," said Stuart. "Do you think it would have been very sordid and sort of pathetic?"

Pat wasn't going to let him think that.

"No. There were probably fabulous birds there. Anyway, older ones are more passionate. She'd probably have had you pinned to the hearth rug the moment we got in the door."

Under a streetlamp, she thought his face looked a bit foolish. As if he had seen how tatty and grubby it might all have been. He was very gentle. In a great wave of affection she realized that indeed she would not have liked sharing him with anyone, and that an evening in bed with a bottle of wine, and a nice spicy donar kebab and all that black and red underwear might be the most exciting kind of thing that she had experienced for some time as well.

Women are so much more sensible about sex, she thought cheerfully as Stuart bought the tickets home. She had forgotten the weeks of anxiety, the endless examinations in the mirror, the ceaseless fears lest anyone should discover. Heady with relief, she even allowed herself the indulgence of imagining what that elderly woman in the car might look like naked, and she smiled at Stuart, who looked like a tiger now that his wife was too rabidly jealous to allow him to indulge in the wife-swapping party to which they had been invited. Horizons had been broadened without anyone having to do anything.

Finsbury Park

Vera hated to see television plays about poverty. She even disliked seeing working-class women, babies in their arms, hair in rollers, explaining some social problem to a concerned television reporter. It reminded her too much of her youth. In those shuffling, whiney women she could see her mother, cigarette always hanging from the corner of her mouth, cardigan held together with a safety pin, the door of the flat never closed since people were always coming in and out, the place smelling of clothes drying . . . clothes that had not been properly washed so it was really dirty clothes drying.

Vera hated to hear women laugh loudly, they reminded her of her mother and her elder sister, cackling away when things were at their worst, cheering each other up with bottles of ginger wine and announcing that they would be dead long enough. Vera never liked to think of anything that reminded her about life as it was lived before she was fifteen.

On her fifteenth birthday she was taken to the hospital with rheumatic fever, and during the long weeks there she got to know Miss Andrews, the gentle schoolteacher in the next bed who changed her life.

"Ask them to bring you lavender water not sweets."

"Ask your school friends for hand cream not comics."

"I'll choose some nice books for you from the library."

"We'll tell the social worker you'd like a hairdo to cheer you up . . ."

The Vera who came out of hospital was slimmer and attractive-looking. And she had changed inside too. Miss Andrews had taught her a very important lesson—even awful things and unhappy times can have their uses, they can be a kind of apprenticeship. Vera must stay at school, she must pass some kind of exams even if school was hell and home was worse than hell.

She had closed her eyes to the dirt and depression around her. She had dreamed of the day she would live in a clean house with no frying pans encrusted with the remains of a thousand meals. She dreamed of having a room to herself where no noise and no shouting could be heard, where no younger sister with nits in her hair would bounce on her bed saying:

"It's half my room, you can't throw me out."

"Don't leave too soon," Miss Andrews had begged. "Don't go until you are sure you can support yourself. It would be too depressing to have to return there. That would break your spirit."

Vera found it difficult to remember the two years she stayed on in her mother's flat. She knew that her father must have come home from time to time . . . the period seemed to be punctuated with screaming and violence. She must have learned something at the school because she had managed to escape with some "O" levels. And during those two years she must have formed the habit of visiting Miss Andrews once a week, some hundred calls must have been made to the quiet apartment with its piano, its dried flowers, its cabinets of china, and its purring Persian cat.

As an apprenticeship it must have worked, but it was blotted out. By the time Vera had finished, she could type, she could take shorthand, she could spell. Miss Andrews had taught her to smile and to speak nicely. Not in actual lessons, but by example. Vera's voice was less shrill, her vowels less extreme, her reactions less speedy— so much so that her mother was totally unprepared for her flight from the tenement. It was done without fuss, without argument, and without heed to the pleas.

"You'll come back often to see us, you'll come home every weekend," begged her mother.

"Of course," said Vera, and never did.

She sent her mother an envelope with a card and a pound in it three times a year, Christmas, birthday, and Mother's Day. No details of how she was or where she was. No plans about coming back for a visit. No inquiries about the rest of the family. They had no way of telling her when Margaret died. And no way of appealing to her when Colin was lifted by the police. And when the pound had reduced to a fifth of its value she still sent it. Crisp and green, attached by a paper clip to a noncommittal card of good wishes. Once her mother tore it up and threw it into the fire. But Vera was never to know that.

Miss Andrews had been too genteel, too ladylike to reveal to Vera what she later discovered to be a major truth in life—that money was the solution to almost every problem. If Miss Andrews had known this she hadn't thought of passing it on, and after Vera had cut her ties with the family she also stopped seeing Miss Andrews. To the teacher she sent more thoughtful cards, and sometimes a lace handkerchief or a little sachet for her drawer. She never said what she was doing or where she was, and soon, or at some time anyway, the lonely teacher put Vera out of her mind. There was a finality about her three-line notes . . . they said good-bye.

Throughout her first five years of freedom, which also meant five jobs and five different bed-sitters, Vera still regarded herself as in apprenticeship. There was no time for dalliances like every other girl she worked with seemed to have. There was no money to waste on silly things—the cinema, yes, sometimes, if it was the kind of film that might teach her something, about style, clothes, manners. Mainly British films, American style was too foreign, it might be outrageous, it might not even *be* style. Lunch hours spent in fashion stores, or in bookshops, reading but not buying the magazines; money, after the rent was paid, spent on evening classes in everything from beginner's French to grooming.

Suddenly she was twenty-three, and nicely spoken and well informed and living in an attractive bed-sitter. She had collected some pretty ornaments, not unlike those that Miss Andrews had in her glass-fronted cabinet. She knew extremely important things about not mixing styles in her decor. She had learned as if by rote some rules of elegant living and if she had ever given herself the opportunity to entertain anyone, she was absolutely confident about how the table should be set and what wines to serve with each course.

She had never relaxed about her background, and was amazed that other girls, the kind she met at work, would talk so freely about the uncouth habits of their parents . . . and joke about the vulgarity of their backgrounds. Vera would never be drawn. Once or twice when people did press she said that it hurt her to talk about the past. And people assumed that there had been some tragedy or some unpleasantness and left it at that.

Because of her interest in china she got a job running the gift shop of a smart hotel and it was here that she met Joseph. Twenty years her senior, with his big anxious eyes and his worried face, he was the ideal catch, one of the giggling receptionists had told her. A lonely widower, no children, pots of money, so broken up after his wife's death that he had sold the house and moved into a hotel. He had been living in this hotel for three years. He was apparently looking for a wife, since hotel life had its drawbacks. Sometimes he called at her little shop to buy gifts for clients, always she advised him with charm and taste. He was very attracted to her. Soon he managed to find the courage to ask her out. Vera's own hesitation was genuine. In her effort to become her own version of a lady, she had given very little time to recognizing that she was a woman. She knew little of men, and was very shy on their first few outings. This pleased Joseph more than anything else she could have done. . . . In a matter of weeks he was telling her of his dream house, but his fears of being lonely in it if he bought it for himself alone. She agreed with him enthusiastically, she thought that a big place was bad if you were alone. That's why she had only a tiny bed-sitter.

Joseph wondered if he could come and call at her bed-sitter sometime. Vera agreed and asked him for afternoon tea the following Saturday. The sunlight caught the beautiful china, and the gentle highlights in Vera's hair, and the shining wood of the one small table . . . and Joseph's eyes filled with tears. He started to apologize for being forty-five, and to excuse himself for his arrogance in supposing that a beautiful young girl could possibly . . . She let him babble on for some minutes and then just as he was about to retract everything he had said from sheer embarrassment, she laid a finger on his lips and said:

"Don't say any more, Joseph. I should love to see your dream house in Finsbury Park, and we'll make it the most wonderful palace in the world."

She had heard dialogue a little like that in some old movie, and it seemed right for the occasion. It was indeed. Utterly right. The months passed in a flurry of inspecting the house, giving in her notice at the hotel, accepting a small marriage settlement from Joseph, a complete refusal on her part to have anything to do with her family, a quiet wedding, an undemanding honeymoon in the sunshine of the South of France, and then Vera's apprenticeship ended and her life began.

The small scullery attached to the great kitchen in Finsbury Park became her headquarters. Here she sat and studied the plans, here she returned after great measuring trips around the rooms, here she studied fabrics, paint charts, samples of tiles, wood pieces. It was in this scullery that the catalogues began to mount up as she debated, and wondered, and frowned, and pouted, and looked at the first ones again. Joseph began to fret after a few weeks.

"Is it proving too much for you, my little darling?" he asked anxiously. "You know we can have a designer, and a consultant if you like. Someone who will take the donkey work from you."

"Donkey work?" cried Vera in genuine amazement. "But this is the best bit. This is what we want, to decide it ourselves, to have it perfect. To have a perfect house which we get for ourselves!" Her eyes looked almost wild with enthusiasm, so Joseph decided not to point out that they slept on a bed in a bedroom and ate meals in the little scullery while a fourteen-room house awaited them. It was like a naked house waiting to be dressed.

It got dressed. Amazingly slowly. It took months for the painting, months for the curtains, the furniture to build up. Two years went by and it still looked as if they had just moved in. Joseph was deeply disappointed.

He worked hard all day as a company lawyer. He had thought that his life had taken a new and almost miraculous turn when the flowerlike Vera had agreed to marry him. True, his evenings were less lonely than when he lived in the hotel. But they were a lot less comfortable. In the hotel he had room to rest, to relax, room to work. In the hotel he had excellent food. At home, in the future palace, he had no room. He lived from a box in their bedroom, since Vera would allow no furniture anywhere until it had been finally agreed and settled and each item took months. The cooking was negligible since they had to wait for all the equipment to be installed. Vera didn't seem interested in food, she didn't seem to think he needed it either. She rushed to greet him on his return each day with a peck on the cheek and a sheaf of leaflets and swathes of fabric.

"Oh there you are, my dear. Dearest, so you think this flower is too large. I'm not quite certain, I'm almost certain but not quite."

He began to try and guess what she wanted him to say, but knew that he had to give the pretence of ruminating over it, otherwise she would not be satisfied. Often, faint with tiredness and hunger after two hours of studying design, he wondered whether she might in fact be having some kind of nervous trouble that he hadn't noticed before. Then he would banish the thought guiltily, and tell himself that he was a selfish swine to expect his young wife to have a glass of scotch ready, a meal cooking, and a lively interest in his day.

Sometimes he called at the hotel and ate before he came home. Vera never seemed to mind. Yes, of course she had plenty to eat, she made herself cups of soup and sandwiches, she said vaguely.

Joseph's hope that they would have children

was also doomed. It was a long time before he realized that Vera had been taking the contraceptive pill. All this time he had been hoping that she would tell him she had conceived.

"But, darling, we can't *think* of children in this beautiful house. I mean how could you have children with this wallpaper?" Her hands caressed the wallpaper almost sensuously.

"But not ever?" gasped Joseph, shocked.

"Perhaps sometime," Vera said, distantly aware she might have gone a little too far.

Vera was twenty-eight, they had been five years married when he dared to say to her that the house was perfect. He had admired every single item, rearranged every piece of furniture with her, and now he hoped that the endless business was over. To his increasing alarm he noted that she didn't seem too anxious to spoil the kitchen by cooking, and she didn't want to fade the colors in the sitting room by letting the light in. There was no comfortable fug in the study she had designed for him, because she begged him not to have the heating too high lest it blister the paint. His cigar smoking was done outside his own home.

That was the unhappiest year of Joseph's life because he now realized that the completion of the house did not signal the start of a normal life together. Her attractive face was still bent over magazines and fabric charts. They had never entertained anyone. He had taken his mother, an elderly woman, there once . . . for a drink before Sunday lunch. Vera said she couldn't possibly cook a huge Sunday roast if they were to show the kitchen at its best.

"But why do we have to show it at its best?" he begged.

"Why spend all this time and money unless we want things at their best?" she answered.

He hoped that if he got her some regular help she might become more relaxed about it. Together they interviewed seventeen applicants, the wages he offered were high. Eventually she settled on a Filipino girl with as much interest in the house as she had herself. Together they cleaned and polished all day. Together Vera and the little Filipino washed woodwork, and held the fitments of glass lights in soft dusters, rubbing gently till they shone. The little girl from Manila saved every penny she earned, and drank packet soups with Vera all day to keep up her strength. At night she went to her own room and watched a portable television. Vera had bought her this in order to keep her at home. She told Joseph that if Anna went out at night she would lose her energy for polishing.

Joseph suggested a cook as well, but Vera asked why did they want someone to mess the place up. She would however like a daily woman to do the heavy work so that Anna and she could be free to do the finer chores.

The cleaning woman came five days a week. She thought Vera was daft and told her so. Vera didn't even listen. She certainly didn't feel insulted.

"If you don't like the job and the money, I'll get someone else," she said reasonably, without any offense in her voice.

The cleaning woman was called Mrs. Murray, and she lived in a block of flats not at all unlike the ones where Vera had grown up. Sometimes

Mrs. Murray, feeling a bit sorry for this poor madwoman she worked for, would tell tales of Life in the Buildings. Vera's face contorted with near spasms. She almost ran from the room if Mrs. Murray began to evoke the life and sounds.

"Please, Mrs. Murray, I beg you, go on with your work. I don't want to delay you. Another time."

Behind her back Anna and Mrs. Murray pointed to their own foreheads and shook their heads.

"I think she must have had nothing when she was young," said Mrs. Murray one day in a burst of confidence to Anna.

"I always think she very wealthy lady," said Anna.

"Wouldn't you feel sorry for her old man?" Mrs. Murray went on. "He'd be better off down with us, coming in to a bit of a laugh and a good meat pie, and a block of ice cream with a glass of port after it, and his slippers. I think that's what he'd prefer, to tell you the God's honest truth."

Anna gave it some thought.

"Yes, and when I think of my family back in Manila . . . where there is little money . . . and little food and little furniture . . . but when the father comes in . . . all stops and there is smiling and welcoming and he is an important man."

Mrs. Murray nodded sagely.

Outside the door, where she had paused not to eavesdrop but to polish the corner of a picture frame which had escaped them all, Vera stood and listened. Her body was flooded with a great pity for them. Two poor women, not much older than herself. One from a drunken Irish family, living now in slum conditions in a London council flat, one a poor Asiatic whose family and country were so wretched they had to export her to clean floors and send them back her wages.

And these two women pitied her. Vera gave a high-pitched little laugh at the wonderful way that nature allows people to bear their burdens so easily by considering themselves better off than others. Happily she moved from the door and knelt down to examine the ball and claw feet of the table, which were known for their ability to trap dust.

Highbury & Islington

"I hope you'll like them all," he said for the fourth time.

"Oh, I'm sure I will," said Heather without looking up.

"I think you'll get on with them," he said, anxiously biting his lip.

Heather raised her eyes from the magazine.

"I said I'm sure I will, funny face. Even if I don't it's not the end of the world. They don't have to live with me, I don't have to live with them." Cheerfully she leaned over and kissed him on the nose. Then she took off her shoes, settled her feet in his lap, and applied herself seriously to her magazine. A very colourful-looking one with a lot of Sin and Passion and Frenzy in capital letters on the cover.

Adam hoped that she might have finished the magazine and, better still, have thrown it away before they got home. He could see his mother's amazement—Frenzy and Sin magazines weren't forbidden at home, it was just that nobody would contemplate buying them. He could imagine his sister's sarcastic comments. Louise was always a little sardonic about strangers but he felt unhappily that Heather might give plenty of ammunition.

"A trifle bookish I see, your Heather?" Louise would shout as she retrieved the offending magazine. And, oh God, would Heather relax so thoroughly that she would actually sit in her stockinged feet as she was doing now?

Adam looked out of the train window and fixed his face in what he hoped was a calm, pleasant expression while he tried to work out some of the more glaring problems which faced him at the weekend. He had explained to Heather that there could be no question of sharing a bed under his mother's roof. She had accepted it good-naturedly.

"No point in terrorizing the poor old darling, is there? I'll wait until they've all had their Ovaltine, then I'll slip along to wherever you are."

He had even managed to tell her that this would not do either. He painted a picture of a home with three women, Mother, Louise, and old Elsie; this was the first time any guest had been invited to stay; there would be enormous excitement. There would be amazing scrutiny. Heather had sounded disbelieving but shrugged.

"Well, two nights' denial won't kill us."

Adam had read a lot about love before he had met Heather. He knew only too well that love was often unreturned—as in the case of his loving Jane Fonda for a while. She had simply been unaware of his existence. And nearer home there had been a severe case of unreturned love when he had yearned for that stuck-up girl in the dramatic society. Of course he, too, had been loved, by that mousy friend of Louise's, the quiet little girl with the irritating cough and nervous laugh. She had loved Adam for a bit and was always pretending that she had been given two theatre tickets and asking him would he like to come to plays with her. He hadn't loved her even a little bit.

Heather was his first experience of Real Love, and Adam frowned as he looked into people's houses from the train window. Real love often ran into problems, well, from Romeo and Juliet onwards. There were cases of families refusing to countenance young lovers. He didn't think this would happen at home. Mother and Louise wouldn't summon old Elsie from the kitchen and face him with an ultimatum. It would be very different and much harder to take . . . they would laugh at Heather, and ridicule his taste. In little ways they would call attention to her shortcomings; they would assume that she was a tasteless little dalliance on his part. They couldn't know that he loved her and wanted her more than he had ever wanted anything in his life.

He moved her feet slightly, she looked up and smiled at him over her torrid magazine.

"Dreaming?" she asked him affectionately.

"A bit," he said, and felt a wave of disloyalty flooding him. Love wasn't meant to be like this, it had nothing to do with trying to get two sets of people to make allowances, to change, to bend in order to accommodate each other. Love was meant to be straightforward. If things got in the way of love, then the Lover had to remove them, honestly and with integrity and dignity. The Lover wasn't meant to sit gnawing his fingers about the confrontation of those that he loved.

He had known Heather for a year and he had loved her for eight months, but this was the first time he had ever raised enough courage to take her home for a weekend. It hadn't been easy.

"But of course you can have a friend to stay, darling," Mother had said. "Who is he? Anyone we know?" Mother had an idea that she might know anyone of substance in London. Among the twelve million people Adam could meet, she felt sure that the one chosen to be a friend might be someone she knew.

"A girl. How dramatic!" screamed Louise, pretending to be a Victorian Lady overcome with shock. Adam could have wrung her neck with pleasure. "Is she a debutante? Do tell, do tell."

Adam had explained that Heather had a bed-sitting room in the same house in Islington. He did not go into the fact that for the past few months they actually shared the same bed-sitting room so as to save rent. To the eager faces of Mother and Louise, and of Elsie, who had come in from the kitchen at the noise of all the excitement, he announced that she really *was* just a friend, and that he would love to invite her for a weekend. He begged them not to ask people around for sherry on Sunday morning. He implored Elsie not to give the place a thorough spring cleaning before young Mr. Adam's young lady came; he said that honestly Louise shouldn't save her supper party for the tennis club people until Heather arrived. Short of going on bended knees, he couldn't have done more to ask for a quiet, normal weekend. It had, of course, been useless.

It was only natural that they should be so interested in his doings, Adam thought, forgiving them, loving them for caring so much. Since Father died he was the only man in their life; Louise was too bookish, too brisk for men. Well, she was nineteen and had never shown any real interest in men. She worked in the local library, she never mentioned boyfriends. She couldn't have any secretly, could she? After all she lived at home. Every second weekend Adam arrived home to the Sussex town and told them tales about his life in London. The work in the bank, his prospects. His squash games, his walks on the heath. The little pub theatres he went to, his French classes preparing for big banking opportunities in the EEC.

He mentioned lots of friends by name, but never Heather. He said nothing about the discos they went to on the Saturdays he stayed in London. He thought Mother might find discos a bit, well, lower class, and Louise would ask in her penetrating voice, "But why, Adam, why do people go to rooms with loud music and funny lights which eventually ruin their eyesight—I mean, do they enjoy it, Adam?" He told Elsie that he was learning a little bit more about cooking, but he didn't explain that it was Heather who taught him, Heather who said, "I made the supper last night, you'll bloody do it tonight, mate, or I'll find myself a bloke who believes in equality."

His worlds were so different that he had put off for as long as he could the date when they had to be brought together. Adam who sat down with a linen table napkin to tasteless, overcooked, plain food served from cracked china plates behind heavy net curtains . . . and Adam who sat on the bed with a great wooden bowl of highly spiced chilli, a bottle of red wine on the floor, his arm around Heather as they laughed and watched television. In the summer evenings the window of their basement flat was often open for all to see . . . He could hardly believe they were the same person.

Heather had invited him to her home several times. Her stepfather had asked Adam for a loan of a pound on each occasion and Heather had cheerfully shouted at him not to be so daft. On one occasion Adam had secretly slipped the man a pound, hoping to buy his affection, but in fact it only worsened relations between them, as Heather had said it would. Heather's mother was a hardworking Scot. She looked Adam up and down and said she hoped that he was a man who could hold down a day's work. Adam explained nervously that although he was still a lowly bank official he was indeed a regular worker and had great ambitions. Heather's mother said she approved of that because she herself had been unlucky in that she had married two wasters and two scroungers and two men who would drink the Thames Estuary dry if they got a chance. "There were only two altogether, Mam," Heather had said laughing. "She always makes it sound as if there were six!"

Adam couldn't understand the casual bond that held the mother to her daughter. It wasn't love, it had nothing to do with duty. There was no need involved, it didn't seem to matter whether Heather went home for months or not. There were no recriminations, no interrogations. There didn't even seem to be a great deal of interest. Heather's mother could hardly remember the name of the department store where Heather worked. Adam marvelled at that; Mother and Louise and Elsie knew the name of every under-manager and a great many of the customers in his bank.

Heather had always seemed amused about his tales of home. But then, Adam wondered with mounting horror as the train was taking them ever nearer, had he told accurate tales? Had he let her know just how very formal Mother could be? Heather hadn't thought of taking a gift for the weekend, so Adam had bought a potted plant.

"You can give that to Mother," he had said.

"Why? I don't know her. She'd think it was silly," said Heather.

"No, first time meeting her, she'd think it was nice," he insisted. "It's what people do, honestly."

Adam was furious. He hadn't taken a plant to Heather's mother because she lived forty minutes away on the tube, because they had gone there for tea one Saturday, because Heather had said that her mother hated airs and graces and he hadn't wanted to be considered a young dandy. Now it was being used against him.

He thought about the kind of weekend they could have had if they had stayed in London. The cinema tonight, perhaps, and a fish and chip supper. Saturday morning poking around antique shops and secondhand stalls. Drink a few pints with some of Heather's friends at lunchtime . . . the afternoon would pass in a haze of doing up the room they lived in, sweeping the leaves away from the basement gutters; they might carry on with that picture framing; they might go and drink a bottle of wine with other friends until they went to the disco; and instead he had this torture ahead.

The train stopped and his heart lurched; they couldn't be there yet. Surely there was another half hour.

"Are we there?" Heather yawned and rooted for her shoes. She hadn't a hint of nervousness or anxiety. She reached for his carefully chosen potted plant.

"Don't forget your geranium," she said.

They hadn't arrived, but they had reached a situation which called for their having to change trains. That was how the guard put it.

"Has this one broken down?" Heather asked him.

"It is a situation where you have to change trains, madam," he said again.

"I'd love it if he was in charge of any crisis," grumbled Heather getting out onto the platform. Her eyes lit on the ladies' room. "I'll take advantage of the change of train situation to have a relief of bladder situation," she said happily and scampered off to the lavatory.

Adam stood glumly wondering why he thought everything that Heather said was funny and endearing at home in London and he thought it was coarse and offensive when he was starting to get into Mother's orbit. He leaned against a telephone box waiting for Heather to come back from the ladies' and for the next train to come and rescue them. On the opposite platform stood lucky people going to London. They would be there in time to go to a theatre perhaps, they might be salesmen coming home from some conference in Brighton. None of them had forty-eight hours of anxiety lying ahead of them as he did. None of them had to worry about Mother asking Heather, "And what school were you at, my dear?" and Louise asking Heather, "You mean you actually sell things to the public? Heavens!" Elsie asking Heather, "Would you like Earl Grey or English breakfast in the morning?" He winced and felt a real pain at the thought of it. And there was no way he could muzzle Heather and ask her to remain completely silent, so she was bound to talk about times when they had both been pissed and to let slip that they had smoked pot, and lived in the same room, and that her father had died in an alcoholics' home and her stepfather was bankrupt. . . .

Adam heaved a very deep sigh.

Love was turning out to be full of problems that the poets and the moviemakers never spoke of.

Suddenly he thought he couldn't stand it. Not now, not yet. He wasn't ready to take the weekend now. Perhaps later when he and Heather were so sure of each other and of their happiness that a weekend like this wouldn't matter. Perhaps later when he didn't seem like a small boy wet behind the ears to the Mummy and the Sister and the Old Retainer . . . perhaps then Adam's bohemian life-style and friends would be much more acceptable. Perhaps when he was more of a man.

He knew he had to act in the next minute if he was going to stop the disastrous visit. A quick phone call . . . he was most most dreadfully sorry but he had just come down with this dreadful flu, and Heather had sent her regrets and would so look forward to meeting Mother and Louise and everyone another time. Yes, yes he could do it now quickly. And to Heather? Well imagine how funny life is! He had just phoned home to explain that they were going to be late and fancy, Mother had come down with this dreadful flu and had been trying to contact him, could they possibly put off the visit? Then he and Heather had only to cross the platform, jump on a London-bound train. In an hour or two they would get off at their tube station and, hand in hand, clutching their weekend bags and the geranium, they would go home . . . there would be no hurts, no confrontations. Love would remain separate and self-contained. He could be a loving son every second weekend until he was mature and manly enough not to care.

With one hand on his ear to cut out the noise of the trains the told the tale first to Elsie and, gritting his teeth, trying to put out of his mind her tones of disappointment, he agreed to tell it all again to Mother.

"We had everything so nice," Elsie said. "We even had a fire in Miss Heather's bedroom. Your mother had the chimney swept during the week."

Mother was concerned about his imaginary flu, but he had the strangest feeling she didn't entirely believe him. She gave the merest of hints that she thought something more exciting and glittering had turned up for Adam and Heather.

"Don't go out to any parties or occasions now, if you have flu."

There was something about the way his mother used the word "occasions" that brought a prickle of tears to Adam's eyes. It was as moving as Elsie being disappointed not to see Miss Heather's pleasure at the fire in her bedroom. Mother thought that bank clerks and shopgirls were good worthy people in service industries . . . but she thought of her son Adam as being "in banking" and she assumed that his nice friend Heather was a young lady who would indeed be invited to glittering functions.

"I'm sorry, Mother," he said.

"Adam my dear, you can't help having influenza," said Mother, and he could hear Louise in the background saying, "Oh no, you don't mean after all this they're not coming. It's too bad."

Fiercely he told himself that it was better this small hurt than two days of misunderstanding and misery. Then Heather came swinging easily along the platform.

"Any news on the train?" she asked.

He told her about his sudden call, his mother's flu, her deep regrets, he added that there had been a fire in her bedroom. Heather looked at him levelly.

"Yes, really, a fire in your bedroom, Mother had got the sweep to come in and do the chimney specially during the week," he said, desperate that she should understand how much welcome had been prepared. After Elsie and Mother's pain he couldn't bear it if Heather were flippant.

"I see," she said at last.

"So, we can just go back, back to London, we can cross the footbridge there," he said, reading the sign aloud.

"Yeah, that's right," said Heather.

"And we're really only losing the cost of the ticket," he said, eagerly looking at her. "That's all we're losing."

"Sure, Adam," she said, but he knew from her

208

voice that he was losing a great deal more. He had known that from Mother's voice too. For once in his life, Adam wondered if there were a danger that he might *never* grow up.

King's Cross

Eve looked around the office with a practical eye. There was a shabby and rather hastily put together steel shelving system for books and brochures. There were boxes of paper still on the floor. There was a dead plant on the window, and another plant with a "Good Luck in Your New Job" label dying slowly beside it. The venetian blind was black—there was so much clutter on the window ledge it looked like a major undertaking to try and free the blind. One of the telephones was actually hidden under a pile of literature on the desk. In the corner was a small, cheap, and rather nasty-looking table . . . which would be Eve's if she were to take the job.

And that's what she was doing now as she sat in the unappealing room . . . deciding if she would take the job of secretary to Sara Gray. Sara had rushed off to find somebody who knew about holidays and luncheon vouchers and overtime. She had never had a secretary before and had never thought of inquiring about these details before she interviewed Eve. She had pushed the hair out of her eyes and gone galloping off to personnel, which would undoubtedly think her very foolish. Eve sat calmly in the room waiting and deliberating. By the time Sara had bounded back with the information, Eve had already decided to take on Sara Gray. She looked like being the most challenging so far.

Sara heaved a great sigh of relief when she heard that Eve would stay and work with her. She had big kind brown eyes, the kind of eyes you often see shown close up in a movie or a television play to illustrate that someone is a trusting, vulnerable character and therefore likely to be hurt. She looked vague and bewildered, and snowed under. She sounded as if she needed a personal manager rather than a secretary—and this is where Sara Gray had hit very lucky because that's what Eve was.

From the outset she was extraordinarily respectful to Sara. She never referred to her as anything but Miss Gray; she called her Miss Gray to her face despite a dozen expostulations from Sara.

"This is a friendly office," Sara cried. "I can't stand you not calling me by my name. It makes me look so snooty. We're all friends here."

Eve had replied firmly that it was not a friendly office. It was a very cutthroat company indeed. Eve had asked Sara how many of the women secretaries called their male bosses by their first names. Sara couldn't work it out. Eve could. None of them. Sara agreed reluctantly that this might be so. Eve pressed home her point. Even the managers and assistant managers on Sara's level were not going to escape, they all called Sara by her first name because she was a woman, but she felt the need to call many of them Mr. After two days Sara decided that Eve must be heavily into Women's Lib.

"There's no need to fight any battles on my

behalf, Eve," she said cheerfully. "Look at how far I've got, and I'm a woman. Nobody held me back just because I'm a downtrodden put-upon female. Did they? I've done very well here, and I get recognition for all I do."

"Oh no, Miss Gray, you are quite wrong," said Eve. "You do not get recognition. You are the assistant promotions manager. Everyone knows that you are far better and brighter and work much harder than Mr. Edwards. You should be the promotions manager not the assistant."

Sara looked upset. "I thought I could say I'd done rather well," she said.

"Only what you deserve, Miss Gray," said Eve, who seemed to have acquired a thorough familiarity with the huge travel agency and its tour operations in two days. "You should have Mr. Edwards's job. We all know that. You *must* have it. It's only fair."

Sara looked at her, embarrassed.

"Gosh, Eve, it's awfully nice of you, and don't think I don't appreciate it. You're amazingly loyal. But you really don't know the score here."

"With great respect, Miss Gray, I think it's you who don't know the score," said Eve calmly. "It is absolutely possible for you to have Mr. Edwards's job this time next year. I'll be very glad to help you toward that if you like. I have a little experience in this sort of thing."

Sara stared at her, not knowing what to say.

"Miss Gray, I'm going for my lunch now, but can I suggest you do something while I'm gone? Can you telephone one or two of the people on the list of references I gave you? You will notice they are all women; I've never worked for men. Ask any one of them whether she thinks it's a good idea to trust me to help. Then perhaps you might add that you will keep all this very much in confidence . . ."

"Eve," interrupted Sara, her good-natured face looking puzzled, "Eve, honestly, this sounds like the Mafia or something. I'm not into power struggles, and office backstabbing . . . I'm just delighted to have someone as bright and helpful as you in the office . . . I don't want to start a war."

"Who said anything about a war, Miss Gray? It's very subtle, and very gradual and—honestly the best thing is to telephone anyone on that list, it's there in the file marked 'Personal.'"

"But won't they think it rather odd. I mean, I can't ring up and ask them what do they think of Eve trying to knock Mr. Edwards sideways so that I can get his job." Sara sounded very distressed.

"Miss Gray, I have worked in five jobs, for five women, I chose them, they thought they chose me. At the very beginning I told them how a good assistant could help them get where they wanted. Not one of them believed me. I managed in a conversation like this to convince them to let me."

"And . . . what happened?" asked Sara.

"Ask them, Miss Gray," replied Eve, gathering her gloves and bag.

"They won't think I'm er . . ."

"No, all of them—except the first one, of course—rang someone else to check things out too." Eve was gone.

Sara wondered.

You often heard of women becoming a bit strange, perhaps Eve was a bit odd. Far too young to be menopausal or anything, heavens Eve wasn't even thirty, but it did seem an odd sort of thing to suggest after two days.

Was there a wild possibility that she might have had a secret vendetta for years against Garry Edwards, the plausible head of promotions, who indeed did not deserve his job, his title, his salary, or his influence, since all of these had been made possible only by Sara's devoted work?

Sara reached for the phone.

"Sure I know Eve," said the pleasant American woman in the big banking group. "You are so lucky, Sara, to have her. I offered her any money to stay but she wouldn't hear of it. She said her job was done. She acts a bit like Superman or the Lone Ranger, she comes in and solves a problem and then sort of zooms off. A really incredible woman."

"Can I . . . er . . . ask you what problem she . . . er . . ." Sara felt very embarrassed.

"Sure. I wanted to be loans manager, they didn't take me seriously. Eve showed me how they would, and they did, and now I'm loans manager."

"Heavens," said Sara. "It's a teeny bit like that here."

"Well naturally it is, otherwise Eve wouldn't have picked you," said the loans manager of a distant bank.

"And how did she . . . um . . . do it?" persisted Sara.

"Now this is where I become a little vague," the pleasant voice said. "It's simply impossible to explain. In my case there was a whole lot of stuff about my not getting to meet the right people

213

in the bank. Eve noticed that, she got me to play golf."

"*Golf?*" screamed Sara.

"I know, I know, I guess I shouldn't even have told you that much . . . listen, the point is that Eve can see with uncanny vision where women hold themselves back, and work within the system without playing the system properly so—she kinda points out where the system could work for us, and honestly, honey, it worked for me, and it sure as hell worked for the woman who Eve worked on before me, she's practically running industry in this country nowadays. In her case it had something to do with having dinner parties at home."

"What?" said Sara.

"I know, it sounded crazy to me, too, and I got real uneasy, but apparently she needed to show people that she could sort of impress foreign contacts by having them to a meal with grace and style and all pizzazz in her country home. Eve sort of set it up for her with outside caterers and it worked a dream. You see, it's different for everyone."

Sara was puzzled. She walked down to the local snack bar and bought a salami sandwich. She ate it thoughtfully on the road coming back to the building. In the lift she heard that Garry Edwards was going to a conference in the Seychelles next week. It was a conference for people who brought out travel brochures, a significant part of promotions for any travel firm. Sara had done all the imaginative travel brochures, Garry Edwards had okayed them. Yet he was going to the Seychelles and she was eating a tired salami sandwich. When she opened her office door Eve was sitting there typing.

"I'll do it," she said. "Whatever it is, play golf, give foolish dinner parties . . . I'll do it. I want his job. It's utterly unjust that he's going to that conference, it's the most unjust thing I've ever known."

"He won't be going to it next year," said Eve. "Right, Miss Gray, I have a few points ready to discuss with you, shall we put this sign on the door?"

"What is it?" Sara asked fearfully.

"It merely says, 'Engaged in Conference,' I made it last night." Eve produced a neat card which she then fixed on the outside of the office door.

"Why are we doing that?" whispered Sara.

"Because it is absolutely intolerable the way that people think they can come barging in here, taking advantage of your good nature and picking your brains, interrupting us and disturbing you from whatever you are doing. We need a couple of hours to plan the office design, and it's no harm to let them see immediately that you are going to regard your job as important. It may only be half the job they should have given you, but don't worry, you'll have the right job very soon."

"Suppose that the really big brass comes along, or Mr. Edwards, or you know, someone important." Sara was still unsure.

"We are having a conference, about the redesign of your office."

"But there isn't any money to redesign it . . . even if they'd let me."

"Yes there is, I've been up to the requisition

department, in fact they looked you up in the book, and wondered why you hadn't applied. Whenever you're ready, Miss Gray, we can start."

Together they worked out how the office should look. It was a big room, but it was in no way impressive; apart from the inferior furniture, its design was all wrong. Eve explained that a separate cubicle should be built for her near the door. Eve should act as a kind of reception area for Sara, she should call through to announce visitors, even though it was only a distance of a few yards.

"They'll walk past and come straight on in," said Sara.

"Not if I walk after them and ask can I help them. They won't do it twice, Miss Gray," said Eve, and Sara realized that most of them wouldn't even do it once.

The costing of the partition was not enormous, and it left a reasonable amount for the rest of the furnishings.

"We'll have the filing section in my part since you shouldn't really have to be looking things up yourself, Miss Gray, but it will of course be kept in a very meticulous way so you can always find anything."

"What will I have in my part of the office then?" asked Sara humbly.

Eve stood up and walked around. "I've been giving it a lot of thought, Miss Gray. You are really the ideas woman here. I'm sorry, I know it's jargon, but that's what you do for the promotions department. You thought up that whole idea about choosing a holiday from your stars in the zodiac and that worked, you thought of having a travel agents' conference in that railway station, which suited them all since they had to come from all over the country and go back again by train. You thought up the scheme of having children write the section for children's holidays, so I think that this is what you should be doing really. Thinking. And let me handle the routine things, you know, the letters about 'Can you trace what we did about Portugal two years ago?' If the filing system works properly then anyone will be able to do that for you. I'll set it up so that at least four fifths of your incoming mail can be handled by any competent secretary. That should give you a great deal more time to do what you are really good at."

Sara looked hopeful but not convinced.

"Me just sit in here with a chair?" She shook her head. "I don't think it's on, Eve, I really don't. You know they'd think I'd gone mad."

"I wasn't suggesting a chair. I was going to suggest a long narrow conference table. Something in nice wood, we could look at auctions or in an antique shop. And about six chairs. Then, for you a small writing desk. Again something from an old house possibly, with your telephone and your own big diary and notebook, a few periodicals and trade magazines or directories you need, that's all."

"Eve, in God's name, what is the long conference table for? Eve, I am the assistant promotions manger, not the chairman of the board. I don't give conferences, call meetings, ask my superiors to come in here with the hope of blinding them about policy."

"You should," said Eve simply. "Listen," she went on. "Remember that children-writing-the-brochure idea? It was marvellous. I've been looking through the files, you got not one word of credit, no letter, no mention, no thanks even. I would not be at all surprised if you, Mr. Edwards, and I are the only people who know you thought it up, and the only reason I know is that I see entries in your diary about going to schools and talking to children and spending a lot of your free time working on it. Edwards got the praise, the thanks, and the job, for not only that but for everything you did. Because you didn't do it right."

"It worked, though," said Sara defensively.

"Miss Gray, of course the idea worked, it was brilliant, I remember seeing those brochures long before I ever knew you, and I thought they were inspired. What I mean is that it didn't work for you, here within the company. Next time, I suggest you invite Mr. Edwards and his boss and the marketing director and one or two others to drop in quite casually—don't dream of saying you are calling a meeting, just suggest that they might all like to come into your office one afternoon. And then, at a nice table where there is plenty of room and plenty of style, put forward your plans. That way they'll remember you."

"Yes, I know, in theory you're right, Eve . . . but honestly, I'm not the type. I'm jolly old Sara Gray, with a nice, jolly, hopeless lover who comes and goes at home—and who is gone at the moment. And they all say to themselves, 'Poor Sara, not a bad old thing'—none of them would take me at a rosewood conference table for one minute, Eve, they'd either corpse themselves laughing or else they'd think I was having a break- down, they'd fire me. And you."

Eve didn't look at all put out. "I wasn't suggesting calling a conference tomorrow, I was suggesting having the furniture right. If you are someone who is valuable to the company for her ideas, you should have a space to think up these ideas, a platform to present them on, and the just recognition for them."

"You're right," Sara said suddenly. "What else?"

"I think you should get into the habit of having Mr. Edwards and others coming to this office, by appointment of course, rather than you rushing to theirs. It makes you more important. That's why we need the right furniture. Mr. Edwards has an office like an aeroplane hangar, and very well laid out, I've inspected it. But yours could have a charm, it could become the place where ideas were discussed, say on one particular evening a week, a Thursday, before people left. It would be relaxing, and pleasant, and *you* would be in control."

As they talked on, it got darker outside, and they switched on the bright neon overhead light.

"That'll have to go for a start," said Eve. "It's far too harsh, there's no style, no warmth."

A few times the door had been half opened, but whenever people saw the two heads bent over the desk and lists, they muttered apologies and backed out.

"I never thought a notice would do that," said Sara admiringly.

"Wait till we get things going properly, you'll be amazed," said Eve.

Eve refused a drink, a girly chat, and the offer of a share in a taxi. Instead she took out her notebook again.

"You should have an account with a taxi firm," she said briskly. "I'll set that up tomorrow, when I'm organizing the flowers and your dress allowance."

Sara stared at her in the windy, wet street as if Eve had gone completely mad.

"*What* are you organizing . . .?" she began.

"Plants, flowers for the office, all the male senior executives have them, and they also get a special expense allowance for clothes because they have to travel, it being a travel company, and . . ."

"Eve, I'm not a senior executive, I can't have free flowers paid for by the office."

"As assistant manager you are technically a senior executive. The other two assistant managers are elderly men who have been pushed upstairs, so if you equate your title with theirs then you can have flowers, nothing extravagant, about six nice flowering plants. I think we can choose them from a brochure, they'll arrive tomorrow."

For the first time for a long time Sara sat back contentedly in her chair at home and didn't think about Geoff and wonder when his new obsession would end. Often she felt lonely and sad during his absences, so that she would hide from the feeling by having the television on or listening to music for long hours. But tonight she just sat calmly drinking her tea and looking into the fire. Eve's arrival meant that a lot of the tension in the office had been eased. It was like someone massaging your shoulders and taking away the stiffness—you didn't know how tense you had been until the massage was over—Eve was going to make things a lot better, and she was going to force Sara to take herself more seriously too. It was a bit exciting in a way.

Next morning was a Friday and Eve wanted to know whether Sara had any important plans and engagements for the weekend. Sara shrugged. "I was going to sort out those figures for Mr. Edwards, you know the ones he wanted on the breakdown of age groups on the coach holidays. We need to know where to direct some of the coach tour promotions this year."

"Oh, that's done," said Eve. "I did it this morning, I saw his note. I've two copies here for you to sign, one for Mr. Edwards and I thought you should send one to the head of marketing, just to let him know that you are alive and well and working harder than Mr. Edwards."

"Isn't that a bit sneaky?" asked Sara, looking like a doubtful schoolgirl.

"No, it's standard office procedure. Mr. Edwards is the sneaky party by not acknowledging your part in all the work that is being done."

With a weekend free Sara agreed happily to go to look at secondhand furniture and office fittings. Eve had already organized the office partition, and it began with great hammering and activity after lunch.

"I suggest you go and check out a few new outfits for yourself, Miss Gray," said Eve. "You can't possibly work here with all this noise."

"Could you come with me, I'm not exactly sure what I . . .?"

"Certainly, Miss Gray. Can you wait five minutes while I tell these gentlemen I shall be back in two hours to see how they are getting on?"

Eve managed to make three large men look as if they knew she was going to have them fired unless the partition was perfect. Then she went to the shop with Sara.

There was a brief objective discussion about what clothes Sara already possessed. Eve explained that she had seen only two tweed skirts and one black sweater in the three days she had been working there. Shame-facedly, Sara said she thought there were a couple of other sweaters and perhaps two more workable tweed skirts.

Eve seemed neither pleased nor put out; she was merely asking for information. In the store she suggested three outfits which could interchange and swap and make about a dozen between them. They cost so much that Sara had to sit down on the fitting-room chair.

"I took the liberty of getting you a credit card for your expenses, Miss Gray," said Eve. "I rushed it through, and what you are going to spend now is totally justifiable. You have to meet the public, you have to represent the company in places where the company may well be judged by the personal appearance of its representatives. What you are spending on these garments is half what Mr. Edwards has spent in the last six months, and you have been entitled to expenses of this kind for over a year and never called on them."

By Monday Sara could hardly recognize either herself or her new surroundings. On Eve's advice she had had an expensive hairdo; she wore the pink and grey wool outfit, put the pink cyclamens on her windowsill near the lovely old table with its matching half-dozen chairs which they had eventually found for half nothing since it was too big for most homes, and nobody except Eve would have thought of it as office furniture.

Eve was living in her purpose-built annex surrounded with files and ledgers. She had just begun to compile a folio of Sara's work so far with the company, a kind of illustrated *curriculum vitae* which would show her worth and catalogue her achievements. Nobody was more surprised than Sara by all she seemed to have done during her years in the company.

"I'm really quite good, you know," she said happily.

"Miss Gray, you are very good indeed, otherwise I wouldn't work with you," said Eve solemnly, and Sara could detect no hint of humour or self-mockery in the tone.

Towards the end of the second week, Eve pronounced herself pleased with the office. She had bought an old coat stand which ideally matched the table and chairs, and on this she urged Sara to hang her smart coat so that the whole place just looked as if it were an extension of her own creative personality. If anyone gasped with amazement at the changes in the room, Sara was to say that there was all this silly money up in requisitions for her to decorate the place, and she did hate modern ugly cubes of furniture so she had just chosen things she liked—which had in fact been cheaper. People were stunned, and jealous, and wondered why they hadn't thought of this too.

Remarks about her appearance Eve suggested should be parried slightly. No need to tell people that she now had regular twice-weekly sessions with a beautician. Eve had booked her a course of twenty.

So on the second Friday of her employment Eve came into Sara's part of the office and said she thought that they were ready to begin.

"Begin?" cried Sara. "I thought we'd finished."

Eve gave one of her rare smiles. "I meant begin your work, Miss Gray. I've been taking up a lot of your time with what I am sure you must have considered inessentials. Now I feel that you should concentrate totally on your work for promotions and let me look after everything else. I shall keep detailed records of all the routine work that I am doing. Each evening I'll leave you a progress report, too, of how I think we have been getting on in our various projects. These I think you should take home with you or else return to my personal file. We don't want them seen by anyone else."

Sara nodded her thanks. Suddenly she felt overwhelmed with gratitude for this strange girl who was behaving not as a new secretary but as if she were an old family retainer blind with loyalty to the young missie, or a kindergarten teacher filled with affection and hope for a young charge.

She felt almost unable to express any of this gratitude because Eve didn't seem to need it or even to like it.

"Are there any, er, major projects you see straight-away?" she asked.

"I think you should look for an assistant, or a deputy, Miss Gray," said Eve.

"*Eve*, you can't go, you can't leave me now!" cried Sara.

"Miss Gray, I am your secretary, not your assistant. I certainly shall not leave you for a year. I told you that. No, you need to train someone to do your job when you are not here."

"Not here?" Sara looked around her new office, which she was beginning to love. "Where will I be, why won't I be here?"

"Because you will be away on conferences, you will be travelling abroad to see the places the company is promoting, and of course, Miss Gray, you will be taking your own vacation, something you neglected to do last year I see."

"Yes, but that'll only be a few weeks at most. Why do I need to have an assistant, a deputy? I mean it's like empire building."

"You'll need to train an assistant to take over when you get Mr. Edwards's job at the end of the year. One of the many reasons why women fail to get promotion is because management can say that there is nobody else to do their job on the present level of the ladder. I suggest you find a bright and very young, extremely young, man."

"But I can't do that. They'd know I was plotting to get Garry Edwards's job."

Eve smiled. "I'm glad you are calling Mr. Edwards by his first name at last, Miss Gray. No, you need an assistant to do your work for you while you are away, of course. Otherwise, if this whole office is seen to tick along nicely without you in your absence, people will wonder why your presence is so essential. If, on the other hand, it turns into total chaos, they will blame you *in absentia*. So you need a harmless, enthusiastic, personable young man to sign letters, which I will write, and to postpone anything major until your return."

"Eve, why do you have to go away in a year?" Sara said suddenly. "Why can't you stay and together we'll take over the whole place. Honestly it's not impossible."

"Oh, Miss Gray, there'd be no point in taking the place over. It's not what either of us want, is it?" asked Eve, accepting naturally that it would be perfectly feasible to take over the largest travel company in Britain if she put her mind to it.

"You never tell me what you want," Sara said, impressed by her own daring.

"I like to see women getting their work recognized. There's so much sheer injustice in the business world—I mean really unjust things are done to women. I find that very strange. Men who can be so kind to stray dogs, lost strangers, their own children, contribute generously to charities, and yet continue appalling unfairness towards women at work."

She stopped suddenly.

Sara said, "Go on."

"Nothing more," Eve said firmly. "You asked me what I wanted. I want to see that injustice recognized for what it is, and to see people fight it."

"You should write about it, or make speeches," said Sara. "I never even saw it in my own case until you came. I do agree now that I've been shabbily treated and now I've got a bit of confidence to demand more. And that's only after ten days with you. Think what success you'd have if you were to go on a lecture tour or on television or something."

Eve looked sad.

"No. That's just the whole trouble. It doesn't work that way, damn it. That's why it's going to take so long."

Politely she extricated herself from further

explanations, from any more conversation, from having a drink at a nearby pub with Sara. She had to go home now.

"You never tell me about your home," said Sara.

"You never tell me about yours, Miss Gray, either," said Eve.

"I would if I got a chance," Sara said.

"Ah yes, but you and I would not get on so well if I knew about your worries and problems!"

Sara took it as a very faint warning. It meant that Eve didn't want to hear about Sara's problems and worries, either. She sighed. It would have been very helpful if Eve could apply her amazing skills to Sara's disastrous relationship with Geoff. He had been gone now three weeks. No, it couldn't be three weeks. It was. She could hardly believe it. The last ten days had passed so quickly she had scarcely missed him. She was so stunned by this that she hadn't heard what Eve had said.

"I was only saying that I left your invitation for the supper party tomorrow night there on your desk," Eve repeated as she gathered up her things. "I hope you enjoy it. I heard that all senior executives were normally invited to meet the chairman and board members so I made sure your name was on the list. Nice chance to wear that black dress, too, Miss Gray, I expect you're thinking."

Sara's eyes were big with gratitude. As if by magic Eve seemed to have known that another lonely weekend was looming ahead. But she knew not to admit to any emotion.

"Great. I'll go in there and knock them dead.

And on Monday we'll be ready to begin the campaign."

"Excellent," said Eve. "I suggest you find out whether any of the board have young and hopefully stupid sons who might want to start in the business. As your assistant, you know. We need someone rather overeducated with no brains."

"What are you going to do for the week-end?" asked Sara.

"This and that, Miss Gray. See you Monday," said Eve.

Sara spent Saturday reading the company's reports, which Eve had left thoughtfully on her desk. She took Eve's advice and wore the black dress to the party where Garry Edwards's surprise at seeing her was as exciting as any romantic flutter. "I can see how people can become obsessed with all this infighting and competitiveness," thought Sara.

She was charming to the chairman, she was respectful to Garry Edwards, and risked calling him Garry once or twice: she caught him looking at her sideways several times. She was very pleasant to a middle-aged and lonely woman who was the wife of a noisy extrovert board member. The woman was so grateful that she positively unburdened her life story. Eve's face came like a quick flash across the conversation; Sara remembered how she had implied that people don't really want to be bogged down with personal life stories, particularly of a gloomy nature. She murmured her sympathy for the details and disclaimers of the woman's tale about neglect and being pushed into the background.

"All he cares about now is our son, he's coming

down from Cambridge soon, with an arts degree—no plans, no interests."

Eve would have been proud of her. She geared the conversation gently to her own office, to how she would be delighted to meet the boy—she even gave the woman her card with a little note scribbled on it. How amazing that she should suddenly find a need for those nice new cards which Eve had ordered for her and produced within days of her arrival. Garry Edwards came across at one stage to find out what she was up to; Sara steered the conversation away again.

"Where's that chap that you are seen with sometimes—and sometimes not?" asked Edwards, determined to wound.

"If he's not here, it must be one of the evenings I'm not seen with him," Sara said cheerfully.

That night she went to sleep in her big double bed hoping that Geoff would not come home. She had too much to think about.

The weeks went by, two more of them. She had already held three successful and supposedly impromptu gatherings in her office. Always she had included several people higher in the pecking order than Garry Edwards.

Everyone had thought it was a splendid idea to have the handsome young son of their important board member and his lonely wife in the department. He worked most of the time in the general promotions department and two afternoons a week he got what was described as a training from Sara. What it really was was an access to her files, permission to sit in her room as she worked out schemes with some of the other promotions executives, and he learned an almost overpowering respect for Miss Gray from Eve, who stood up

229

and expected him to do the same. Eve almost lowered her voice in awe when she spoke of anything Sara had done, and the well-meaning, overeducated, and not very bright Simon did the same.

Simply because Eve kept him under such an iron rule, Simon did learn something. So much in fact that his parents were utterly delighted with him, and the head of marketing, who had opposed his appointment as the nepotism it undoubtedly was, had to admit that that young Miss Gray was able to do the most extraordinary things. He took to dropping in to her pleasant office occasionally, and once or twice that strange colorless secretary had told him very firmly that she couldn't be disturbed. When he implied that he was more important than whoever she could be talking to, the secretary had said very flatly that her instructions were to ask everyone to make appointments, or at least to telephone in advance if they intended to drop in. Since the head of marketing had been saying long and loud that too much socializing and twittering went on in his department in the name of work, he could not be otherwise than pleased.

Geoff came back. His latest lady decided that she must go back to her husband and children. This she said was where her duty lay. She said it when all Geoff's money had run out. Geoff had shrugged and come back to Sara. Amazingly she wasn't at home. He let himself in one night with a bottle of champagne, a single rose, and a long explanation, but there was nobody to receive any of these things so he just went to bed.

She wasn't there in the morning either. He checked her wardrobe, most of her sweaters and skirts seemed to be there. The place looked neater somehow, and there were no work files strewn about. She had a lot of much more expensive cosmetics in the bathroom too. He wondered what had been happening. He couldn't have been gone more than a month. She hadn't run out, surely? She couldn't have decided to end with him, surely? After all she hadn't changed the lock or anything. His key still opened her hall door.

He called her next morning, and a very cool voice that was not Sara's answered him. "Miss Gray's office."

"Oh, we have gone up in the world," giggled Geoff. Loyalty to Sara and building her up to her colleagues was never his strong suit.

"I beg your pardon?" said the voice.

"Listen, it's Geoff here, can I talk to Sara?"

"Can I know who wants to speak to Miss Gray please?" asked Eve.

"Hell, I've just told you. It's Geoff. Sara's chap, Geoff. Put me onto her will you, sweetheart."

Eve answered very pleasantly. "I'm afraid you must have the wrong number."

Geoff sounded annoyed. "Sara Gray's office, right?"

"Yes, this is Miss Sara Gray's office, now will you kindly tell me who this is speaking?"

"Geoff. Geoff White, for Christ's sake, who is that?"

"I am Miss Gray's secretary. Mr. White, can you please tell me your business? You're taking up a lot of time."

She didn't actually lie when Sara asked had Geoff phoned. She said that a totally inarticulate man had called but it could hardly have been

Geoff. Sara had paused only momentarily to wonder. She had spent five days at a sales conference in Paris, and had told Eve excitedly how she had been asked to address the meeting twice about new brochure ideas. Mr. Edwards—or that buffoon Garry as she was now calling him—looked positively yellow with rage. He had tried to make a pass at her which she had rejected with amazement and something akin to distaste. Eve was full of praise.

Next day Sara said, "The inarticulate man must have been Geoff. His things were in the flat, but I couldn't bear to be woken at three A.M. with champagne and tears and all, so I bolted my door and didn't hear whether he called or not."

Eve nodded in her cool way. She wanted to hear no more, not one word of Sara's private life. Yet she looked pleased. Things were going as hoped for. Sara was now too busy to worry about Geoff, and soon she would be too confident to accept his amazing behaviour, which was already a legend in office gossip. The new Sara would either throw him out or make him behave in a civilized way. Very satisfactory.

The weeks passed again. By now it was already office gossip that Sara would shortly take over from Garry Edwards. People who hadn't rated her much before were saying now that she had been holding back. Others said that she was always brilliant and that it was only a matter of time before it was recognized.

Garry Edwards blew it. He tried to drop Sara into great trouble for one of his own mistakes. Unlucky Garry Edwards that he had joined battle with Eve's filing system, the relevant documents were produced in a matter of minutes; quite obviously Sara had dealt with the problem; had recommended a correct course of action.

It was shortly after this that Eve asked Sara to come into her small cubicle and go over the filing system with her.

"Let's do a test," Eve said. "Suppose you had to find press comment on Senior Citizen Campaign, where would you look?" Sara checked first under "Publicity" then under "Senior Citizens." It took her five minutes.

"It's too long," said Eve firmly. "Perhaps you should have a look for something every day for the next month or so. Just to familiarize yourself."

"You're going to leave me, aren't you?" asked Sara.

"I think so," said Eve.

"It's not the year, it's not even half a year," Sara complained.

"But there's nothing left to do, Miss Gray. We get you a new efficient typist, we both explain to her and to Simon what the routine is, you'll be leaving shortly anyway for Mr. Edwards's job, we'll just make sure that any changeover here goes smoothly."

"Can't you come with me, upstairs?" Sara nodded in the direction of the promotions manager's office. "Please."

"No, you can do it better on your own really. And it's better for you." She was like a swimming instructor encouraging a bright but apprehensive pupil.

"The office, Eve, how will I do up the office so that it's like this . . . I mean I hate his furniture, I hate his style."

"You choose, Miss Gray. A few months ago

233

you wouldn't even have noticed his office or his style."

"Eve, a few months ago you know very well nobody would have noticed me."

"You underestimate yourself, Miss Gray. Shall I advertise for a secretary, I'd be happy to advise you on any points during any interview."

"God, yes, Eve." Sara looked at her. "I won't keep asking you but you know there's no problem about salary."

Eve shook her head.

Sara put her face into a bright smile. "In a few months I suppose I'll get a telephone call from some bewildered woman asking me do I know Eve and can I possibly recommend her insane notions."

Eve looked solemn. "Well, yes, if you don't mind. I should like your name as a reference."

"And I'll say Miss whoever you are . . . Eve is not from this planet. Let her have her way with you and you'll be running your company in months."

Eve stood up briskly. "Yes, if you think it was all worth it."

Sara put out her hand and held Eve's arm.

"I know you hate people prying but why, just why? You're far brighter than I am, than the woman in the bank, than the other woman—the one you told to have dinner parties. I mean, why don't *you* do it? Why don't you do it for *you*? You know better than any of us how to get on. It's like a kind of crusade for you but you stay in the background all the time. I don't know what you're at. What you want."

Eve shrugged politely. "I like to see you do well, Miss Gray, that's enough reward for me.

234

You deserve it. You were being passed over. That wasn't just."

Sara nodded. "Now I promise, all the rest of the time you are here, I'll never ask again. Never. Just tell me. Why this way? If you feel there's discrimination against women there must be better ways to fight it."

Eve leaned against the beautiful table and stroked it. "If there are I can't find them. I simply know of no better way to fight it than from within. You have to use the system. I hate it but it's true."

Sara didn't interrupt. She knew that if Eve was ever going to say anything it would be now. She let the pause last.

"How do you think I, as a feminist, like asking intelligent, sensitive women like you and like Bonnie Bernstein in the bank and Marrion Smith in the ministry to dress properly? As if it mattered one goddamn whether you wore woad to the office . . . all three of you are worth more than any man I ever met in any kind of business. And I could say that for seven or eight other women too. But women don't have a chance, they don't bloody know. . . ."

Sara sat breathless.

"It's so *unjust*." Eve stressed that word heavily. "So totally unjust. A married man has a woman to look after his appearance and his clothes and his meals and his house, a woman does not. A single man has a fleet of secretaries, assistants, manicurists, lovers, to look after him. A single woman is meant to cope. A man is admired for sleeping with people on his way up, a woman is considered a tramp if she does. A man . . ." She paused and pulled herself together, almost physi-

235

cally. "Miss Gray, you must excuse me. I really don't think I should be taking up your time with all this. I do apologize. I feel ashamed of myself."

The moment was gone, the spell was broken.

"I don't suppose you'll tell me why you feel like this? I mean was there some experience in your life, Eve? You are so young, too young to be bitter about things."

Eve looked at her. "No, of course I'm not bitter, I'm very constructive. I just try to get some justice for strong, good women who deserve it. When I've got it I move on. It's very satisfying. Slow but satisfying. Now, about this advertisement. I don't think we should phrase it 'travel business,' it will attract the kind of woman who thinks in terms of cheap flights and free holidays."

Sara played along. She owed Eve that much.

"Oh yes, of course. Let's word it now, and put it in whenever you want to. The later the better of course. You know I don't want you to leave here ever."

"Thank you very much, Miss Gray. But I think really if you agree I'll get it into tomorrow's papers."

Sara looked up.

"So soon?"

"There's a lot to be done," said Eve.

Euston

At the beginning of December, Mary decided to forgive them and go home for Christmas. She saw this documentary on television about people who held grudges and people who took stands and did things for a principle but still the principle only made everyone else unhappy and meant nothing to anyone. It was as clear as daylight to her: she would forgive them and go home. She looked up the plane times, and decided to go on the Wednesday. That would give her a day in Dublin, she would travel home by train on Thursday night.

She felt years younger, once she had decided to forgive them. She wondered whether anyone else who saw the television programme had got such a clear insight. She might write to them afterwards and tell them about it. People said that television folk loved to hear from people that programmes were good. She walked around her little room hugging herself. She hadn't felt so lighthearted for years.

She must tell them in plenty of time, too, no point in all this surprise business, arriving, long-lost prodigal on the doorstep, on Christmas Eve. It was fine in the parable, but she'd always felt sorry for the Prodigal's brother, the one that had been there all the time and nobody killed a scrawny chicken for him, let alone a fatted calf. No, they must have time to think about it. Because obviously they would need to adjust to the relief of it all, just as she would. She would write to her mother tonight.

Her mother would be so happy; Mary could almost see the way she would hold the letter to her chest as she did whenever she got good news. In the old days she had suspected that a letter meant bad news and it was always opened in fear. It would be funny to see her mother as an old woman—she would be seventy-five on Stephen's Day. Imagine her mother being like one of the old women she saw in the supermarkets here; imagine, her mother probably had a stick, and glasses. Her mother, who used to be so tall and strong. And so convinced that she knew everything. So sure of herself, and her notions.

But of course all that had changed now. There had been none of that sureness and accusation in the letters she had written begging Mary to come back. Oh ho, no. There had been different words. "Life is very short," "families shouldn't fall out," "it's very hard to have you turn your heart against us."

Mary remembered the letters, she had filed them neatly in a box that had once contained a rotary whisk. She had written on each envelope the date it had arrived. She had read them once and placed them in neat rows. She had answered none of them—there was nothing to say. She didn't mind that they were saying an extra decade of the Rosary for her, she didn't get any satisfaction out of the grudging admission that her father might have let himself go much too far. She knew that her father had let himself go much too far. She knew that there was no way she would forgive them because they didn't want to have anything to do with Louis.

Louis had said that she should be patient, that she should be sensible, they would see things differently in time. But Mary Brennan didn't think there was enough time. Louis had said that her mother and father were kind to worry so much; he wished that he had someone to worry about him, he had no one, but if he ever had a daughter he'd be careful who she went off with. Mary told her mother this one night, with tears running down her face.

"He's all for us to wait, Ma, he says we'll wait two years if you like, just if we can get engaged. See how sensible he is. Ma—how can you call him a fly-by-night?"

To Mother and Father this was further evidence of Louis's cunning. That proved that he must be after her money. But what money? Mary used to throw her eyes wildly up to the heavens; Lord God, they were talking about a few hundred pounds. Twelve hundred pounds. How could they be so stupid and so cruel as to think that Louis wanted to marry her so that he could get his hands on twelve hundred pounds?

Ah, but her father had said, does he want to marry our Mary? That's the point. Doesn't he just want to go off and live with her until the money was spent? What was all this nonsense about not wanting a big wedding because he had nobody to ask? What kind of trickery was that? What kind of a man had nobody to ask for a wedding, had appeared from nowhere in the town with no background, no recommendation. Wasn't it funny that he had picked a girl that nobody else had seemed to make much of a run for? Answer him that. How was it that none of the other young fellows in the town had seen fit to run and propose to Mary Brennan when it was time for them to pick a wife? No, only a fellow from God knows where, running from God knows what, picking the town's settled spinster because she had a few pounds in the post office.

★   ★   ★

239

Mary Brennan had been twenty-nine the year she had met Louis; he had come to work in Lynch's grocery for the summer. He had cut ice creams and the children liked him because he made the fourpenny ones big and put a little extra in the threepenny cones. The Lynches liked him because he was always smiling and he didn't mind staying open late after the cinema crowds, or even until they came out from the dance when he'd sell crisps and minerals and he always knew how to move on anyone who was a bit noisy. They made more money that summer that ever before. He used to tell them to go in and listen to the wireless; he didn't mind sitting in the shop.

Mary Brennan had been dreading the end of the summer but no, the Lynches kept him on. Then when all the tourists had gone, Mary used to have him to herself. They walked the cliffs in autumn and when the winds got cold in October he put his coat around her shoulders and told her that she was lovely. Nobody had ever kissed her, except two drunks at the dance, and she thought it was great to have waited so long for it because it was even better than she had ever hoped. Then people started to tell her that he was making a fool of her.

Her father had been the worst, even her mother and Nessa and Seamus had tried to stop her father when he got into one of his attacks. Nessa had looked away when her father had said to Mary that she should look in the mirror and have some sense. How would a young ne'er-do-well like Louis, six years younger than she . . . how could he want a woman like her?

The winter days had melted into each other, Mary could remember only a blur. She used to go to work in the post office every day, she supposed. She must have come home for her tea, but did she have it on her own or were there rows every single night with them all? She remembered that Louis was always shivering, they used to talk on the street. They couldn't come home; her father wouldn't let him into the house, he couldn't ask her into the Lynches' house . . . it would be setting them up as enemies of her parents. Sometimes they talked in whispers in the back of the church, where it was warm, until once Father O'Connor had said it wasn't very respectful to the Lord to come into his house and talk and skitter in it like a couple of bold children.

The night that Louis had said maybe he was only being a cross for her to bear, she made up her mind. Louis had said maybe he was bringing her more bad luck than happiness, and that he should go off and she should forget him. Mary Brennan made up her mind firmly. She was very calm. It was three days before Christmas, and she filled in all the forms about transferring the money from her post office account. She tidied up her little section of the counter and told the postmistress that she should look for someone else in the new year, and then she walked home and told her mother and father and Nessa and Seamus that she was leaving on the bus, and they would catch the train and they would go to England.

She left the house in an uproar and went to Lynch's and told Louis. He said they couldn't go now. She said simply:

"You have to come with me, I'm cleaving to you like it says in the New Testament—you know, about a man cleaving to a wife and leaving father and mother and all. That's what I'm doing. Don't leave me to cleave all by myself."

Louis had laughed and said of course he couldn't do that; he packed his case, he told the Lynches that they needn't pay him the Christmas bonus because it wouldn't be fair. He came and stood outside the Brennans' house with his suitcase in his hand, a bit like he had looked when he arrived at the beginning of the summer but colder, and waited until the door opened and all the crying and the noise came out into the street and Mary came down the steps slowly, but without any tears.

They had never cried on that journey, they laughed and thought what great times they would have and they found a room near Paddington station and, though they pretended to be married, they slept in separate beds until they were married by an Italian priest three weeks later, with two Italians as witnesses.

She wrote one letter home. Early in that year, in the spring of 1963. She said that they had been married in a Catholic church and that they had used her £1,200 to buy a share of a small corner shop. They thought the business should be very good.

They were both prepared to work long hours, and this was how you built up good trade in a neighborhood like this. She said she had nothing more to say, and she didn't really expect to hear from them, she thought they had said all they ever wanted to say that last day. But still Louis had been very keen that she should let them know where she was. Louis sent them cordial wishes. She was merely pleasing him by writing this once.

They wrote, they tried to write letters

explaining what had been done was done with the best motives. Nessa wrote and told her about the visit of President Kennedy and how they had all gone on the excursion to see him. Seamus wrote and said it was a bit dead at home now, and you'd sort of feel sorry for the old fella. But Mary never wrote back.

Once, when she was combing her hair, Louis said she should look in the mirror. "Look at yourself in the mirror, there's a bit sticking up there," he said good-naturedly. Mary had burst into tears. She never looked in the mirror. She was afraid she might see a mare like her father had seen.

When he knew the result of his exploratory operation, Louis wrote to Mary's parents. "She is very proud and she feels always that to open up her heart to you . . . is to let me down somehow. She thinks that it's further loyalty to me if she cuts you out. But when it's all over I'm sure she'll need you. Please let her know that this is what I wanted. I'll leave her a letter myself."

They had tried to contact him at the hospital, but it was too late. Mary had sent them a black-edged printed card, thanking them for their condolences.

As she had worked for ten years in the little shop as a wife, so she worked ten years as a widow. Other little shops were bought by new immigrants, hard-working Pakistanis who were prepared to work equally hard hours. Once or twice an elderly Pakistani had made her a good offer for her little corner business, saying he wanted to set his nephews up in a good trade. That day she remembered that she, too, had nephews. Nessa had three sons, and Seamus had

243

two. She wondered what they heard of their Aunt Mary in London.

The night she forgave her family Mary looked at herself in the mirror. Nearly fifty, she didn't feel it; perhaps she looked it. She didn't really know how she looked nowadays. No Louis for many years to admire her, or tell her she was frowning too much, or that she had beautiful big gray eyes. Her father was nearly blind now, and her mother's yearly letter seemed to imply that he was no longer able to leave the house. Her mother seemed to go to the church even more than she had done all those years ago; there was a lot of mention of Nessa's family, she had married the son of the pub owner, which was a good thing to have done. They had three boys and three girls.

Nessa had her own car. Not much mention of Seamus. His wife was hardly mentioned at all. Perhaps she had been another Louis in their eyes, a no-good, mad for the Brennan money. The poor Brennan money. It was laughable. Within two years she and Louis had gathered more than her father had gotten in his lifetime. But she mustn't speak like that when she got home.

No, no triumphant tales of how well it had all gone, what a good man Louis had turned out to be, how wrong, how very wrong they had been to say that he had been anything less. No, if you forgive, you must forget a lot too.

They had obviously been able to forget, too, no words of apology these days. Not since Louis had died, and they had sent her his letter and asked her to come back. Begged her.

Excitedly, she wondered what it would be like. She would stay for a week, young Mr. Patel, who was her assistant in the shop, could easily run the place. His family didn't celebrate Christmas anyway. She could even stay for two weeks. She wondered where she would sleep. In her old room? She supposed that Nessa would want her to stay in her house, too . . . and she'd make a great effort to go and stay with Seamus and the wife and make a fuss of them. She would be like Santa Claus for all the children . . . she must look through the letters again to see how old they were. It would be desperate to bring them all the wrong things. Lord, Nessa's eldest would be seventeen now. A grown man nearly.

What would he have to say to his aunt, his new aunt, or rather his old aunt? Her gaiety left her for a moment. What would any of them have to say?

There was a nagging voice which wondered would they like to be forgiven . . . or might it all be a bit too much trouble now? Perhaps they all had their own Christmas planned. Perhaps the priest was coming to lunch on Christmas Day, and old Mrs. Lynch from the shop where Louis had worked. Perhaps Nessa and her fellow had to go to the pub people for Christmas. Who knew what Seamus was like now?

She touched her grey hair as she looked in the mirror. She was a stranger to them all. It didn't really matter whose fault it had been . . . or who had said what . . . the main thing was that they didn't know her. They didn't know what her life had been like with Louis; they'd never heard that she and Louis took a train to Rome one year and had picnics with Italians all the time. They didn't know what her little flat was like here, and how

245

she had made a patchwork quilt and how she had gone on a holiday to an old hotel with a lot of other people who wanted to learn about antiques.

Her mother and father didn't know that she had had her gall bladder out three years ago, and that she had given up smoking three times and the last time it seemed to be working. They didn't know she could make pickles and that she had a friend, Phyllis, whom she went to a show with every week. They would look up the papers and choose what seemed suitable.

They both had the same taste. Phyllis had been going to book them a Christmas lunch in a hotel . . . she had probably made the booking by now. She would understand, of course. But still.

No, perhaps it would be foolish to rush into it. She might do more harm than good. Perhaps this year she should just pave the way. Send them a card. Let them know that she was holding no more grudges. Yes, that would be the way, and when they wrote and thanked her . . . then, little by little. And next Christmas. *That* was it. Not immediately, people don't like to be forgiven too quickly.

She found a card and put a second-class stamp on it. There was still plenty of time—no point in wasting first-class postage. She thought for a while. People mustn't be rushed.

After a lot of thought she wrote, "Seasonal Wishes to one and all. Mary."

She put it on the little table to post early next morning, on her way to the shop. She thought that it would give them all a nice warm glow to know that she had forgiven them, and she was glad that it had happened at Christmastime.

Warren Street

Nan had had another god-awful day. Nobody seemed to use any underarm deodorant anymore. She had been wincing from whiffs of sweat all day, as people flung off their garments to try on her designs.

That maddening Mrs. Fine had, of course, noticed the seam that wasn't exactly right; while that stupid, stupid woman—who apparently worked in some important position in an estate agent's—had forgotten again what she wanted made out of the woollen material but was absolutely certain that it wasn't the poncho that Nan had cut out for her.

"Why would I have said a poncho, when I have one already?" she asked, wide-eyed.

"That's what I asked you at the time," hissed Nan.

But the thing that was making Nan's heart leaden was that she had had a row with Shirley.

Now nobody had rows with Shirley. She had a face so like the rising sun you expected rays to stick out from her head like in a child's drawing. If Nan had rowed with her, it had to have been Nan's fault and that was that.

Shirley had been coming to Nan for two years now, ordering maybe five garments a year. Nan remembered the first day she came she had been pressing her nose against the window rather wistfully, looking at a little bolero and skirt outfit on display. The skirt wouldn't have gone over Shirley's head, let alone made it to her waist.

Nan pulled back the curtain and waved her inside—she still wondered why she did it. Normally she never encouraged customers. She had enough enquiries she couldn't deal with, and this was obviously not a fashion-conscious girl whom it would be a pleasure to dress.

Shirley's great, happy face and bouncing, bulging body arrived in Nan's little shop.

"I think I have the wrong place," she began. "Lola, who works with me and who's eight months pregnant, said she got her smocks here, and I was wondering if you have any more smocks. I mean, they might fit me, even though I'm not pregnant."

Nan had liked her cheerful face so much she'd encouraged her.

"Sit down. I'll go and see. I've very few things really—I mainly make clothes up for people, you see."

"Oh, are you a designer?" asked Shirley innocently.

She had touched on something very near to Nan's heart. She would have liked to think of herself as a designer and she had a flair for ideas and style. She sold things to classy boutiques from time to time. But something about Shirley's face made her answer, to her own surprise, "No, more a dressmaker."

"Oh, that's great," Shirley had said. "I thought that they'd disappeared. I wonder, would you be able to make me a smock . . .?" She broke off, seeing a refusal beginning to form itself on Nan's face.

"Oh, please, please do!" she said. "I can't find

anything in the shops that doesn't have white collars or tiny, thoughtful mum-to-be prints on it."

"It's just that I'm very busy . . ." Nan began.

"It would be very easy to do," said Shirley. "You wouldn't have to put any shape in it, and you wouldn't have to waste time wondering if the fit was right." She grinned encouragingly, and that did it. Nan couldn't bear her to go around the world as vulnerable as that, and indeed, as badly dressed in that hideous, diagonally striped garment she had on.

"You win," Nan had said, and they spent a happy half hour planning what Shirley would wear for the winter.

Away went the belted grey army issue-type coats—the only ones that fitted Shirley—and on came a cape. Away, too, the men's warm sweaters and on with a rosy-red dress and a warm pink one.

Nan also made her a multicoloured evening dress, which had all the shades of the rainbow in it. It was, she thought, a pleasure to design a dress for Shirley. She was so grateful, so touched and happy when it was finished. Sometimes she would whirl around in it in front of the mirror, her fat little hands clasped excitedly like a child.

Shirley was one of the few clients who didn't seem to have a list of complaints and personal problems, which was another bonus. Nan thought of Mrs. Fine, always running down her husband. Shirley never complained about men at all.

Miss Harris was always bitching about traffic or work, or how you couldn't get a taxi or a waiter who spoke English, or proper whole-meal bread.

Shirley never seemed in the least upset by such deprivations.

In fact, Nan knew little of Shirley's life, except that she fancied her boss in an advertising agency. Or maybe she didn't—Shirley was always so jokey. The last garment she had made Shirley was a really lovely dress. Nan had spent hours on the very fine wool, with its embroidery, ruffs, and frills, its soft blues and yellows. Shirley looked like an enormous, beautiful baby.

It was for some gala evening and Shirley had said, "If he doesn't tear the clothes off me when he sees me like this, he never will."

Nan worked on a system of appointments that meant you had to come and see her on the hour, and she saw only eight people a day. That way, she said, the job was manageable. People didn't stay longer than twenty minutes at the most. The rest of the hour Nan worked away, with her quiet little machinist burring on in the background.

She would never be rich, never be famous, but it was a living. She couldn't see a life where she would be finishing buttonholes at 3 A.M. for a show next day. Her own life and her own lover were far too precious for that. Colin and she had lived together happily for ages and often thought of getting married but they'd never actually got the details organized.

That's what they said. The truth was that Colin would have disappeared very sharply if Nan had suggested marriage. She didn't mind much, although sometimes she felt he had it all ways since they both worked. She did the housework and paid the rent; but then it was her place, and he did share the bills.

And he loved the fact that she worked downstairs. Sometimes if he had a day off he would come in and give her a rose in the workroom, and on one never-to-be-forgotten occasion he had asked the machinist to go for a walk, locked the door, and made love to her there and then, to the accompaniment of Miss Harris pounding on the door.

One day Colin had seen Shirley leaving with a finished dress. "Who on earth was the beach ball bouncing out a minute ago?" he asked. Shirley wasn't the usual mould of Nan's clients.

"That's our Shirl, whom I talk about sometimes," Nan said.

"You never told me she looked like a technicoloured Moby Dick," said Colin. Nan was annoyed. True, Shirley was enormous; true, she was dressed extremely brightly—mainly at Nan's insistence. But because she had such a lovely face, she looked well in colourful clothes and Nan didn't like Colin's joke.

"That's a bit uncalled for, isn't it?" she said sharply. Colin was amazed.

"Sorry to tease her—let me hold out my hand for a smack," he mocked. "Yes, it was very uncalled for, teacher, nobody called for it at all."

Nan retorted, "It's cruel—to laugh at somebody's shape!"

"Aw, come on, come on," said Colin reasonably. "You're always saying someone's like a car aerial or the Michelin Man or whatever. It was just a remark, just a joke."

Nan forgave him. "It's just that I feel, I don't know, a bit protective about her. She's so bloody nice compared with almost anyone who comes in here, and she's literally so soft—in every way. I just feel she'd melt into a little pool if she heard anyone making a remark like that about her, honestly."

"She was halfway down the street before I opened my mouth," said Colin.

"I know—I suppose I just hope that nobody says such things whether she hears them or not," said Nan.

That conversation had been a few months ago, Nan reflected, as she sat, head in hands. Funny that it all came back to her now. She did remember exactly how protective she had felt, as if Shirley had been her favorite sister and their mother had entrusted Nan with the care of seeing that nobody ever laughed at the fat girl.

Nan could hardly believe that, not half an hour ago, Shirley had banged out of the door and shouted from the street that she would never come back. It was like a nightmare where people behave completely out of character.

Shirley had come along for a final fitting for the wedding outfit. Her best friend was getting married and Shirley and Nan had been through reams of ideas before settling on the emerald-green dress and matching hat.

Nan had been delighted with it and Shirley's face was a picture of happiness as they both looked at the outfit in the mirror: the tall, slim, slightly wary-looking dressmaker in her elegant grey wool tunic and the short, mountainous client in her metres and metres of glittering emerald.

"You'll need green eye shadow, not blue," said Nan. "I'll lend you some for the wedding if you like." She looked around for her bag. "Do you know, I was running out of some, and then I thought of you and this color, so I asked Colin to get me some. He's in the trade, you know, so it's a little perk. I can't find the wretched thing anywhere." As she hunted for the parcel, which wasn't in her handbag after all, Nan felt a strange, unnatural silence descend behind her.

"Is that it?" asked Shirley, holding up an envelope that was on a table. The envelope had writing on it. It said "Green eye shadow for burly Shirley."

The two women looked at the inscription in silence for what must have been only four seconds or so, but seemed never-ending. Nan could think of only one thing to say.

When it was obvious that Shirley was going to say nothing either, she tried, but her voice only came out like a squeak. What she had been going to say was, "I didn't write that," and that didn't seem a very helpful thing to say at that moment.

She thought she would kill Colin. She would physically hurt him and bruise him for this. She would never forgive him.

Shirley's face had turned pink. Her fat neck had gone pink, too, which didn't go very well with the emerald.

"Is that what you call me—'Burly Shirley'? Well I suppose it has the advantage of rhyming," she said. She was so hurt she was almost bleeding.

Nan found her words finally. "Colin has rude, destructive nicknames for all my clients. It amuses him—it's childish, immature, and senseless," she snapped fiercely.

"How does he know I'm . . . burly? He's never met me," said Shirley.

"Well, you see he makes up these nicknames without knowing who people are. You do see that it's not an insult and it's not a comment. He could have written anything." Nan nearly laughed with relief. How marvellous to get out of it in this way. But Shirley was looking at her oddly.

"So I expect he just chose the word because it rhymes with your name. If you had been called Dotty he might have said Spotty." Nan was very pleased with herself, at the unknown powers of invention that were suddenly welling up within her.

Shirley just looked.

"So now that's cleared up, why don't you take the eye shadow and put a little on to see how it looks with the outfit?" urged Nan.

Shirley politely started to put it on, and Nan released her breath and foolishly didn't leave well, or nearly well, enough alone.

"I mean it's not as if anyone would deliberately make a joke about fat to anyone, not that you are very fat or anything, but one wouldn't mention it even if you were."

"Why not?" asked Shirley.

"Why? Well, you know why—it would be rude and hurtful to tell someone they were fat. Like saying they were ugly or . . . you know . . ."

"I didn't think being fat was on the same level as being ugly, did you?"

Desperately Nan tried to get back to the comparatively happy level they had just clawed their way to a few moments ago.

"No, of course I don't think being fat is the same as being ugly, but you know what I mean— nobody wants to be either if they can possibly avoid it."

"I haven't hated being fat," said Shirley. "But I wouldn't like to think it was on a par with being ugly—something that would revolt people and make them want to turn away."

"You're not very fat, Shirley," Nan cried desperately.

"Oh but I am, I am very fat. I am very short and weigh sixteen stone, and no normal clothes will fit me. I am very, very fat, actually," said Shirley.

"Yes, but you're not really fat; you're not fat like . . ." Nan's inventive streak gave out and she stopped.

"I'm the fattest person you know, right? Right. I thought it didn't matter so much because I sort of felt I had a pretty face."

"Well, you do have a very pretty face."

"You gave me the courage to wear all these bright clothes instead of the blacks and browns . . ."

"You look lovely in . . ."

"And I didn't worry about looking a bit ridiculous; but you know, ridiculous was the worst I thought I ever looked. I didn't think it was ugly . . ."

"It isn't, you misunderstood . . ."

"It's always disappointing when you discover that someone hasn't been sincere, and has just been having a bit of fun, that she's just been pitying you."

"I don't pity you . . . I wasn't . . ."

"But thanks anyway, for the outfit." Shirley started to leave. "It's lovely and I'm really very grateful. But I won't take the eye shadow, if you don't mind."

"Shirley, will you sit down . . .?"

"The cheque is here—that *is* the right price, by the way? You're not doing it cheaply just for me, I hope."

"Please, listen . . ."

"No, I'm off now. The life has gone out of it here, now that you pity me. I suppose it's just silly pride on my part, but I wouldn't enjoy it anymore."

"Shirley, let me say something. I regard you as my most valued customer. I know that sounds like something out of a book, but I mean it. I look forward to your coming here. Compared with most of the others, you're a joy—like a friend, a breath of fresh air. I enjoyed the days that you'd been. Now don't make me go down on my knees. Don't be touchy . . ."

"You've always been very friendly and helpful . . ."

"Friendly . . . helpful . . . I regard you as some kind of kid sister or daughter. I had a fight with Colin about you not three months ago, when he said you looked like Moby Dick with stripes or something."

"Oh yes."

"Oh God."

Shirley had gone. The bang of the door nearly took the pictures off the walls.

"I'll miss her dreadfully," thought Nan. "She was the only one with any warmth or life. The rest are just bodies for the clothes." To hell with it. She would telephone Lola, the friend who had sent Shirley to her in the first place.

"Listen, Lola, this sounds trivial, but you know that nice Shirley who worked with you . . ."

"Shirley Green? Yeah, what about her?"

"No, her name is Kent, Shirley Kent."

"I know it used to be till she married Alan Green."

"Married?"

"Nan, do you feel okay? You made her wedding dress for her, about a year ago."

"She never told me she got married. Who's Alan Green? Her husband?"

"Well, he's my boss, and was hers. Nan, what is this?"

"Why do you think she didn't tell me she got married?"

"Nan, I haven't an idea in the whole wide world why she didn't tell you. Is this what you rang up to ask me?"

"Well have a guess. Think why she mightn't have told me."

"It might have been because you and Colin weren't getting married. She's very sensitive, old Shirl, and she wouldn't want to let you think she was pitying you or anything."

"No, I suppose not."

"Anyway, it was the most smashing wedding dress—all that ruffle stuff and all those lovely blues and lace embroidery. I thought it was the nicest thing you've ever made."

Green Park

They had both sworn that they would not dress up. They had assured each other that it would be ridiculous to try to compete with Jane after all these years and considering all the money she had. Very immature really to try on fine feathers and glad rags—like children dressing up and playing games. Yet when they met at the station

257

they were almost unrecognizable from their usual selves.

Helen had bought a new hat with a jaunty feather, and Margaret had borrowed a little fur cape. Both of them wore smart shoes, and their faces, normally innocent of powder, had definite evidence of rouge and even eye shadow. After much mutual recrimination they agreed that they both looked delightful and settled themselves into the train to London with more excitement than two schoolgirls.

How extraordinary to be heading off for tea at the Ritz with Jane. Helen whispered that she would love to tell everybody in the railway compartment that this was where they were heading. Margaret said it would be more fun to let it fall casually in conversation afterwards: "How nice you look today, Mrs. Brown, what a sensible colour to wear, lots of people in the Ritz last week seemed to be wearing it."

And of course they giggled all the more because, in spite of sending themselves up, they actually were a little nervous about going to somewhere as splendid as the Ritz. They were overawed. The very mention of the Ritz made them nervous. It was for perfumed, furred people, not people who had dabbed some of last Christmas's perfume behind the ears and borrowed a sister-in-law's well-worn Indian lamb.

In some way both Helen and Margaret feared they might be unmasked when they got there. And they giggled and joked all the more to stifle this fear.

None of their fear was directed towards Jane. Jane was one of their own. Jane had trained to be a children's nanny with them all those years ago. You don't forget the friends made during that kind of apprenticeship. It was far more binding than the services were for men. It was almost like having survived a shipwreck—the eighteen girls who survived that particular obstacle race in the school for nannies, which had long since closed down, had forged a friendship which would last for life. Some of them had gone to the Gulf states and they wrote regular newsletters saying how they were getting on. Some, like Helen and Margaret, had married and applied their nanny training to their own children; only Jane had become spectacular and famous. But because she was Jane from the nanny training school it didn't matter if she became head of the United Nations, Helen and Margaret would never be in awe of her.

They changed trains, twittering happily at Euston, and took the underground to Green Park.

"Perhaps people think we are career women, dropping into the Ritz for a business conference," whispered Helen.

"Or wealthy wives up for a day's shopping," sighed Margaret.

Neither Margaret nor Helen were wealthy. Margaret was actually married to a vicar and lived in a draughty vicarage. She was so much the vicar's wife now that she felt quite guilty about wearing the Indian lamb in case any of her husband's parishioners saw her and wondered about her showiness. Helen, too, was far from wealthy. Jeff, her husband, had a flair for backing things that went wrong and that included horses. Yet never had a hint of envy been spoken or indeed felt by the two women about the wealthy friend they were en route to meet.

Jane was the mistress of a very eccentric and extraordinarily wealthy American industrialist. He had bought her many gifts, including a ranch and a small television station; she was one of the world's richest and best-known kept women.

For the twentieth time Margaret wondered if Jane could possibly look as well as she appeared in the photographs, and for the twentieth time Helen said it was quite possible. If you didn't have to do anything each day except make yourself look well, then it was obvious you could look magnificent. Suppose each day when Margaret got up she didn't have to clean the vicarage, take her children to school, shop, cook, wash, go to coffee mornings, sales of work, cookery demonstrations, and entertain the doctor, the curate, the headmaster—think how well she could look. Margaret had a very good bone structure, Helen agreed grudgingly, she could look very striking if only she had time to lavish on herself. Margaret felt a bit depressed by this; she knew that Helen meant it as a compliment but it left her feeling as if she were in fact a great mess because she didn't have this time, and that her good bone structure was wasted.

As they came up from Green Park tube station into the sunlight of Piccadilly the two women giggled again and reached for their powder compacts before they crossed the road to the Ritz.

"Aren't we silly?" tittered Helen. "I mean we're forty years of age."

"Yes, so is Jane of course," said Margaret as if that was some kind of steadying fact. Something that would keep their feet on the ground.

Jane had been attractive twenty years ago, but she was a beauty now.

"You look ridiculous," gasped Helen. "Your face, your whole face, it's the face of a twenty-year-old. You look better than when we were all teenagers."

Jane gave a great laugh showing all her perfect teeth.

"Aw, for Christ's sake, Helen, I bought this face, and bloody boring it was, I tell you. It's easy to have a face like that. Just give it to someone else to massage it and pummel it and file the teeth down and put caps on, no the face isn't any problem."

Margaret felt that she wished the foyer of this overpowering hotel would open and gulp her into the basement area. She had never felt so foolish, in her ratty, overdressed, overdone bit of Indian lamb.

"Come on, we'll go to the suite," Jane said, an arm around each of their shoulders. She noticed how impressed Helen and Margaret were with the tea lounge and the pillars and the little armchairs beside little tables where only the very confident could sit waiting casually for their friends. She knew they would love to sit in the public area and drink it all in with Jane herself there to protect them.

"We'll come back and do the grand tour later, but now we go and meet Charles."

"Charles?" Both women said it together with the alarm that might be generated at a dorm feast if someone mentioned that the headmistress was on her way. It was obvious that neither of them had thought that the ordeal of meeting Charles was included in the invitation to tea.

261

"Oh yeah, the old bat wants to make sure I really am meeting two old chums from the college. He has a fear, you see, that I'll have hired two male go-go dancers from some show. I want him to get a look at you so that he can see you are the genuine article, not something I made up. Come on, we'll get it over with, and then we can settle down to cream cakes and tea and gins and tonics."

Because Jane had shepherded them so expertly towards the lift, Margaret and Helen hadn't even had time to exchange a glance until they found themselves outside a door where two tall men stood.

"Are they bodyguards?" whispered Margaret.

"They speak English," laughed Jane. "I know they look like waxworks, but that's part of the qualifications. If you came in here with a machine-gun to kill Charles you wouldn't get far."

They were nodded in by the unsmiling heavies at the door, and Charles was visible. He stood by the window looking out at the traffic below. A small, old, worried man. He looked a bit like her father-in-law, Helen thought suddenly. A fussy little man in an old people's home who didn't really care when she and Jeff went to see him, he only cared about what time it was, and was constantly checking his watch with clocks.

When Charles did give them his attention he had a wonderful smile. It was all over his face, even his nose and chin seemed to be smiling. Margaret and Helen stopped being nervous.

"I'm a foolish old gentleman," he said in a Southern States drawl. "I'm jes' so nervous of my Jane, I always want to see who she goes out with."

"Heavens," said Margaret.

"Well, I see, how nice," stammered Helen.

"You ladies jes' must understand me. I guess you know how it is when you only live with someone, you aren't so sure, it's not the same binding thing as marriage." He looked at them winningly, expecting some support.

Margaret found her vicar's wife's voice: "Honestly, Mr. . . . er . . . Charles . . . I'm not in any position to know what you're talking about. I don't know any couples who live together who are not married."

She couldn't in a million years have said anything more suitable. Jane's mouth had a flicker of a smile and in two minutes Charles had taken his briefcase, his personal assistant, and his bodyguards and, having made charming excuses, he left for a meeting that had been delayed, presumably until he had satisfied himself about Jane's activities and plans for the afternoon.

"Is the place bugged?" Helen whispered fearfully when he had gone. Her eyes were like big blue and white china plates.

Jane screamed with laughter. "Darling Helen, no of course not. Hey, I'm really very sorry for putting all that on you both but you see the way he is."

"Very jealous?" suggested Helen, still in a low voice.

"A little paranoid?" Margaret offered.

"No, dying actually," said Jane flatly, and went to get a jeweled cigarette box. "Yeah, he only has two months, poor old bat. He's half the size he was six months ago. They said well under a year, now it's getting quicker."

She sounded as if she were talking about a tragedy in some distant land, a happening in a country where she had never been. Everyone is sad about far floods and droughts but they don't concern people like near ones do. Jane spoke of Charles as if he were a figure she had read about in a Sunday paper, not a man she had lived with for ten years. She seemed neither upset nor relieved by his terminal illness, it was just one of the many sad things that happen in life.

"I'm very sorry," said Margaret conventionally.

"He doesn't look as if he had only a short time to live," said Helen.

"I'm sure that if he's not going to get better it's all for the best that it should happen swiftly," said Margaret, being a vicar's wife again.

"Aw shit, that's not what I wanted to see you about," said Jane. She looked at their shocked faces.

"Look, sorry, sorry for the language, and this, well, lack of feeling. I *am* sorry for the old bastard, he's been very brave, and he's very frightened, you know. But hell, Margaret, Helen, we are not fools. I mean, be straight. He's hardly the love of my life."

There was a silence. Whatever they had expected from afternoon tea with Jane in the Ritz, it certainly was not this.

Jane appealed to them: "I thought that being in the nanny school was blood brothers, you know, for life? I thought that those of us who survived could say anything, anything, and it wasn't misconstrued."

264

Margaret said, "Jane, of course you can say anything to me, but remember we've all lived a life since we came out of nanny school. Mine has been very sheltered. I'm a vicar's wife for heaven's sake. What can be more sheltered than that? I ask you. It's the kind of thing people make jokes about, it's so, well, so different from yours. Can you really expect me to take all this in my stride?"

"All what?" Jane wanted to know.

"Well, your wealth, your life-style, the fact that your husband, your common-law husband, is dying of cancer and you say awful words and . . ." Margaret looked genuinely distressed. Helen took up the explanation:

"You see, Jane, it's not that either Margaret or I are trying to be distant. It's just that we don't really live in the same world as you anymore and I expect after a few minutes or an hour we'll all settle down and be the same as we used to be. It's just hard to expect us to act on your level."

Jane walked around the room for a moment or two before she replied:

"I guess I was taking things a bit too much for granted. I guess I was reading too much into all that solidarity we had twenty years ago."

She was silent, and looked perplexed. She looked young, beautiful, and puzzled, the two matrons stared up at her from their sofa in disbelief. It was as if they were watching a film of their youth where only Jane had stayed young. She used to look just like that when she was nineteen and thinking of a way to avoid detection by the nanny college principal.

"You needn't think the friendship isn't there," said Helen. "In fact it is, enormously. I can tell Margaret things about my private life, my worries

265

with Jeff and money. Susie was back from Kuwait and when we met she was telling us all about how she discovered she was lesbian and she could tell nobody." Helen looked like a big innocent schoolgirl trying to join the senior girls by revealing secrets and showing herself to be mature.

"Oh I know, Susie wrote to me," said Jane absently.

"I feel we've let you down, Jane," said Margaret. "I feel there was something you wanted us to do for you, and just by racing the wrong way at the outset we've made that impossible."

Jane sat down.

"You were always very astute, Margaret," she said. "There was indeed something I wanted to ask you. But now I don't know whether or not I can. You see I can only do it if I am utterly frank with you. I can't go through any charade with anyone from nanny college. There are rules I break in life but never that." She looked at them.

"Of course," said Helen.

"Naturally," said Margaret.

"Well, you see, I wanted to stay in England until Charles kicks it. No, sorry, if we are going to be frank, I simply will not use words like 'passes away,' he's dying, he's riddled with cancer, he's not going to see Christmas. I don't wish him any more pain, I wish he were dead. Dead now."

Their faces were sad, less shocked than before but still not understanding.

"So if we stay here till the end, I want Charles to see that I have friends, good decent normal friends like you two. I want to take him to your homes. He'll probably insult you and buy you

266

new homes but we can get over that. I mean he'll buy you and David a new parsonage certainly, Margaret, possibly the bishop's palace, and as for Jeff, he'll either buy him a book-making business or he'll send him to a Harley Street specialist to have what he will consider compulsive gambling cured in some clinic at three hundred quid a day."

There was a ghost of a smile passing over the faces of the two on the sofa.

"I wanted to ask your support in these last weeks. There's nobody else I could trust, and I've worked so goddamn hard for ten years I can't lose it all now."

"What will you lose?" Margaret asked. "You've already said you won't miss him. I don't see how our inviting him to our homes can help anything at all."

"Don't you see?" Jane cried out. "He is going mad, he has premature senility, he's paranoid. He thinks I'm unfaithful to him, he thinks I'm cheating on him. He's busy trying to dispossess me of everything."

"He can't do that," Helen gasped.

"You can't think that," Margaret gasped at the same time.

"He can, he can do a lot of it, and I can and do think it because I know it," said Jane.

In simple terms she told them a tale of stocks and companies, of the properties she owned absolutely which could not be repossessed, of the shares that had been bought back. The two women sat mutely listening to companies which were merged and stock transferred. They heard of the invalid wife whom Charles would never divorce because in his part of Georgia only cads and men who were not gentlemen divorced invalids. They heard of his suspicions, none of them founded on any truth, that Jane was in fact using his riches to buy herself young lovers.

"Even so, even if he does dispossess you," said Helen, trying to find a word of consolation, "you'll still be very rich."

Margaret thought of the corridors upstairs in the vicarage which would never have a carpet on them because they could afford to carpet only to the top of the stairs.

"You'll still be young, Jane, and wealthy compared to almost everyone," she said. "I can't see how anything will be so terrible."

"It's terrible to be denied over ninety percent of what I could have had," said Jane. "If the old bat had stayed sane. That's why I want to try and recoup as much as I can. I can't chain him to his bed. The lawyers for his various trusts are slobbering with greed. They're helping him each bloody hour to get more away from me. My lawyers say it's an unequal struggle. They even want to be paid in advance in case I'm left with nothing at the end."

She looked like a thwarted child.

"How would coming to visit us help?" Helen asked, trembling at the thought of bodyguards and Charles and huge cars in her small terraced house.

"He'd see I was normal; came from some normal sinless background. He's so heavily into sin now that he can't commit any anymore. He'd see heavy respectability in your homes. We could act out a pantomime till he snuffs it."

Margaret gave her a look of great distaste.

"You can't mean it, Jane."

"I do."

Helen looked at her as if she had been someone apologising for a drunken scene.

"You can't have been aware of what you were asking us to do. That's why you feel you can no longer ask it," she said.

Jane looked at them slowly.

"I'm asking you to join in a little deception with me, I'm telling you the whole score, I'm explaining why, and why I need it."

"But, Jane, it's so dishonest, it's so phoney, so high-powered," said Margaret.

"I think it's only because you imagine it's *high-powered* you're asking me to drop it," said Jane. "We went in for a lot of things that were phoney and dishonest in the old days. No holds were barred when you two were landing your men, but now that we're older and the stakes are higher, it's high-powered as well as dishonest, we can't do it."

With a very swift movement she lifted a telephone and cancelled afternoon tea, asking room service to make sure it was set for them downstairs instead.

"My guests will prefer to eat in the tea lounge instead," she said crisply.

Her eyes were bright, she dismissed any further discussion of the matter, she shepherded them neatly downstairs, past another bodyguard at the door who plodded discreetly after them and eventually positioned himself in the hotel lobby where he could see them at all times.

As she poured tea Jane insisted on hearing of all their happenings, and little by little the guard relaxed sufficiently for them to talk about their homes and lives. She told them, too, about some of the things she had done. Nothing relating to Charles and his short future or his pathetic paranoia.

She told how she had met a famous film star, and she described what it was like to have a beautician arrive every morning at 7 A.M. and not to allow you to face the world until after nine. She ate no cream cakes but urged the others to finish the plate.

They parted at the door under the admiring glance of many people who thought Jane quite startlingly attractive, and under the watchful glance of the bodyguard who had instructions not to let Jane out of his sight. There were little kisses and assurances of further letters and visits and meetings, there were clasps and grins and pronouncements that it would all turn out fine in the end.

Helen and Margaret went down into the tube again. Green Park station looked less full of promise and giggles and a day out.

"Everything they say about money not bringing happiness is true," said Helen as she fumbled in her shabby purse for the coins for her ticket.

"You would have thought that with all that money and high life she would have been contented, but no, it's more, ever searching for more," said Margaret.

They were very silent going home. It was unlike them to be silent. Such a long friendship meant that they could say things which others wouldn't broach. But even the apprenticeship in the nanny college and all that it involved was no help to them now.

Helen thought about how Jane had helped her to raise the money for her wedding to Jeff, when

270

Jeff had lost the whole three hundred pounds on a horse. Jane had been efficient and practical and dishonest. She had sold tickets for a charity that did not exist. She delivered the money to Helen without a comment.

Margaret was thinking of the early days when she had fallen for Dave, the handsome divinity student. Jane had helped her then, so well had Jane helped her that David's fiancée had been dislodged. There was just a rumor here and tittle-tattle there so that poor David thought that he had become engaged to a Jezebel. While the same process in reverse was worked about Margaret. A blameless innocent was how Margaret appeared.

In those days it had seemed the normal thing to do, to support your friends. After all, everyone knew that men were notoriously difficult and could cause all kinds of hurtful problems. They were always misunderstanding things. It was only right that friends should help each other when there was a problem of that sort. Those were their thoughts, but they didn't share them.

Victoria

Rose looked at the woman with the two card-board cups of coffee. She had one of those good-natured faces that you always associate with good works. Rose had seen smiles like that selling jam at fêtes or bending over beds in hospitals or holding out collecting boxes hopefully.

And indeed the woman and the coffee headed for an old man wrapped up well in a thick over-

271

coat even though the weather was warm, and the crowded coffee bar in Victoria Station was even warmer.

"I think we should drink it fairly quickly, Dad," said the woman in a half-laughing way. "I read somewhere that if you leave it for any length at all, cardboard melts into the coffee and that's why it tastes so terrible."

He drank it up obediently and he said it wasn't at all bad. He had a nice smile. Suddenly, and for no reason, he reminded Rose of her own father. The good-natured woman gave the old man a paper and his magnifying glass and told him not to worry about the time, she'd keep an eye on the clock and have them on the platform miles ahead of the departure time. Secure and happy, he read the paper and the good-natured woman read her own. Rose thought they looked very nice and contented and felt cheered to see a good scene in a café instead of all those depressing, gloomy scenes you can see, like middle-aged couples staring into space and having nothing to say to each other.

She looked at the labels on their suitcases. They were heading for Amsterdam. The name of the hotel had been neatly typed. The suitcases had little wheels under them. Rose felt this woman was one of the world's good and wise organizers. Nothing was left to chance, it would be a very well planned little holiday.

The woman had a plain wedding ring on. She might be a widow. Her husband might have left her for someone outrageous and bad-natured. Her husband and four children might all be at home and this woman was just taking her father to Amsterdam because he had seemed in poor spirits. Rose made up a lot of explanations and finally decided that the woman's husband had been killed in an appalling accident which she had borne very bravely and she now worked for a local charity and that she and her father went on a holiday to a different European capital every year.

Had the snack bar been more comfortable she might have talked to them. They were not the kind of people to brush away a pleasant conversational opening. But it would have meant moving all her luggage nearer to them, it seemed a lot of fuss. Leave them alone. Let them read their papers, let the woman glance at the clock occasionally, and eventually let them leave. Quietly, without rushing, without fuss. Everything neatly stowed in the two bags on wheels. Slowly, sedately, they moved towards a train for the south coast. Rose was sorry to see them go. Four German students took their place. Young, strong, and blond, spreading German and English coins out on the table and working out how much they could buy among them. They didn't seem so real.

There was something *reassuring* she thought about being able to go on a holiday with your father. It was like saying "Thank you," it was like stating that it had all been worthwhile, all that business of his getting married years ago and begetting you and saving for your future and having hopes for you. It seemed a nice way of rounding things off to be able to take your father to see foreign cities because things had changed so much from his day. Nowadays, young people could manage these things as a matter of course; in your father's day it was still an adventure and a risk to go abroad.

She wondered what her father would say if she set up a trip for him. She wondered only briefly, because really she knew. He'd say, "No, Rose, my dear, you're very thoughtful but you can't teach an old dog new tricks."

And she would say that it wasn't a question of that. He wasn't an old dog. He was only barely sixty, and they weren't new tricks, since he used to go to Paris every year when he was a young man, and he and Mum had spent their honeymoon there.

Then he would say that he had such a lot of work to catch up on, so it would be impossible to get away, and if she pointed out that he didn't really have to catch up on anything, that he couldn't have to catch up on anything because he stayed so late at the bank each evening catching up anyway—well, then he would say that he had seen Europe at its best, when it was glorious, and perhaps he shouldn't go back now.

But he'd love to go back, he would love it. Rose knew that. He still had all the scrapbooks and pictures of Paris just before the war. She had grown up with those brown books, and sepia pictures, and menus and advertisements, and maps carefully plotted out, lines of dots and arrows to show which way they had walked to Montmartre and which way they had walked back. He couldn't speak French well, her father, but he knew a few phrases, and he liked the whole style of things French, and used to say they were a very civilized race.

The good-natured woman and her father were probably pulling out of the station by now. Perhaps they were pointing out things to each other as the train gathered speed. A wave of jealousy came over Rose. Why was this woman, an ordinary woman perhaps ten years older than Rose, maybe not even that, why was she able to talk to her father and tell him things and go places with him and type out labels and order meals and take pictures? Why could she do all that and Rose's father wouldn't move from his deck chair in the sun lounge when his three weeks' holiday period came up? And in his one week in the winter, he caught up on his reading.

Why had a nice, good, warm man like her father got nothing to do, and nowhere to go after all he had done for Rose and for everyone? Tears of rage on his behalf pricked Rose's eyes.

Rose remembered the first time she had been to Paris, and how Daddy had been so interested, and fascinated, and dragging out the names of hotels in case she was stuck, and giving her hints on how to get to them. She had been so impatient at twenty, so intolerant, so embarrassed that he thought that things were all like they had been in his day. She had barely listened, she was anxious for his trip down the scrapbooks and up the maps to be over. She had been furious to have had to carry all his carefully transcribed notes. She had never looked at them while there. But that was twenty and perhaps everyone knows how restless everyone else is at twenty and hopefully forgives them a bit. Now at thirty she had been to Paris several times, and because she was much less restless she had found time to visit some of her father's old haunts—dull, merging into their own backgrounds—those that still existed—she was generous enough these days to have photographed them and he spent happy hours examining the new prints and comparing them with the old with clucks of amazement and shakings of the head that the old bakery had gone, or the tree-lined street was now an underpass with six lanes of traffic.

And when Mum was alive she, too, had looked at the cuttings and exclaimed a bit, and shown interest that was not a real interest. It was only the interest that came from wanting to make Daddy happy.

And after Mum died people had often brought up the subject to Daddy of his going away. Not too soon after the funeral, of course, but months later when one of his old friends from other branches of the bank might call.

"You might think of taking a trip abroad again sometime," they would say. "Remember all those places you saw in France? No harm to have a look at them again. Nice little trip." And Daddy would always smile a bit wistfully. He was so goddamn gentle and unpushy, thought Rose, with another prickle of tears. He didn't push at the bank, which was why he wasn't a manager. He hadn't pushed at the neighbours when they built all around and almost over his nice garden, his pride and joy, which was why he was now overlooked by dozens of bed-sitters. He hadn't pushed Rose when Rose said she was going to marry Gus. If only Daddy had been more pushing then, it might have worked. Suppose Daddy had been strong and firm and said that Gus was what they called a bounder in his time and possibly a playboy in present times. Just suppose Daddy had said that. Might she have listened at all or would it have strengthened her resolve to marry the Bad Egg? Maybe those words from Daddy's lips might have brought her up short for a moment, enough to think. Enough to spare her the two years of sadness in marriage and the two more years organizing the divorce.

But Daddy had said nothing. He had said that whatever she thought must be right. He had wished her well, and given them a wedding present for which he must have had to cash in an insurance policy. Gus had been barely appreciative. Gus had been bored with Daddy. Daddy had been unfailingly polite and gentle with Gus. With Gus long gone, Rose had gone back to live in Daddy's house. It was peaceful despite the blocks of bed-sitters. It was undemanding. Daddy kept his little study where he caught up on things, and he always washed saucepans after himself if he had made his own supper. They didn't often eat together. Rose had irregular hours as a traveler and Daddy was so used to reading at his supper, and he ate so early in the evening. If she stayed out at night there were no explanations and no questions. If she told him some of her adventures there was always his pleased interest.

Rose was going to Paris this morning. She had been asked to collect some samples of catalogues. It was a job that might take a week if she were to do it properly or a day if she took a taxi and the first fifty catalogues that caught her eye. She had told Daddy about it this morning. He was interested, and he took out his books to see again what direction the new airport was in, and which areas Rose's bus would pass as she came into the city centre. He spent a happy half hour on this, and Rose had looked with both affection and interest. It was ridiculous that he didn't go again. Why didn't he?

Suddenly she thought she knew. She realized it was all because he had nobody to go with. He was, in fact, a timid man. He was a man who said "Sorry" when other people stepped on him, which is what the nicer half of the world does, but it's also sometimes an indication that people might be wary and uneasy about setting up a lonely journey, a strange pilgrimage of return. Rose thought of the good-natured woman and the man who must be ten or fifteen years older than Daddy; tonight they would be eating a meal in a Dutch restaurant. Tonight Daddy would be having his scrambled egg and dead-heading a few roses, while his daughter, Rose, would be yawning at a French restaurant trying not to look as if she were returning the smiles of an aging lecher. *Why* wasn't Daddy going with her? It was her own stupid fault. All those years, seven of them since Mum had died, seven years, perhaps thirty trips abroad for her, not a mention of inviting Daddy. The woman with the good-natured countenance didn't live in ivory towers of selfishness like that.

Almost knocking over the table, she stumbled out and got a taxi home. He was actually in a cardigan in the garden scratching his head and sucking on his pipe and looking like a stage representation of someone's gentle, amiable father. He was alarmed to see her. He had to be reassured. But why had she changed her mind? Why did it not matter whether she went today or tomorrow? He was worried. Rose didn't do sudden things. Rose did measured things, like he did. Was she positive she was telling him the truth and that she hadn't felt sick or faint or worried?

They were not a father and daughter who

278

hugged and kissed. Pats were more the style of their touching. Rose would pat him on the shoulder and say, "I'm off now, Daddy," or he would welcome her home clasping her hand and patting the other arm enthusiastically. His concern as he stood worried among his garden things was almost too much to bear.

"Come in and we'll have a cup of tea, Daddy," she said, wanting a few moments bent over kettle, sink, tea caddy, to right her eyes.

He was a shuffle behind her, anxiety and care in every step. Not wishing to be too inquisitive, not wanting, but plans changed meant bad news. He hated it.

"You're not *doing* anything really, Daddy, on your holidays, are you?" she said eventually, once she could fuss over tea things no longer. He was even more alarmed.

"Rose, my dear, do you have to go to hospital or anything? Rose, my dear, is something wrong? I'd much prefer it if you told me." Gentle eyes, his lower lip fastened in by his teeth in worry. Oh what a strange father. Who else had never had a row with a father? Was there any other father in the world so willing to praise the good, rejoice in the cheerful, and to forget the bad and the painful?

"Nothing, Daddy, nothing. But I was thinking, it's silly my going to Paris on my own. Staying in a hotel and reading a book and you staying here reading a book or the paper. I was thinking wouldn't it be nice if I left it until tomorrow and we *both* went. The same way, the way I go by train to Gatwick, or we could get the train to the coast and go by ferry."

He looked at her, cup halfway to his mouth. He held it there.

"But why, Rose dear? Why do you suggest this?" His face had rarely seemed more troubled. It was as if she had asked him to leave the planet.

"Daddy, you often talk about Paris, you tell *me* about it. I tell *you* about it. Why don't we go together and tell each other about it when we come back?" She looked at him; he was so bewildered she wanted to shout at him, she wanted to finish her sentences through a loudspeaker.

Why did he look so unwilling to join? He was being asked to play. Now don't let him hang back, slow to accept like a shy schoolboy who can't believe he has been picked for the team.

"Daddy, it would be nice. We could go out and have a meal and we could go up and walk to Montmartre by the same routes as you took in the Good Old Days. We could do the things you did when you were a wild teenager."

He looked at her frightened, trapped. He was so desperately kind, he saw the need in her. He didn't know how he was going to fight her off. She knew that if she were to get him to come, she must stress that she really wanted it for her more than for him.

"Daddy, I'm often very lonely when I go to Paris. Often at night particularly I remember that you used to tell me how all of you . . . ."

She stopped. He looked like a hunted animal.

"Wouldn't you like to come?" she said in a much calmer voice.

"My dear Rose. *Sometime,* I'd love to go to Paris, my dear, there's nothing in the world I'd like to do more than to come to Paris. But I can't go just like that. I can't drop everything and rush off to Paris, my dear. You know that."

"Why not, Daddy?" she begged. She knew she was doing something dangerous, she was spelling out her own flightiness, her own whim of doubling back from the station, she was defining herself as less than level-headed.

She was challenging him too. She was asking him to say why he couldn't come for a few days of shared foreign things. If he had no explanation, then he was telling her that he was just someone who said he wanted something but didn't reach for it. She could be changing the nature of his little dreams. How would he ever take out his pathetically detailed maps and scrapbooks to pore once more with her over routes and happenings if he had thrown away a chance to see them in three dimensions?

"You have nothing planned, Daddy. It's ideal. We can pack for you. I'll ask them next door to keep an eye on the house. We'll stop the milk and the newspaper and, Daddy, that's it. Tomorrow evening in Paris, tomorrow afternoon we'll be taking that route in together, the one we talked about for me this morning."

"But, Rose, all the things here, my dear, I can't just drop everything. You do see that."

Twice now he had talked about all the things here that he had to drop. There was *nothing* to drop. What he would drop was pottering about scratching his head about leaf curl. Oh Daddy, don't you see that's all you'll drop? But if you don't see and I tell you, it means I'm telling you that your life is meaningless and futile and pottering. I will not tell *you*, who walked around the house cradling me when I was a crying baby,

281

you who paid for elocution lessons so that I could speak well, you, Daddy, who paid for that wedding lunch that Gus thought was shabby, you, Daddy, who smiled and raised your champagne glass to me and said, "Your mother would have loved this day. A daughter's wedding is a milestone." I won't tell you that your life is nothing.

The good-natured woman and her father were probably at Folkestone or Dover or Newhaven when Rose said to her father that of course he was right, and it had just been a mad idea, but naturally they would plan it for later. Yes, they really must, and when she came back this time they would talk about it seriously, and possibly next summer.

"Or even when I retire," said Rose's father, the colour coming back into his cheeks. "When I retire I'll have lots of time to think about these things and plan them."

"That's a good idea, Daddy," said Rose. "I think that's a very good idea. We should think of it for when you retire."

He began to smile. Reprieve. Rescue. Hope.

"We won't make any definite plans, but we'll always have it there, as something we must talk about doing. Yes, much more sensible," she said.

"Do you really mean that, Rose? I certainly think it's a good idea," he said, anxiously raking her face for approval.

"Oh, honestly, Daddy. I think it makes *much* more sense," she said, wondering why so many loving things had to be lies.

Pimlico

Olive sat in her little office making her weekly lists. First she balanced her books. It didn't take long. Her guests paid weekly and usually by banker's order. Her staff bills were the same every week. The laundry was always precisely the same—thirty-two sheets, thirty-two pillowcases, thirty-two towels, seven large tablecloths, seven smaller teacloths. Olive had costed the business of getting a washing machine and a dryer and in the end decided that the effort, the space, and the uncertainty in case of breakdowns were simply not worth it. Her food bills were fairly unchaninging too; she hadn't been twenty years in the hotel business for nothing. And other bills were simple as well; she transferred a regular amount weekly to meet the electricity, telephone, gas, rates, and insurance demands when they arrived. Olive could never understand why other people got into such muddles about money.

Then she made her list of activities for the notice board. This involved going through the local papers, the brochures from musical societies and theatres, appeals from charitable organiza- tions for support for jumble sales. When she had a good selection she would pin them up on her cork board and remove those which had become out of date. She took care to include some items that none of her guests would dream of choosing, like Wagner's Ring or a debate about philosophy. But she knew that they liked to be thought the kind of people who might want to patronize such things and it flattered them.

Then she would take out her loose-leaf file, the one she had divided into twelve sections, one for each guest, and in her neat small handwriting Olive would make some small entries under each name. It was here that she felt she could find the heart of her hotel, the memory, the nerve centre. Because Olive knew that the reason her twelve guests stayed with her was not the great comfort, the food, the value, the style; it was simply because she knew all about them, she remembered their birthdays, their favourite films, their collar sizes, the names of their old homes or native villages. Olive could tell you quite easily the day that Hugh O'Connor had come to live there, all she had to do was open Hugh's section in the file. But it warmed him so much to hear her say "Oh, Hugh, don't I remember well the day you arrived, it was a Wednesday in November and you looked very tired." Hugh would beam to think that he was so important that his arrival had seared itself into Olive's mind.

She never saw anything dishonest or devious about this. She thought it was in fact a common courtesy and a piece of good sense in what people nowadays called "communications and relating." In a way it was almost a form of social service. After all, if she was going to go and spend a half hour with Annie Lynch on a Saturday afternoon, with Annie retired to her bedroom with what looked like the beginnings of a depression, then Olive thought how much more considerate to look up Annie's file and remember the little farm in Mayo and how it had to be sold when Daddy took to the drink, and how Annie's mother, who was a walking saint, had died and the boys were all married and the only sensible thing for Annie to do was to come and work in London. Olive had filed the kind of things that seemed to cheer Annie up, and would trot them out one by one. Yes, perhaps she should remember everything without writing it down, but really she lived such a busy life. It would be impossible to manage without her little Lists.

Nobody knew of Olive's filing system; they weren't even aware that she seemed to have a better than average memory. Each one of her guests simply marvelled at his or her own good fortune at having found a woman who ran such a comfortable place and who obviously understood them so well. Even the three Spaniards who had been with Olive for five years thought this too. They didn't question their money or their small living quarters, they just appreciated that she could remember their names and their friends' names and the village in the south of Spain where they went back once a year when Olive closed for her two-week break. She was determined that nobody would ever know and had even made preparations that after her death her executor should arrange to have her private records of her years in the hotel business destroyed unread. A solicitor had told her that such a request was perfectly in order.

She was only thirty years of age when she bought the small and then rather seedy hotel in Pimlico. Everyone had assured her that she was quite mad, and that if clever boys who knew about making money hadn't made a go of it, how could an innocent Irish girl with ten years' experience working in a seaside Irish boardinghouse hope to do any better? But Olive was determined; she had saved since her teens for the dream of a hotel of her own, and when her uncle's legacy made it actually within her reach she acted at once. Her family in Ireland were outraged.

"There's more to it than meets the eye," said her mother, who foresaw gloomy summers without Olive's considerable help in the boardinghouse.

"Maybe she'll find a fellow in London, she hasn't found one here," said her sister cattily.

Olive's father was enthusiastic that she should try working in London for a little bit before actually committing herself to the buying of a hotel. He had worked there himself for ten years and found it a lonely place.

"When you've seen Piccadilly Circus and Buckingham Palace and you've said to yourself, this is me here sitting listening to Big Ben strike, well that's it. You've seen it then. It's time to come home. It's a scaldingly lonely place."

As determined as any young woman about to enter religious life and take vows as a nun, Olive went ahead with her plans.

Ten years in a third-rate boardinghouse had given Olive more of an insight into the psychology of hotel work than any amount of professional courses. She saw the old and the lonely who could barely endure the sea winds and the bracing air and who hardly left the sun lounge during their two week visit. She knew they came for company, and that the anticipation was much better than the holiday. She saw the couples with their children hoping that the two-weeks vacation would be a rest, a bit of peace, a time to get to know each other again, and she saw her mother disappointing them year after year by frowning at the children, complaining about noise, and in general making the parents much more anxious than they would have been had they remained at home in the normal daily round. Oh, the number of times Olive would have loved to be in charge, she knew what she would have done. She would have had a special room for the children with lino on the floor, a room where it didn't matter if they kicked the furniture or made a noise. She would have offered the guests a welcoming drink when they arrived instead of making an announcement about what time she expected them to be in.

But in the years of watching the visitors come and go, Olive gained what she thought was an insight into the returned emigrants, those who lived the greater part of their life in big English cities. What they seemed to appreciate so much when they came back was the smallness of the place, the fact that people saluted other people and knew all about them. These might have been the very things that they fled to London and Birmingham and Liverpool to avoid, but it certainly seemed to be something their souls cried out for now. Olive knew that when she had enough money she would run a place for Irish people in London, and she would make a small fortune. Not a big fortune, she didn't want that, just a little fortune. So that she could live in comfort, and could surround herself with nice furniture, nice pictures, so that she needn't worry about having two bars of the electric fire on. The kind of comfort which would mean she could have a bath twice a day, and take a taxi if it was raining.

And in her terraced house in Pimlico she built up the hotel of her dreams.

It had taken time. And a great deal of effort. For a year she lost money—heavy, frightening sums, even though she regarded it as an experiment. She advertised in local papers in boroughs where there were large Irish populations, she attracted lonely people, certainly, but not the ones she could help. Too many of her guests turned out to be out working-on-the-Lump men who had forgotten their real names because they used so many in so many different jobs, men who appeared on no social welfare list, men who knew that if they got a bad dose of pneumonia or broke a leg the other lads would pass a hat round for them, but there would be no pension, no insurance, no security.

They didn't stay long in Olive's little hotel, and she made them uneasy, asking where they were from and what they did.

"Sure the police wouldn't ask me that, ma'am," a man had replied to her once when she had asked some simple and, she thought, courteous question about his origins.

Then she had the con men. The charmers, the people who were expecting money shortly, who cashed checks, who told tales. It was an apprenticeship, she was learning. Soon she thought she was ready and she advertised again. By this time she had the hotel the way she wanted it. Not splendid, nothing overawing, but comfortable. There wasn't a hint of boardinghouse about it, no sauce bottles appeared with regularity on stained cloths. She arranged a weekly rate which included an evening meal, with no refund if the meal was not taken. She knew enough about her future clients to know that they were the kind of people who would like to be expected home at a quarter to seven. They could always go off out again afterwards.

She implied that those she was accepting were people of good manners and high standards. This was done very cunningly and without any hint of appearing restrictive. Whereas her mother would have said, "I want no drink brought into the bedrooms," Olive said, "I want you to consider this house very much as your home. I know you don't want to be in the kind of place where people have bottles in bedrooms."

She chose the guests carefully. Sometimes after several interviews where she always gave them tea and managed to explain that it was simply a matter of having promised the place to somebody else who was to let her know by Thursday. It took her a year to build up to twelve and she sat back satisfied. They were right. They were the correct mix. They depended on her utterly, they needed her, and for the first time in her life she felt fulfilled. She felt she had got what other people got from teaching or nursing or maybe the priesthood. People who needed them, a little flock. She never included marriage and children in her list of fulfilling life-styles. She had seen too many less than satisfactory marriages to be impressed by the state. And anyway she was too busy. You didn't run the perfect hotel without a lot of work.

There had been a question of marriage two years ago. A very nice man indeed. A Scot, quiet and industrious. She had met him at a hoteliers' trade fair, when she was examining a new system of keeping coffee hot. He had told her that it didn't really work, he had tried one in his own hotel and it had been wasteful. Their friendship got to a stage where her twelve guests were rustling and ruffled like birds in a coop fearing the intrusion of an outsider. Alec came to tea so often on Sundays that there were definite fears he might either join the establishment or else spirit Olive away. The ruffled feelings were balm to Olive, the ill-disguised anxiety among those men and women who paid her hefty sums of money to live with her was almost exhilarating. Olive kept them and Alec in suspense for some weeks and finally sent Alec away confused, wallowing in the luxuriating relief and happiness of the civil servants, bank clerks, bookkeepers, shop assistants, and bus driver who were now her family.

She finished her list of entries in the ring file with the information that Judy O'Connor, the nice girl who worked in the chemist shop, had a brother who was a missionary and that he was coming back from Africa and through London on his way home to Ireland for Christmas. Olive thought it might be a nice occasion to have a Mass in the hotel.

Well, why not? They were all Irish, they were all Catholic. Even the three little Spaniards, José, his wife, Carmen, and her sister Maria, they were Catholics, they would love a Mass in the dining room. It would make it all much more like home. She must start putting it in Judy's mind soon. Olive was careful for people not to think that all the good ideas came from her. She let the guests think that it was their idea to strip their own beds on Monday mornings and leave all the dirty linen neatly ready for the laundrymen. The guests thought that they had suggested pooling fifty pence a week each to have wine with Sunday lunch.

Hugh O'Connor was absolutely certain that *he* had broken off his engagement to that rather forward hussy who had no morals and wanted to come in and share his room saying that it was perfectly all right since they were engaged. Annie never realized that it was Olive who suggested that she should break her ties with Mayo, she thought she had done it herself. The guests thought that it had just come about that they all stayed in the hotel for Christmas, they saw nothing odd about it. Olive had carefully managed to distance herself from those who had been rash enough to go to relations or friends. They had felt lacking in some kind of spirit and had felt deeply jealous when they returned afterwards to hear about the wonderful turkey and the presents and the carols by the Christmas tree and the Pope's blessing in the morning and the Queen's speech in the afternoon—a combination of what was best about both cultures.

The last thing that Olive did on her List day was to write home. Her father was in hospital now, her mother almost crippled with arthritis. She sent them regular small contributions with pleasant cheering letters. She had no intention of returning home. They were nothing to her now. She had a real family, a family that needed her.

Stockwell

Mona had vomited when the news was given to her. It was the last thing she had expected would happen and she was very ashamed. She helped the doctor and his young aide to clean the carpet, brushing aside any of their cries that she leave it alone.

"I wouldn't hear of it. These things have to be done quickly. Have you any borax? Good, and then I find a quick squirt with a soda syphon is good. I really am most frightfully sorry."

The doctor finally got her to sit in a chair again. Gave her a glass of water, a pill, and his hand.

"I didn't put it well. I probably gave you a far worse impression of the situation . . . you must excuse me, Mrs. Lewis. I have been very crass."

His hand tightened on hers and his kind brown eyes were filled with concern. Mona Lewis looked at him gratefully.

"Dr. Barton, I can't thank you enough. You have been exactly what I needed in every way. You could not have been more supportive. It's not your fault that the diagnosis was so bad. You must realize that I am completely in your debt."

The doctor took off his glasses and wiped his eyes. He looked at this handsome woman in front of him again and marvelled. He had told her that she had inoperable cancer of several glands. In response to her calm question, he said that he had been told it was a matter of months and probably not as many as six months. It was when he had added "before Christmas" that her stomach muscles had reacted even though her face had not.

How could he have been so heavy-handed, so thick-skinned, so leaden? Why did he have to mention Christmas to this glowing woman? Why remind her of the one most emotive date in the year and let her picture a family scene without her? He could have cut out his tongue.

But she encouraged him to talk calmly. She had talked calmly throughout their whole odd professional relationship. She had come to him four months previously saying that she was staying with friends in Stockwell and giving a local address. After her third visit, however, she explained that she really lived in a different part of London, it was just that she wanted a doctor far away from her friends, far away from people who might know her business. Mona Lewis lived in Hampstead and all her friends went to the same doctor. It wasn't that she didn't trust him, of course she did, but if what she suspected was wrong with her was indeed true, then she didn't want his pity, his sympathy, his concern, until she knew how she was going to cope with it.

It had seemed reasonable. He had referred her for all the tests, he had liked her breezy matter-of-fact ways. He had even had nice little chats with her which were rare for him to have with patients, since his was a largely immigrant practice and much of his work seemed to him to consist of trying to understand worried young Indian mothers who could not come to see him on any matter without the husband there to interpret and act as chaperone. Mona Lewis with her light-hearted sense of mocking him was a special treat.

She had told him that her fingers were simply itching to repot the tired busy lizzies and ferns in his waiting room. She had even bought him some plant food and left him a book on simple plant care which he had read to please her. Even when she had gone for the biopsy she had remained cheerful. He had got her into a local hospital.

"Where does your family think you are this week?" he had asked, worried.

She had mentioned a husband and twin daughters of sixteen.

"I've told them I'm on a course."

"Why?" he had asked gently. "Why don't you tell your husband? He'd want to know."

"Don't be ridiculous, Dr. Barton, nobody would want to know that his wife was having a biopsy. Come now, that's not worthy of you."

"Very well, let me put it another way. He would like to share these things with you, if they have to be undergone, he will want to be part of them."

"I want to go through the first bit by myself," she said. "Later, later I'll talk to the others. Please let me do it this way."

He hated having to give her the news, but there was no ethical way he could involve anyone else. He was, as she said, being supportive.

She finished her glass of water, examined the damp patch on the carpet, and shook her head ruefully, as if a favorite puppy, not herself, had made the mess.

"I am sorry again about that, Dr. Barton, very shaming. Now, can I just settle up with you as usual, and then I'll leave you to the rest of your waiting room."

She had established early on that she would like

to be considered a private patient even though she always came in surgery hours and she paid in cash. He hadn't liked the whole arrangement, and particularly as her diagnosis looked worse and worse. Today for the first time he was adamant about the money.

"Please, Mrs. Lewis. Just pause and think about me as a human being, not just a doctor with a hand out for money from a private patient. I have given you distressing news today."

She looked at him politely, her hand already on her wallet.

"It's quite bad enough for me to know that a charming and vital woman like you has a terminal disease and it is doubly hard to have to be the one who tells you this, can you please let me have the dignity of telling you and seeing you to a taxi or telephoning your husband, or calling a friend for you, without having to take your goddamn bank notes?"

She snapped her bag shut.

"Of course. And how considerate of you. I didn't pause to think. But no, I'd prefer to walk. I usually do walk around here, when I come to you. And take buses. I'd like to do that today. Please."

As he shook her hand, and she assured him that she felt perfectly fine, he knew he was seeing her for the last time. She would not now come back to him. She didn't want to discuss remissions, radium treatment. She wanted to know nothing of drugs or palliatives. She implied that if anything were to be done, it might be done back in Hampstead.

"You have been exceptionally good to me. I know that professional people hate things to be irregular, and you have been wonderful at hiding your irritation that I didn't go through the more conventional channels."

The doctor didn't know why he said it but it was uppermost in his mind so it just came out:

"People often try to . . . you know . . . beat it, get there first. It's not a good idea. They bungle it, and even if they don't . . . well . . . you know, nature does it in its own rotten way. It would be a pity to take your own life . . ."

"Oh no." She smiled at him. "No, I agree it would be a mess. Anyway, why would I go to all these measures to find out if I were going to do something so feeble as take a bottle of pills and a bottle of vodka?"

"I'll keep feeding those plants in case you come back to see me." He grinned, taking his tone from hers. She liked that.

"Of course I'll come back to see you." She smiled. "One day when you least expect it, when all the shoots need to be trimmed."

He watched until she had turned the corner, then he pressed his buzzer and saw a malingering workman who claimed he had a bad back, and barked at him so fiercely that the man left in terror demanding to know when Dr. Barton's relief doctor would be on duty.

Mona felt dangerously calm. It was a sunny July afternoon, and everything looked quite normal. Like it often looked in this strange part of London, less planted, less cared for than her own neighbourhood. Funny that she liked it so much. She was certain that Jerry would like it, too, but it was something she would never share with him. What she had to do now was go through the whole sham of tests again. It seemed silly and wasteful, but this was how she had planned it. Tomorrow, tell Jerry that she felt below par, fix an immediate appointment with Franz, allow Franz to send her for tests at the clinic, follow through, slowly and remorselessly, everything she had just done.

And at every step of the way now she could be clear-sighted and calm because there was going to be nothing hanging in the balance, no doubts, no waiting to know. Because she now knew the very worst she could behave with her customary calm. Reassuring everyone, allowing no panic, being utterly fatalistic. She even had a little sentence ready: "Don't be silly, darling, it's not a question of knowing that I'm going to die, after all we all know we are going to. I just know *when* I'm going to die. That gives me the advantage over all of you."

She was going to be perfectly frank with the girls also. There was no hiding and whispering and pretending as there had been when her own mother had died. Six months of confusion, and hope and counter-hope, and bewilderment. Mona was going to be authoritative in death as she had been in everything in life. It was sad, it was obviously very regrettable since she was only forty-six. But to look on the bright side, she had had an excellent life, she would leave behind not a dependent unsupported family, but a husband whose every comfort had been catered for, whose house ran smoothly and easily, two attractive sixteen-year-olds who had always been able to discuss their future plans with their mother and who would not cease to do so now. She would redouble her efforts to get Marigold into art school, and to direct Annabelle towards a career in social work. She would see that they both had advisors, separate ones, and contacts. She would also establish a proper social life for Jerry so that he wouldn't be left high and dry. If only she could persuade him to learn bridge. He had withstood it so long, and yet as a widower it would be his instant passport to people's houses. Nobody would say, "We must have poor Jerry around, poor chap is utterly broken up since Mona's death," instead they would think more positively and say, "We need a fourth for bridge. How about Jerry?"

Mona hated the thought of telling Sally, her dearest friend. Sally was so utterly sentimental and emotional, she could ruin everything by arriving around at their house with flowers and autumn bouquets saying that she wanted Mona to see one more bunch of dahlias or a last autumn crocus.

She had several plans also for the school where she taught. She would explain to the principal that a new teacher must be found for the autumn term, but she would ask if she could stay on as an advisor for the first two months or so, or until her strength gave out. She also felt she should like permission to discuss some aspects of death and facing it with the older girls, since they were unlikely to have the chance again of meeting someone who was going to face it as calmly as Mona was about to do.

And as for dear Jerry, she was going to try to explain to him how essential it was that he should marry again, lest he become eccentric and absent-minded and his whole lovely antique business fall apart. If she could find the right words to explain that posthumous jealousy cannot exist. She would be in a great sleep and nothing could hurt her or touch her. Mona realized that not everyone else felt as peaceful about facing death as she did, and she wondered whether she should give talks on the subject on the radio or to women's groups.

Thinking of women's groups reminded her of old Vera North, her mother's friend of many years, now bedridden and in a wheelchair. Mona usually went to see her once a month, but with all the tests and waiting and examinations she hadn't seen Vera for some time. I'll go today, she thought. It will give everyone an explanation of why I was out all day, and should my face look a bit gloomy in spite of myself then they'll think it was because of seeing Vera.

Vera called for tea, she had a faithful slave who had looked after her since childhood. Mona always admired the setup, they needed each other, Vera and the old retainer Annie. She didn't think it was shameful to have a maid, not if you were Vera, not if you were kind and considerate, and paid Annie a just wage.

"I've been busy," she explained to Vera.

"I know," Vera said. "You look more cheerful now. You looked worried when I saw you last. Were you having a medical examination?"

"How on earth did you know?" asked Mona, amazed.

"Is it a hysterectomy?" asked Vera.

"No, lymph glands," said Mona before she realized.

"Poor Mona, you are so young, yet so courageous." Vera did not look put out.

"I am brave, but by other people's standards, not my own. I just feel that we should take the mythology out of cancer. I mean, people are afraid to mention its name. They call it silly names, they won't acknowledge it. Such huge strides have been made in, say, attitudes to mental illness, it seems strange that we cannot admit to cells going rogue, which is all that cancer is."

"I know, Mona," said Vera gravely.

"So as a last gesture, as some kind of, I don't know, some kind of statement I suppose—I'm going to talk about it, I'm going to make it normal. Acceptable even."

She smiled triumphantly at Vera. She just got a steady glance in return.

"You see since I *am* going to be gone by Christmas at least I know that there's some end to my courage, some defined end. It's not going to be all that hard . . . and it will make it so much easier for everyone else."

"Do you think it will make it easier for other people?" Vera asked mildly.

"Well, it stands to reason . . . if they see that I'm not terror-stricken, if they see that if the one who has the bloody disease can accept it, then they will too. It will save so much time, it will cut through all that pretence, we needn't make all those absurd plans for holidays next year, when everyone knows that I won't be around next year . . ."

She was rather put out by Vera's refusal to be impressed, her unwillingness to admire such amazing bravery.

"They'll prefer to pretend. And they will definitely prefer you to pretend," Vera said firmly.

"But that's nonsense. I'm doing it for them, I'm not going to have them go through what we went through with Mother. Vera, you must remember that, how dreadful it was." Vera sat very still.

"How old were you when Clare died . . . seventeen, eighteen?"

"I was eighteen, Vera, and I won't put my family through such an experience. We were constantly going to the church and lighting candles in front of statues so that Mother's illness should turn out not to be serious. The word *cancer* was simply not allowed to be mentioned, there was no honesty. All the things I would like to have said to my mother but never did because we were prevented from admitting it was goodbye by some confused code of keeping quiet. If Mother even knew she was dying, which I doubt, none of us had a chance to ask her if she had any last things to discuss."

"Oh she knew," said Vera. "She knew very well."

"Did she talk to you about it?" Mona was startled.

"She began by wanting to talk to everyone, you are so like her it's uncanny. She wanted to face it . . . do all the things you want to do."

"But *why* did she not do that?"

"It caused too much pain. Simply that," Vera said. "She saw after a couple of days that people couldn't take it. Your father for one—'Clare, stop this, there is hope, nothing is definite. I won't have you speaking as if you are a condemned woman.'"

"And other people?"

"Just the same. Me too. I wouldn't look her in the eye and discuss the fact that her body was rotting, no, even though she wanted to laugh and tell me that it was nothing special, mine would rot too. I wanted to believe there was hope. I wanted not to see her getting thinner and comment that the disease was taking its toll. I wanted to say, 'Yes you have lost a lot of weight and it does suit you.' You see, Mona, you're going to find the same thing. I know what I'm talking about."

"But that was nearly thirty years ago," Mona pleaded. "Things have changed now. They must have."

Vera touched her gently. "Go and see if you like, and if they haven't changed, come back and talk to me."

Mona looked at her stonily.

"I mean it, Mona, my brave young girl. Really I do. I wasn't able to do it for your mother, and I don't want to do it for you. But if I couldn't face one generation being brave, if I let her go to her death with hypocritical exclamations of how well she looked, I won't do it a second time."

Mona smiled at her and stood up to go.

"I mean it," Vera said. "Come back anytime. And think before you bare it all to the others. You and your mother are unusual in this world, the rest of us aren't so strong."

Mona kissed her good-bye. The first time she had done that.

"And I'll tell you more about Clare, too . . . you'll like her," said Vera.

"I'll come back anyway," Mona said. "You don't have to bribe me. And, Vera, I'll try and tell the others, it would be very good if someone made a stand. Wouldn't it?"

"Clare wanted me to marry your father," said Vera.

"I wish you had," said Mona.

302

"Perhaps I'll marry Jerry instead," said Vera with a tinny little laugh.

And Mona left quickly before she saw the tears that were going to come from it.

Brixton

The woman in personnel was about fifty and had a silly perm, all grey bubbles like an aging Harpo Marx. Sandy looked at her without much hope.

"Well, of course, I can try and fix you with hostels or shelters or organization addresses, Miss Ring. But quite frankly I feel sure you would do better just to find accommodation for yourself."

"How can I do that?" Sandy asked. It was so very different to the hospital where she had trained. There the rules about where nurses had to live were still strictly enforced. There had been a list of approved lodgings and apartments, and only in these were the nurses permitted to stay.

"The nurses seem to play musical chairs with each other," said the Harpo Marx personnel officer disapprovingly. "You'll be very unlucky not to see about a dozen tattered notices on the board downstairs offering accommodation."

"That sounds great," Sandy said eagerly. "And if I share with someone who works in the hospital, then I'll learn the ropes a bit more quickly."

She got a watery and unenthusiastic smile. The personnel officer obviously found as little satisfaction in her job as she had found success with her hairdresser.

There were eight notices offering accommodation. Four were too expensive, two specified that the applicant must speak Spanish. That left two. One of them had a phone number, so Sandy dialed it at once. In her hand she had her *A to Z* so that she could identify where the place was.

"It's SW9," the girl said.

"Clapham?" asked Sandy, studying her map intently.

"More east of it," the girl said.

"Near the tube?"

"Yeah, four minutes."

"How many of you in the flat?"

"Just me."

"That's not a bad rent for a flat for two."

"You ain't seen it, lady."

"Shall I come over and look, and let you look at me?"

"Sure. Come now. I'll make you tea."

"That's very nice, I'm Sandy Ring."

"That's funny. I'm Wilma Ring."

"Hey, we might be cousins."

"Yeah. Are you black?"

"Err . . . um . . . no. Are you?"

"Yeah, we most likely ain't cousins. See you for tea."

It was certainly shabby, though nothing that paint and a new hall door could not have cured, Sandy thought to herself, but the street didn't have too much smart paint and new hall doors. There were three bicycles in the hall and a lot of very loud music came up from the basement.

What the hell, Sandy thought, I'm not going to be on nights for the first six months, and if I can't sleep after a day's hospital work because of a few bars of music I must be in bad shape. Wilma was standing at the door.

"Come in, cousin," she called with a laugh. "Have some nice English tea to get you over the culture shock of a walk through the Brixton West Indies."

It was agreed in ten minutes. The room, the rent, the life-style.

"I don't have friends in, because I'm studying, see," Wilma said. "But I study in my own bedroom, so you can have people in so long as they don't shout through the walls. And if your guys don't eat all the food in the fridge and take all the hot water, they can stay all night."

"What are you studying?" Sandy wanted to know. She didn't feel like telling Wilma yet that there would be no guys for a long time, not after the guy in Wales, the one she was running away from.

"Open university. I am reading for a university degree," said Wilma. "When you come back tonight, remember to get yourself a lamp and bulb for your room, there's only a centre light, it makes it even worse than it need be."

"I can come back tonight?" Sandy said.

"I can't see why you should pay a hotel and pay me. You've got only one body and it can sleep in only one bed."

For a few weeks they rarely saw each other. Wilma worked strange hours on the admission shifts, so that she could have appropriate time off for her studying and to watch the programmes on television. Sandy worked a day shift on the neurosurgical ward. It was demanding and sometimes depressing. She often wished that Wilma were there to chat to when she got back. Bit by

305

bit she got used to the area; they even joked with her in the corner store as she refused akee and salt fish and other Jamaican treats.

"I only like the patties," she said firmly.

"You wait till you go out to the island and have goat curry," Nelson, the good-looking man who ran the shop, used to say to her. "Then you never eat anything else."

"I can't imagine going to Jamaica," she said truthfully. "It must be such a contrast between the rich tourists and the poverty of the people who live there."

"What makes you think that?" Nelson wanted to know.

Sandy was about to say that if so many Jamaicans came to Britain to live in what she considered relative poverty, things must be in a very bad state back home. But she was unsure if that would be offensive, so instead she muttered vaguely about something she had seen on television.

"You don't take no notice of that Wilma," Nelson had said. "Wilma is a no-good communist, she is always finding something wrong with every society."

The day she heard this new slant on her flat-mate Sandy climbed the stairs and found Wilma at home. She had washed her hair and was sitting in an unaccustomed relaxed mood with her feet on the window box, a towel around her head, and a beer in her hand.

"Come on, pretend we're in the sun-soaked Caribbean. There's a beer for you in the fridge," she called to Sandy and they sat in the summer evening listening to the sounds from the street below, the planes overhead, the distant traffic, and the general hum of city noises.

"I hear you're a communist," Sandy said lightly.

"That pretty boy Nelson has a big mouth an' no brain," commented Wilma, unperturbed.

"I think he fancies you. He always mentions you," probed Sandy.

"Yeah, he should fancy Margaret, the mother of his three children. She works sixteen hours a day for him. He should discuss her politics and her tits, not mine," retorted Wilma, this time with more spirit.

"But *are* you a communist?" persisted Sandy. In a way she hoped Wilma was. It was quite outrageous enough to share with a Jamaican woman, which had them all whispering back in Wales, but a Jamaican communist would be over the top.

"Of course not, dope," said Wilma. "Would I be lying here talking chicken shit to a silly little nurse like you, drinking beer, if I were a communist? No, I would be fighting the good fight somewhere and overturning things. Not planning to become rich and middle class and have a university degree."

"I think you are mad to try and do all that studying," said Sandy, stretching her tired muscles. "It's bad enough doing what we do. I only want to sleep and look at telly when the day is over. Study! I couldn't even think of it."

"I had always heard they were ambitious in Wales," Wilma said.

"They may be. I'm not anymore. Anyway, being a nurse isn't that far below being a teacher, you know, they rate about the same. And teachers don't get all that much more money. I don't know why you're killing yourself if all you'll do is teach in the end."

"I'll do both," said Wilma.

"How can you do both?" Sandy became suddenly irritated at the calm way this tall girl had everything planned. Even her short burst of leisure was carefully planned, hair shampooed, fresh air by the window, lounging in a robe, instead of sitting there, tired and hot, like Sandy was.

"I'll be a teacher during the day, and then some nights a week I'll do a night shift, and I can work full-time nursing in the long holidays. Teachers have vacations of three to four months, you know, when you add it all up. It is a ridiculous life . . . they get paid . . . I don't know." She shook her turbanned head from side to side in amazement.

"My sister married a teacher in Wales. They don't get well paid I tell you, and he's knackered come the summer when the exams are over. You've got it wrong," Sandy said. She didn't like to hear of people doing two jobs. She felt quite proud of herself, having managed to drag herself unwillingly from Wales, from a man who walked out on her, to a big strange city and find a job and a flat. She thought that Wilma was pushing it.

Wilma got them more beer.

"Ohh," she sighed. "Ohh, Sandy girl, if only you knew what my mother had to do for me, and what she and her sisters have had to do for all our family. I'll *never* stop getting degrees, every letter I have to my name is a shaft of sunlight for them. It's a reason to go on scrubbing floors, to go into offices and shops at five A.M. where the air is stale and the baskets are full of yesterday's sour milk cartons, but the letters after my name will make it worthwhile."

"Oh, for heaven's sake, Wilma, you're far too intelligent to go along with that crap," cried Sandy, annoyed now and tactful no longer. "If you really wanted to help your mother, then you'd give her money, for God's sake. I mean, I send my mother money each week, not much, but a little, for her to get herself something nice, maybe a hairdo or a night at the bingo and a fish supper. My dad keeps her very short."

"Oh yes?" said Wilma.

"Yes, bloody yes. And that's what you should do instead of filling your poor mam's head up with ideas and nonsense, and degrees and airy-fairy letters after your name. If you can't bear her being down on her knees then take her off them. You can send her ten quid a week—better, you can go and give it to her. She lives only an hour away. I can't understand why you don't go to see her more. My mam lives hundreds of miles away, otherwise I'd go and take her out on a Saturday night for a bit of a laugh. That's what a daughter is for."

Wilma sat up and looked at her.

"No, Sandy my little sister, that is *not* what a daughter is for. A daughter must never be for that. That means the system never ends. A daughter must be something better, something stronger, she must give hope and reason for what is being done. She must make some sense out of all the scrubbing, bring some logic to all that lavatory cleaning. Otherwise a daughter is just yourself again, on and on forever."

Sandy saw why Nelson thought that Wilma wanted to overturn society.

And because she thought of Nelson she mentioned him.

"But the other Jamaicans don't feel that way, Nelson and those girls in the store for example, they have a laugh and they go to parties and they sing songs, and they say it's not too bad. Isn't that better for a mother, to see she has happy children?"

Wilma stood up and rested her hands on the window box. She looked as if she were about to make a speech to a crowd below but instead she spoke in a very gentle voice.

"My mother told me that before she came here she never knew that white women were poor, too, when she saw poor white women in Britain she thought they had done something bad and were being punished. She came from a family where the women were strong.

"*Her* mother remembered being a mammy and remembered having to lie down and let a white boss screw her. But that had all gone by my mother's time, she had five jobs, five different jobs to get her fare to England, and when she came here she had six jobs to make the money for us to come, but she didn't mind having six jobs because she lived in luxury. She had electricity, not kerosene, she had water in a tap, down the corridor but in a tap. She had a house where the food didn't melt, or rot, or go bad, she didn't have to buy expensive ice to keep food fresh for twenty-four hours. And one by one she sent for us. One by one we came."

Her voice began to sound a little like a

preacher's. Sandy could imagine her putting a few "Yea, verilys" into her conversation.

"You see, what was so wonderful was that we knew she would send for us. I was only nine when she went, only a child of nine when she got on the bus to Kingston that day, and I knew she would send for us one by one. That when I came first, part of her sending for Sadie and sending for Margaret and the others was that I should work hard at school. It was team work, it was solidarity like you've never known. If we had the homework done and our mother's supper ready when she came in from one job, that gave her strength to go out to another. If she didn't have to worry about us, if we cleaned the house, then she could stay healthy, in her jobs, and not fret. You have to scrub a lot of floors and get a lot of bonus and overtime to pay five airfares from Jamaica and for a home for them to live in."

Wilma smiled seraphically.

"But we were a lucky family because it was the woman who came. No danger of the woman finding a fancy man and forgetting us like happened to some of the men who came. A woman with five children will not forget them. That Nelson you admire so much in the corner store, he has a wife and two children in Ocho Rios, as well as Margaret and the three children here. Nice for Nelson to be chatty and to have a laugh and a drink and a song. Very nice. My mother would spit on him. A disgrace to Jamaica, every song and every bit of a laugh which you said I should be having is a mockery."

"But, Wilma, surely you can have both. I mean the pride in your doing well *and* a bit of a laugh, that's all I was suggesting. That's all I was saying, your mam has to have some relaxation, some happiness."

"I write to her and I tell her what I am studying, sometimes she looks at the television when the open university programmes are on. She can't understand them, but that's her happiness."

"What does she do on her time off?"

"She sleeps. And when she wakes to work again she remembers that her mother couldn't read but she can read and write, and she knows that even though she can read and write she will never have qualifications but I will have a university degree, and that sends a big surge of happiness right through her and she is glad that she didn't just sit and laugh with her mother while the chickens ran around the dusty yard, and that I did not sit and laugh with her while we both went out to play bingo."

"I see," said Sandy, who didn't see at all.

"You don't see, because for you it has always been a possibility, a good life. You don't have to prove anything to your mother nor she to hers."

"Oh I don't know. I've had more education, a better job, more freedom, than she did." Sandy didn't want anyone to think that there had been no progress. Life hadn't been a bed of roses in the small Welsh town.

Wilma sighed. Sandy was by far the nicest of the girls who had shared her flat, but she would leave, she would leave soon. Without a proper explanation. And Nelson would say that she left because she was too toffee-nosed for the area, and Old Johny, the man from Barbados two floors down, would say that it was good riddance to that young whitey anyway, and only Wilma would know that it had nothing to do with colours of skin or area, or smells of curry or steel bands in the basement. It had everything to do with life being short and most people wanting to have a laugh and a good time.

IF YOU HAVE ENJOYED READING THIS
LARGE PRINT BOOK AND YOU
WOULD LIKE MORE INFORMATION
ON HOW TO ORDER A WHEELER
LARGE PRINT BOOK, PLEASE WRITE
TO:

WHEELER PUBLISHING, INC.
P.O. BOX 531
ACCORD, MA 02018-0531